Suspended Matters

Suspended Matters

Witches of Willowbrook

Book Two

Alena Orrison

SUSPENDED MATTERS

For information, address Spirited Ink Press, spiritedinkpress@gmail.com

spiritedinkpress.com

ISBN 979-8-9880131-3-6

Cover Design by Get Covers

1st edition 2025

Printed in the United States of America

DEDICATION

To my best friends, Emily and Nicole, who are always there for me. I don't know what I would do without you.

AND

To all the women who have ever felt lost and alone.

Table of Contents

Chapter 1: Messages

I hung the navy wrap dress on my closet door and looked at it critically. It flared gently at the waist, and the cape sleeves gave it an elegant touch. I nodded in approval. The dress was perfect for Jessica's cocktail party for her boyfriend, Zane—formal yet comfortable enough for setting up and cleaning up afterward. As I was on my hands and knees digging out a pair of low-heeled pumps from the back of my closet, I heard my phone ring. Grunting, I pushed myself to standing and fumbled for my phone that was partially buried in the blankets on my unmade bed.

"Hi, Jessica," I answered.

"Hannah, are you still able to pick up the cake? You can use my car."

"Of course. Anything else?" I plopped down on the side of my bed.

I heard paper rustling and envisioned my friend sorting through papers on her desk to find her party-planning list.

"Stan is bringing the sandwiches and fruit at three, Jewels is there now putting up decorations, and I'll go put on the finishing touches after I pick up the flowers. I have the wine. Evan is getting the dishes from the rental company. But I feel like I'm forgetting something."

"The banner?"

"Oh, right! It arrived the other day, and I put it under my bed to hide it."

I laughed. "It will be an amazing party, Jess."

She sighed. "I hope so. His parents will be here, and they come from money."

"So do you," I pointed out. Her parents had been very well-off.

"Not like this. I'm worried they will assume he's too good for me."

"He's a sweetheart, which means his parents aren't conceited. What are you wearing?"

"My burgundy dress."

I knew her closet almost as well as my own. "The one with the spaghetti straps that's the color of a wonderful red wine?"

"That's the one."

"You're going to look amazing."

"What about you?" she asked.

I glanced at the dress hanging on the door. "My navy wrap-around. Will that be okay?"

"Absolutely," she gushed. "That's a great color on you."

"Thanks. I'll see you at three?"

"Yep, that should be great. I'll leave the keys in the car for you."

"Sounds good. If you think of anything else you need, let me know."

"You're the best."

We hung up, and I found my shoes. I put them on the floor next to the bed and went to the jewelry box on my dresser to choose a necklace. My phone chimed. "Now what are you worried about?" I said with a smile. I placed the gold and diamond heart necklace on my nightstand and picked up my phone again. But when I looked at the screen, it wasn't from Jessica.

A notification from Messenger displayed in the center of my lock screen.

Jamison Stewart wants to send you a message.

"Who is Jamison Stewart?" I muttered. "Perhaps a cousin?"

I knew very little about my extended family. My mother had a sister but didn't talk to her much. I only saw her a few times, and I couldn't remember if she had children or not. I clicked through to open the message and read.

Hi, Hannah. I know this will be a shock, but I'm your dad.

This had to be a hoax. Scammers made social media profiles like I made coffee on a busy day at Over the Moon.

I've wanted to reach out for years, but your mother forbade it. I'd like to get to know you.

My heart pounded. I tapped a few more times on the screen to bring up his profile. There wasn't much there, not even a photo. Another message popped up.

It's understandable if you don't believe me. I can prove it, though.

Okay, I'll bite.

How do I know you're telling the truth?

I gripped my phone, my palms sweaty, as I watched the typing bubble appear.

You were born on January 5th at 3:49pm.

My eyes narrowed as I read. He could have found that somewhere. Hospital records or an old newspaper. I remembered my mom saying all the birth announcements were in the paper back then.

Your first word wasn't mama or dada like most babies. It was baba, for sheep. You had a stuffed toy sheep that you loved. You carried it with you everywhere.

A heaviness settled in my stomach, and I sank to the floor as my knees went weak. I still had that stuffed sheep. My eyes drifted to it sitting on the top of my dresser. The love of my little hands had flattened the fleece, and the yellow ribbon around its neck had frayed ends. My first instinct had my finger hovering over Jessica's number. I desperately wanted to talk to her, but I didn't want to ruin today for her. Zane choosing to stay here in Willowbrook instead of returning to the city meant their relationship was serious. I decided to wait until after the celebration to tell her.

Hannah, please. I want to explain why I left.

I hesitated, then shot off a reply.

I'm going to talk to my mom first.

I waited until I saw him read the message, and when he didn't respond after a few minutes, I assumed he would give me some space. I wrapped my arms around my stomach and squeezed my eyes shut, willing the sudden dizziness to stop. Taking a deep breath, I opened my eyes. Jessica would know what I should do; I only had to get through the party.

Going into the bathroom, I groaned at the sight of my hair. Rummaging at the bottom of my closet had not been friendly to my curls. The dark strands had a level of fizziness usually only reserved for high-humidity days. With a sigh, I methodically applied product and coaxed my dark brown hair into cooperation. I checked my makeup and smiled with relief. Somehow, I hadn't smudged it. With a pale pink lip gloss and jasmine oil behind my ears, I reached a greater sense of calm. I put the pair of nude pumps into a canvas bag, dropped the lip gloss into my clutch, and slipped on the dress, adjusting the wrap to ensure it didn't show too much cleavage. Satisfied, I slid my feet into a pair of comfortable sandals for the walk to Jessica's house to get her car.

Refusing to think about the Jamison Stewart's messages and what they might mean, I put my earbuds in my ears and chose a pop mix playlist on my phone to listen to. I stepped out onto the sunny street, firmly closing and locking the cottage door behind me. The music drowned out my thoughts and provided a pleasant rhythm for my walk, making me slightly winded by the time I reached Jessica's house. I was thankful for the ocean breeze; its gentle touch carried the scent of salt and seaweed, keeping me from overheating.

"Wouldn't that be great? Arrive at a fancy party covered in sweat and smelling like a horse." I snorted, pulling the car door open and tossing my bags onto the passenger seat.

I pulled the visor down and caught the keys as they dropped. The car started easily, and I backed out of the driveway. The short distance to the ferry seemed silly in a car, but I would need it in the city to get to the bakery. Once on the ferry, I stayed in the vehicle instead of standing by the railing like I usually would. I didn't want to have to wrangle my hair into submission again. As the ship pulled away from the dock, my thoughts about the man claiming to be my dad started tumbling again, so I turned the car key to Accessory and blasted the radio, tapping my hand on the steering wheel to the beat. Four songs later, the deckhand waved at me to pull forward, and I gratefully drove off the boat.

It took all of my concentration to drive in the heavy weekend traffic. The late fall heat seemed to have the city people on edge. One angry driver almost sideswiped me when he pulled out of a side street. I jerked the wheel and swerved, barely avoiding getting hit, and the car next to me honked. Then, as I made a left turn, someone coming from the other direction ran the red light. I slammed on the brakes, causing the car behind me to brake hard and honk.

"This is why I don't like the city," I grumbled to myself.

Finally, I arrived safely at Thistledown Bakes. I found a parking spot near the front door and entered.

A cheerful woman with pink cheeks and white hair greeted me. Her eyes wrinkled when she smiled, and her back was straight despite her obvious age.

"Welcome in. I'm Betsy Thistledown. What can I help you with today?"

"I'm here to pick up a cake for Jessica Barnes."

"Oh, of course. It's already paid for. I'll bring it right out." She disappeared into the back.

As I waited, I studied the cakes in the display case. A small, white-frosted cake with a bride and groom topper and delicate pink roses and green vines around the base caught my eye.

"That's a topper," Betsy said, noticing my gaze as she came around the counter with a large box. "It's just an example of what the tiers could look like. Are you planning a wedding?" She smiled cheerfully and placed the box on a nearby table.

I straightened and shook my head. "No, just admiring your work." I cast a wistful glance back at the cake.

"A pretty girl like you?" She gently lifted the lid of the box.

"I'm not seeing anyone."

"Ah, but you would like to. You look to me like you want a family of your own."

My cheeks heated, and I glanced away from her knowing gaze. "It's not in the cards for me yet."

She patted my hand. "Soon, I'm sure. Here, will this be okay?" She gestured to the sheet cake in the box.

I gasped when I saw it. Jessica had gotten one of the high schoolers to take an aerial photograph of Willowbrook with his drone, and the baker had somehow printed it onto the cake. The words "Welcome Home" swirled in a color that matched the hazy blue of the north beach.

"It's beautiful," I said. "I did not know you could print with frosting."

She chuckled. "My daughter does these. Did you know there is a thing called an edible ink printer?" She shook her head. "I prefer making the cakes by hand, but this brings in good business." Closing the lid on the box, she continued, "Be sure to keep it flat and don't let it slide. Don't take corners too fast. When you want to serve it, fold the lid back and the box sides can come down, so you don't have to lift it out."

"Thank you. I'll go open the car, then come back for the cake."

"Good plan. And be sure to come back and see me when you are planning that wedding, eh?"

I smiled and shook my head, amused. Once I settled the cake safely on the back seat with a blanket tucked under and around it for stability, I made the return trip to the island. To avoid jostling the cake, I drove slowly, causing several drivers to swerve to avoid me. Once on the ferry, the tension in my shoulders eased.

I considered what Betsy had said. For as long as I could remember, it was just me and my mom. I didn't have siblings like Jessica had Evan. And my mom was always distant, also unlike Jessica's family. Her parents welcomed me in as one of their own. I never told Jessica, but their loss affected me almost as much as it did her. They were the parents I needed, and I wanted a family like that.

But first, I needed a husband, and that required a boyfriend. I hadn't had a date in almost two years, not since Randy Park. He broke up with me when he found out I had a degree in early childhood education, and he had a GED. Jessica suspected he felt threatened by my superior intelligence.

I rolled my eyes. As if I'd ever judge someone's intelligence by their schooling. Their choices, however, were fair game. And Randy's decision to walk away from something good just for his pride? Not exactly a smart move. I flipped the visor down and reapplied my lip gloss, admiring the way the sunlight brought out the mahogany in my hair.

"He could have had all this," I muttered. "His loss."

The ferry docked, and I followed the deckhand's directions to leave the ship. I drove the few blocks to the coffee shop and parked on the street in front of the entrance. Jewels walked up as I carefully lifted the cake from the car.

Jewels had replaced her usual 80s punk-rocker look of miniskirts and legwarmers with a neon green sheath dress and low slingback heels. She had twisted her pink-streaked hair into a braid that somehow showed more of the blond than pink.

"You look great! Last-minute things?" I asked, nodding at the bags she carried.

She grinned. "Of course. Jess wanted more napkins and some other snacks." She held the door open for me, then followed me inside.

"Hi," Jessica greeted me. Her red hair hung in loose curls down her back, and the burgundy dress showed off her perfect figure and green eyes. "Thank you for doing this." She took a few bags from Jewels as I placed the cake on the counter.

"No problem. It's gorgeous, by the way." I lifted the lid.

"Zane will love it," Jessica said with a smile. "Thanks again."

As we unpacked the grocery bags, I said, "I don't want to overshadow his big day, but I've got some news to tell you later. Maybe tomorrow?"

She paused in the act of setting out plates to study me. "You can tell me now, Han. I'm always here for you."

I shook my head. "No, it's okay. It can wait."

"Okay, sure." Jessica looked skeptical, but smiled. "Whatever you're worried about will be fine."

She pulled me into a hug. I allowed myself to rest against her for a moment. Then I took a deep breath, pulled away, and gave her what I hoped was a confident smile.

"Let's go make some magic," I said, gesturing to the half-emptied bags.

Chapter 2: Welcome Party

Once we finished setting up, we stood back to admire our work. We had transformed the entire coffee shop into an elegant yet festive space, complete with streamers, balloons, gold pompoms, and hanging swirls. Fairy lights twinkled along the bookshelves, and the banner proclaiming "Goodbye and Welcome" hung across one of the large front windows.

A few minutes later, the bell over the door sounded and Zane walked in, wearing a black suit and white shirt without a tie. He wore his jacket open and had undone the top button of his shirt collar, giving him a smart-casual look.

"Wow, you ladies outdid yourselves," he said.

Jessica tugged on Zane's hand, and he followed her to the counter. "What do you think?" she asked, gesturing at the cake.

"That's fabulous. More than I expected."

"What, you expected me to bake you one and use canned frosting?" Jessica teased.

"Of course not. But this is stunning. Thank you." He pulled Jessica close and kissed her gently on the lips. "Don't want to smudge your lipstick," he said with a wink.

The moment was so intimate that I turned away, only to lock eyes with Evan as he walked in.

Jessica's brother looked sharp in black slacks and a forest-green button-down shirt that brought out the flecks of green in his hazel eyes. My cheeks heated at the sight of him. He gave me a mischievous grin before turning and holding the door open.

An elegant couple walked in and enthusiastically greeted Zane, who introduced them as his parents, Eloise and Benjamin. They both hugged Jessica and shook hands with the rest of us. After that, a steady stream of people entered, and I kept busy pouring wine and refilling the water carafes. I exchanged smiles with Jessica as she mouthed "thank you."

Then the bell jingled again, and Donna swept in.

She wore a sleek black dress, her shoulder-length brown hair styled in soft waves. She gave the room a polite smile, her eyes lingering on Jessica for a beat longer than the others.

"Donna," Jessica said, her voice carefully polite.

"Jessica." Donna offered a small, practiced smile. "This looks beautiful."

Jewels brightened and waved her over. "Donna! Glad you could make it." She crossed over and gave her a warm hug.

"Thanks, Jewels," Donna said, relaxing slightly. "I managed to get away after the charity board meeting. Sorry I'm a little late."

"You're right on time," Jewels said, pulling her toward the drinks table.

I watched as Donna selected a glass of wine and Jewels leaned in to chat easily with her, complimenting her dress and making her laugh.

Jessica tapped her spoon on her glass, gaining the attention of everyone in the room. She hated being in the spotlight. She must really love this guy to be the center of attention voluntarily, even for a few moments.

"Thank you all for coming," she said. "As you know, we're here to celebrate Zane Matthews's decision to stay in Willowbrook as the new director of the *Chronicle*, Willowbrook Island's only and most prestigious newspaper." A smattering of applause and laughter went around the room, and Jessica smiled.

Now she's making jokes? Love really changes a person.

"This is sad news for the *Seattle Sun,* though," Jessica continued. "Steve Alcott from the *Sun* is here to say his goodbyes. Steve, would you like to say a few words?"

Jessica stepped to Zane's side as a short, balding man in his forties moved to the front of the crowd.

"Well, Zane, as you know, everyone at the *Sun* will miss you. I'm going to miss you the most, though. You're one hell of a reporter and always find the truth in the stories. It looks like you've found more than that this time, and I'm happy for you. Even if it means I have to interview some college kids for your job." He raised his glass in a toast. "To Zane and finding our place in the world."

"To Zane," we echoed.

"And to my retirement!" Dave Brown called out.

"What are you going to do with all of your free time?" someone asked.

"I'm going fishing." Dave reeled in a pretend fish.

"Take care of our boy," Steve said to Jessica.

She smiled, and pink tinged her cheeks. "I will."

Jewels and I efficiently passed out plates of cake, and I finally had a few minutes to sit. I perched on a stool at the counter, savoring the rush of sugar as I took a bite of cake.

"Hey," Evan said behind me.

I inhaled abruptly, then coughed as a crumb went down my throat.

"Easy." He patted me on the back.

I managed a breath and sipped my wine before turning to him, hoping my eyes weren't red from choking. Did I have frosting on my lips? I licked them, trying to look seductive, just to be sure. "Enjoying the party?" I asked.

His gaze shifted from my lips to my eyes. "Yeah, you three did a great job."

I shrugged. "Jessica planned it all. Jewels and I just helped put it together."

"It counts. I came over to ask what you were doing after this. Sorry about startling you."

My cheeks heated, and I prayed he thought it was because of the wine. "Jewels and I are cleaning up so Jessica and Evan can go to dinner with his parents."

He gave me that slow smile of his that made my heart flutter and all thoughts flee my brain. "Maybe we can get something to eat besides tiny sandwiches and cake afterward?"

I laughed. "Cocktail hors d'oeuvres not enough for you, big guy?"

"When Jessica said there would be food, I expected something more substantial." He rubbed belly as if it were growling.

I resisted the urge to pat his flat stomach as I said, "I'm sure we can grab something to eat after we put all of this away."

"It's a date," he said, and strode off as Jessica called to him.

Did he mean it as a date, or was he using the phrase like people do when they make plans? I shook my head. "Stop overthinking, Hannah," I muttered to myself. "He's your best friend's brother."

I surveyed the room and noticed some of the guests had already left, including Steve. Jessica and Evan stood with Zane and his parents near the door. I couldn't hear their conversation, but Jessica looked slightly surprised as Eloise spoke before gliding to the door with Benjamin in her wake.

That seemed to be the cue for the rest of the town, who came to welcome the new newspaper director, and the bell over the door jingled almost continuously as people took their leave.

"We can clean up. You should get ready for dinner with the parents," I told Jessica. "Evan, you'll stay and help, won't you?"

"Sure," he said.

"We have time. I'm just going to freshen up." Jessica replied. She leaned closer to me and whispered, "What did Evan say to you earlier?"

I glanced around to see where he was. He strode to the back room to get the crates for the dishes, so I quickly whispered back, "He asked me to get something to eat after we clean up."

"Finally! A date!" Jessica crowed.

I shushed her. "I don't know if he meant it as a date. We are friends, after all."

"What's a date?" Evan asked, returning to the main room and carrying three crates stacked together. I pretended not to look at the way his arm muscles flexed as placed the crates on the counter and unstacked them.

"Oh, um…" I stammered.

"Zane asked if I wanted to go to a football game in the city. It's not really my thing, but it's a date," Jessica said smoothly.

I shot her a grateful glance, then moved to gather the scattered glasses and plates.

"I thought that went really well," I said to Jessica, picking up the wine glasses off the tables. "Zane's parents seem nice."

"They are nice. Not quite what I expected. His mom is so graceful," Jessica replied, methodically corking the opened wine bottles that weren't empty.

I noticed Donna lingering near the door, watching Jessica quietly.

After a moment, she crossed the room.

"Jessica," Donna said, her voice even but a little stiff.

Jessica straightened from wiping the counter, brushing a strand of red hair behind her ear. "Donna. Thanks for coming tonight."

Donna gave a small, polite smile. "Of course. I wouldn't have missed it." She hesitated, then added, "I'm happy for you, really. You seem… settled."

Jessica's expression softened slightly, but there was caution in her eyes. "Thank you. That means a lot."

Donna glanced briefly toward Zane, who was laughing with Evan across the room, then back at Jessica. "He seems like a good man."

"He is," Jessica murmured.

There was a brief pause, the kind where old friendship and old fractures sit together in the same breath.

"Well," Donna said, shifting her coat. "I should go. Jewels, I'll call you next week?" She added over her shoulder.

"Definitely," Jewels called from the back.

Jessica gave a small nod. "Goodnight, Donna."

"Goodnight."

As Donna left, Jessica let out a slow breath, then caught me watching. She offered a wry smile. "That was... almost normal."

I grinned. "Progress."

I balanced a wine glass on top of a teetering stack of dessert plates, edging carefully toward the plastic crates. My toe snagged on the leg of a chair—a sharp, sudden catch—and before I could even gasp, gravity yanked me forward. The plates slipped, the glass tilted, and everything burst from my hands in a helpless spray.

"No!" I cried. I thrust one hand out, as if I could catch them before they crashed to the floor.

They froze. The dishes froze in midair.

Chapter 3: Afterparty

"**W**hat the hell?" I whispered, staring at the plates and wine glasses suspended in the air.

"It's okay, Hannah," Jessica said, hurrying over to me.

Evan gently grabbed my elbow, guiding me into the chair I'd tripped over. My knees buckled as I sat, stunned. I couldn't tear my gaze from Jessica and Jewels, who plucked the dishes from the air with ease and set them in the crate.

My hands shook violently. I shoved them under my thighs, gripping the chair's edge hard enough to make my arms ache. Evan held out a bottle of water toward me, but I could only shake my head, too dizzy to drink.

"How did that happen?" I croaked. I didn't expect an answer, but the question clawed its way out of me anyway.

"Magic, my dear."

I jerked my head toward the doorway. Sofia stood there with a sympathetic smile on her face.

What is she doing here? She hadn't come to Zane's party as she disliked formal events.

"I'm sorry, what?" I asked, certain I'd misheard. She'd always been a little eccentric, but showing up out of nowhere and talking about magic?

The older woman ambled closer, her flowing green top rippling with her movement. Zane pulled out a chair for her. The chair creaked as she settled into it.

"Magic," she repeated, slower this time. "You're a witch."

"Welcome to the club," Jewels said brightly.

She sounded as if she were happy for me. The room tilted. I fought to stay upright.

"I don't understand," I said, looking around wildly. Everyone wore identical expressions of encouragement, as if this was some casual Friday night conversation.

Zane murmured something in Jessica's ear, gave me a pat on the shoulder, and left.

"He's going to meet his parents," Jessica said, but the words barely registered.

"You should go, too," Jewels said. "We can handle things here."

"I'll meet up with them later," she responded. She pulled out another chair and sat across from me.

Jewels hopped up to sit on a nearby table, swinging her feet like a child.

Evan remained standing close to me.

"Can someone please explain?" My voice cracked. "How did I do that?"

"Magic is real. Witches are real. You're a witch, and your powers just manifested," Sofia said calmly. "I can help you learn to control them."

"Sofia is basically the Council's hound dog," Evan quipped.

"Pardon me?" Sofia arched an eyebrow at him.

"I just mean that you seem to sniff out the new witches and then teach them how to use their magic." He shrugged. "Am I wrong?"

"No, you're not wrong. I suppose I do find the new ones quickly. I've just never had anyone call me a dog before." She tucked a wisp of her gray hair behind one ear.

Evan grinned unapologetically, and the others chuckled. But I felt like the floor was sliding out from under me.

Sofia turned back to me. "Let me start from the beginning. You know how Willowbrook was founded, yes?" When I nodded, she continued. "Well, the families that originally settled here were all witches. They came here to get away from the Mundanes—non-magical folk—who were afraid of them. People do horrible things to each other when they are afraid, and sometimes fear creates anger as a defensive mechanism. Anyway, those founding families formed the Council. It's three or five witches, most of the time three, who act as a governing body for the Circle. The Circle is the rest of us." She gestured to include my friends.

I looked at them one by one. They each nodded when our eyes met.

"The weather? That's me," Jessica said. "I think I finally have it mostly under control."

"Yes, dear one, you're doing well," Sofia confirmed.

"I'm empathic and, I guess, a little clairvoyant. Although I usually don't see visions. Mostly it's impressions about people." Evan smiled at me.

Jewels leaned forward a little. "I have visions of the future. I'm called a precog, for precognitive."

The conversation blurred at the edges. As they spoke, pieces of the past slammed into me. Jessica's odd reactions to sudden rainstorms. Jewels's eerie guesses about things that hadn't happened yet. Evan's uncanny ability to calm a room with just a glance.

I had missed it all. Or I hadn't wanted to see.

I nodded slowly, then shook my head. "This is all crazy," I whispered.

"I thought that too when things started happening to me," Jessica said. "No one else really knew, or at least I thought they didn't know. You're not alone."

"We'll help you learn your magic," Jewels said. The rest of them nodded in agreement.

Sofia's voice cut through the haze. "I need to ask you something. Did anything happen recently that might have triggered this?"

My mind scrambled. "What do you mean?"

"A great loss?" Sofia prompted.

"When Evan's and my powers manifested, it was after our parents died." Jessica said.

"No one's died," I replied.

"It can be something else," Sofia said. "Did you get some bad news? Or lose something precious to you?"

I inhaled sharply. "I got a message..."

"Go on," she prompted.

"A man claiming to be my dad contacted me on Facebook. He wants to meet me and explain why he's never been around." I looked at Jessica. "This was the news I mentioned before Zane's party."

"Oh, Hannah." She looked stricken. "Did you reply?"

I nodded. "I think it's real. He knows the time of my birth and my first word. I don't think that stuff is floating out there on the internet." I gestured vaguely in the air.

"What are you going to do?" I could almost feel Evan's protectiveness radiating out from him. He had always acted as if he were my big brother, too. Until recently, that is. I closed my eyes for a moment to refocus my thoughts on the current situation.

"I wanted your opinion. And then I thought about talking to my mom, but I'm pretty sure she'll say the same things she's said before. She'll say he abandoned us, and she had to raise me alone, and if I ask why he left, she'll wave it off as if she doesn't know. But he made it sound like they talked about it and decided together."

Sofia tilted her head and regarded me. "This is definitely a large enough emotional shock that it is probably the trigger for your magic. It appears you have suspension magic, meaning you can suspend objects in time. I'll include you in the lessons with Evan and Jessica, as I think having them around will help. I can't tell you what to do about your father, but I am here if you want someone else to talk to."

"We're all here for you," Jessica stated.

"Thank you," I whispered.

"If you want to go home, we can clean up here," Jewels said.

I shook my head. "I don't want to be alone right now. Besides, Jessica has a dinner date with her boyfriend and his parents."

"Ugh, don't remind me! They're so...classy. And I'm just a small town girl. I have no idea what we'll talk about."

"Zane is classy, too, yet you're not intimidated by him," Jewels reminded her.

"True." She flashed her a grateful smile, then looked back at me. "But after dinner, I'm coming over and we can talk more about your dad."

She left, and I looked at Evan, worried he had to go as well.

"Don't worry. I'm not leaving." He slung one arm around my shoulder and gave me a wink. "After all, someone has to supervise so you don't freeze the dishes again."

"Funny."

"Since you're staying, Evan, go ahead and shield Hannah. I'm sure she'll be relieved to know her powers won't cause any damage, at least for today." Sofia gave me a sympathetic smile.

"What does that mean?" I croaked out.

"Part of my abilities allow me to block emotions from other people, and that extends to magical powers. And I can shield someone else as well as myself. Basically, put an impenetrable bubble around you so your magic doesn't leak out." He shrugged. "It comes in handy sometimes."

My eyebrows raised, and I'm sure I looked like a deer in headlights. Heat suffused my skin, and I finally took the water bottle from Evan, gulping down several mouthfuls. "Ah," was all I could manage.

"You won't feel or see anything," he reassured me. "I'm shielding you right now, in fact."

I didn't feel any different. Nothing looked odd, and there wasn't a shimmer or glow around me or Evan like in the fantasy movies I watched late at night when I couldn't sleep. I would have to trust him.

"I will be in touch, Hannah. You're in good hands. As I said, you can start doing lessons with Evan and Jessica. We're meeting again on Tuesday." Sofia stood and patted me on the shoulder again. Her touch was oddly comforting, coming from someone I barely knew.

I couldn't think of anything I'd rather do less, but I knew I needed help. "Okay, I'll be there."

Sofia nodded as if she expected nothing less before taking her leave, the bell above the door jingling softly.

"It'll be okay." Jewels said with a smile. "And now we don't have to hide our magic from you."

I scoffed. "This is a lot to take in. And I'm not sure how much I believe it."

She nodded. "That's understandable. But how else would you explain the dishes just hovering in midair?"

"I'm exhausted and seeing things?"

She laughed. "Yeah, okay. You can tell yourself that."

I frowned and bit my lip, trying to gather my thoughts.

"Hey," Evan said, gently touching my shoulder so I would focus on him. "It really will be okay. I promise."

I took a deep, shuddering breath. "Okay. I've got this."

He grinned. "You do. Only a few short months ago, my sister and I came into our powers, and it was very confusing and overwhelming. But we came through."

"These dishes aren't going to pack themselves," Jewels said, moving to one of the tables. "Hannah, can you help me here?"

Relieved to have something else to focus on, I stood and brushed off Evan's steadying hand. "I'm okay."

He nodded and stepped back. Despite their reassurances to me, I couldn't help but notice that Evan kept shooting glances my way as he stacked crates by the door, almost as if he thought I would bolt if he didn't keep an eye on me. Jewels worked next to me as we packed dishes, wiped tables, and swept floors.

"It gets easier," she said as she watched me carefully putting the plates in the plastic rack for transport. "The magic, I mean. I don't know about the dad thing. My parents are less than supportive of me."

"I'm sorry." I slid the last plate into place and turned to look at her. "My mom has always been there for me. She's refused to talk about my dad, though, so I can't imagine she'll want to talk about magic." Just the thought of my business-minded mother discussing something like magic made me cringe. If she couldn't buy it, negotiate with it, or use it, she avoided it.

Jewels tilted her head, frowning. "It used to be that magic was solely hereditary, but over the last few generations, more and more people manifest it without any ancestral connection. So, it's possible she doesn't have a clue."

"Or she's been hiding it from me. She won't talk about her past, and she barely tells me anything about when I was a baby. It wouldn't surprise me if she hid magic from me, too."

"Witch etiquette," Jewels said solemnly. "What happens in witch club stays in witch club."

A surprised giggle escaped me, and I clamped a hand over my mouth. "I'm sorry. I don't know why I thought that was funny."

Jewels' grin reassured me. "It does sound like something out of a fantasy movie. But really, one of the rules is we can't tell people if they aren't part of us." She surveyed the room. "I think that's it for tonight. Evan, did you say you would take the dishes back in the morning?"

"Yeah, and I can load them in my truck tonight. You ladies should head home. Jessica may use a 'friend in distress' as a reason to get out of dinner early if it's not going well."

"I don't think she'll really want to come by tonight. It's Zane's big day, after all. Wouldn't she rather be with him?"

Evan gave me a pointed look. "You've known my sister since grade school, and you're questioning if she meant what she said?"

A smile tugged at my lips. "You're right."

"Come on," Jewels said. "We can stop at the store for ice cream if we hurry. It closes in about ten minutes."

Chapter 4: Girl Talk

I followed Jewels out the front door and onto the dimly lit street. Stan's Grocer was only a few blocks away, but knowing it was near closing time had us half-jogging up the sidewalk. We raced the last few yards and entered the store, laughing.

"I totally beat you!" Jewels declared.

"By about an inch. I could have taken you."

"You'll have to prove it next time."

The physical exertion pushed the darker thoughts from my mind. I sucked in a breath and remembered how I used to love running. Maybe I should get back into it. Taking Evan's self-defense classes provided some cardio when we were sparring, but I could probably do with some more.

"What will it be, ladies?" Stan's voice boomed across the store.

"We're here for the one thing that cures all ills," Jewels replied.

Stan nodded gravely as he made his way toward us, his large frame moving with a type of grace. Maybe the rumors that he used to be a dancer were true. "You know where to go, then. We have a new flavor: Sunburst Berry. I haven't tried it myself, but I'm told it tastes like rainbow sherbet with chunks of strawberries."

"That sounds amazing." I trailed Jewels to the back of the store to the frozen foods section. "I was thinking about chocolate fudge brownie, but now I want to try Sunburst Berry."

"Have both." Jewels shrugged. "I mean, it's not every day you find out you're a witch," she whispered.

"True. It's a cause for celebration or misery. Something. Ooh, we should get pizza, too."

"Frozen or delivery?"

"Delivery. It takes just as long, but we won't have to do as much."

"Done. I'm having this." Jewels twisted the pint container around so I could read the label.

"Wow. I didn't know they made a Reese's peanut butter cup ice cream."

She gasped in mock horror. "My friend, they make a Reese's peanut butter cup ice cream and brownie mix and practically every junk food that's worth eating. You're going to have to try some of this. And, of course, cookie dough for Jess. I think that's everything we need here."

"This looks like you're in it for the long haul," Stan said. A smile creased his round face, making his dark mustache twitch, as he rang us up.

"It's been a rough day," I replied.

"Well, you've got the supplies now to make it better. I hope whatever it is works out."

"Thanks, Stan. Why are you here alone tonight?"

"Oh, Duke took Larissa out for dinner, and I gave the rest of them an early night. If I can't close my own store by myself, I don't have any business being in business." He guffawed, handing us a paper bag with our goodies inside. "You two take care now."

"Thanks," we chorused.

As we made our way home, Jewels called Ironwood Tavern and placed our order. I texted Jessica to let her know we had treats, but to take her time at dinner. Her reply came swiftly.

I'm skipping dessert. Zane's parents are very understanding.

"Jessica will probably be over soon," I said, walking up the stairs and unlocking the door to the small cottage I shared with Jewels.

"Good. Why don't you take a shower in the meantime?"

"What, do I stink?" I cautiously sniffed my armpit.

Her laugh bubbled and made me grin in response, despite the evening's events. "No, but it might help to clear your head a little. I'll make a fire."

"Then I'm definitely putting on my cozy clothes after my shower."

Jewels was right, I thought as the warm water flowed over my skin. The citrusy scent of my body wash was uplifting and refreshing. I inhaled deeply and closed my eyes. The ordinary action of taking a shower made the intensity of the day slightly distant. I hadn't realized just how frazzled I felt between my assumed-father's message and this magic thing.

I turned off the water, grabbed a towel from the hook next to the shower, and wrapped it around my hair. Wrapping another towel around my body, I stepped onto the plush green rug. I wiped the steam from the mirror and gazed at my reflection. My round face looked ruddy from the heat of the shower, despite my dark complexion. I leaned closer to the mirror to peer at the worry lines in the corners of my eyes. When did those appear? Sighing, I squirted some moisturizer into my hand and massaged it onto my face, adding a little extra to the area around my eyes. Twenty-eight was too young to need eye cream, but maybe I should pick some up anyway.

Once I had combed my hair, adding some leave-in conditioner to help tame the frizz, and pulled on an oversized sweatshirt and soft jogger pants, I entered the living room, following the scent of warm gooey cheese.

"Hi," Jessica said when she saw me. She sat on the sofa with her feet tucked under her. "Feel better?"

I nodded. "Still confused, but not panicking."

Two boxes of pizza sat stacked on the table. Jewels came in from the kitchen, holding some paper plates and napkins.

"Perfect timing! Jessica showed up moments after the pizza, and now you walk in just as I find the plates. I wonder if that's a witch thing, too." She winked.

Of the three of us, Jewels was the most light-hearted despite her hard past. She almost had a childlike quality. When she first came to Willowbrook, I was hesitant to take her on as a roommate, but did so as a courtesy to Jess, who told me Jewels was homeless. Jessica had met Jewels when she was attending group therapy after her parents' deaths. That, combined with the very colorful way Jewels liked to dress, had me wondering if she would burn my little cottage down in the first week. But Jewels turned out to be an excellent roommate.

"Thanks for this. And the shower suggestion." Plopping down on the other end of the sofa, I accepted the plate Jewels handed me and reached for the pizza. The top box was a loaded supreme, which meant the bottom was chicken garlic. I lifted a piece of the supreme on my plate and passed the box to Jessica, who also took a piece.

"What, didn't Zane's parents feed you at dinner?" Jewels asked as she took her own slice and put the box back on the coffee table.

"Oh, they did. But this is comfort food. We ate at Rosita's. I had chicken enchiladas but couldn't finish them. I was too worried about you." She reached out and squeezed my hand.

"I'm fine. Everything will be fine," I said. I took a large bite of pizza. Sausage, cheese, and crust blended together on my tongue, and I sighed with contentment.

"That's what people say when they aren't fine."

Jewels nodded agreement. "It's okay to be scared or angry or sad or whatever. It's normal. Tell us about this guy who says he's your father."

I took a deep breath and let it out slowly. "Well, earlier today, I got a message request. I usually ignore them since most of them are scams or creepers. But it started off with, 'Hi Hannah. I know this will be a shock,' so I opened it. His name is Jamison Stewart. He said he's been wanting to contact me for a long time but hadn't before because my mom forbade him. I asked him how I knew he was telling the truth, and he told me I was born at 3:49pm and my first word was baba for sheep."

"Why would your mom forbid him from contacting you, even as an adult? Shouldn't that be your choice?" Jessica's eyes narrowed, a sure sign she spotted injustice.

"I'm sure my mom has a good reason for it."

"Maybe you should talk to your mom," Jewels suggested. "Get her side of the story before you decide if you want to meet this guy."

"Yeah, that's what I was thinking. She hates coming to the island, so I'll have to go to her." I scrunched my nose in disgust. "Ugh, the city. I do my best to avoid it, and today's traffic reminded me why."

"Do you want backup? I could wait in the car or something."

"Thanks, Jess, but I don't think I'll need it. I'll probably take the ferry over and then walk to her office."

"Well, let me know if you change your mind. Or Jewels can go. She's a city girl."

"Not so much anymore," Jewels protested. "Oh, I love the shops there, but I much prefer this quieter life."

"Yeah, it's so quiet with unruly witches and crazy weather." Jessica chuckled.

"Speaking of witches," I began. They both looked at me, and I shrugged helplessly. "I don't even know what to ask."

"Well, we already told you the basics. About the Council and how magic is traditionally hereditary, but that's been shifting lately."

"Right. But how did you two learn how to control your powers?"

Jewels laughed, a bright ringing sound. "I didn't!"

"What?" Jessica and I both stared at her.

"I didn't learn how to control them. I just accepted them. At first, I thought I was crazy from grief, which is why I went to group therapy. But once I accepted my visions and allowed them to happen, it wasn't so scary. But I don't have the same kind of magic you two do. I don't control the weather or freeze items in midair. I just get visions. Some are clearer than others, but all of them have to do with me somehow. I'm at the scene of the crime, so to speak; otherwise, I can't see anything. So, before you ask, I can't see what's going to happen when you meet your mom, Hannah, unless I'm supposed to be there, too."

"Oh." Disappointment stabbed my chest. When Jewels said she was precognitive, I had hoped she could see something about my situation.

"And sometimes, I don't get the visions in time to warn anyone or do anything, or they're super vague. More like impressions of things. But I don't try to bring them about or stop them. At least, not anymore. I just ride the wave."

"That makes sense, I guess."

"You already know I control the weather. Well, 'control' is a stretch. It's more like I influence it. That big storm earlier this year was my fault. When I have strong emotions, my power comes out in the form of weather."

I nodded, remembering that storm and what we talked about afterward. "So, when you heard Zane on the phone and thought he was just using you to get a story, your hurt and anger manifested as lightning and wind?"

"Exactly. I've learned how to acknowledge and accept my feelings instead of trying to control them, which helps. I can also do little things on command, such as bring a cool wind on a hot day. That helps to keep my magic from building up until it blows up. Besides the weather, I can also start fires. I'm not sure how that helps anyone unless we're roasting marshmallows, but Sofia said all magic is used to help others. She claims that the first witches came into existence because of a great need to help the people they loved."

I sighed. "That's a romantic notion." I paused, considering what my friends had said. An idea nudged its way to the front of my mind. "Wait. Jewels, you said you accepted your visions, and Jess, you just said you accepted your feelings. So, accepting the magic is the key to controlling it?"

Jessica grinned. "You are way ahead of the curve. It took me months to figure that out."

My thoughts whirled. "All I have to do is accept that I can freeze things?"

Jessica shook her head. "That's the beginning. You'll have to learn how your power manifests and how to keep it from accidentally freezing things when you don't want to. It's very important to keep Mundanes from realizing we're witches. Although I'm still not sure why when it seems like most of the people on the island are either witches or know about us. Sofia never really explained that to my satisfaction."

"I'm honestly surprised you kept it from me for this long. We've been best friends since grade school." My chest tightened, and I looked away from Jessica. "I have noticed some strange things, like how you always looked sad when it rained. Or the one time you were furious, and the power went out at Over the Moon. But I just figured they were freak accidents."

"I'm sorry. It was so hard to keep it a secret. I almost told you a few times, but it's against the rules. The Council determines who can know about us, and I haven't had a chance to ask them about you."

"But that doesn't matter now," Jewels said brightly. "You're a witch, too. And we're all friends and will be friends until the end of time."

"That's a long time," I said.

"I saw it in a vision," Jewels quipped.

Chapter 5: Sparring

The mats didn't feel intimidating anymore. That was new.

Three months ago, I'd walked into this class expecting to fumble through it, unsure if I could ever throw a punch without flinching. Now, my footing was solid. My stance came naturally. And while I wasn't about to enter a cage fight, I'd learned enough to think twice before backing down.

The room smelled faintly of rubber mats and industrial cleaner. Fluorescent lights buzzed overhead as half a dozen women trickled in, chatting nervously as they set down their bags. I spotted Evan kneeling beside a crate of red foam pads, pulling them out with practiced ease. He'd worn the same kind of t-shirt and joggers every class, but somehow, he still looked unfairly good doing it.

I dropped my gym bag by the back wall and joined Jessica as she adjusted her ponytail beside me.

She gave me a pointed once-over, then smirked. "Is that lip gloss?"

I blinked. "What?"

"Lip. Gloss." She leaned in slightly. "You really expect me to believe you're here to break noses and not hearts?"

I rolled my eyes, heat blooming in my cheeks. "It's tinted lip balm. My lips were dry."

"Sure, and I wear eyeliner to impress the punching bags." She elbowed me lightly. "Just saying, he is looking extra coachy tonight. Maybe he's wearing cologne."

I snorted a laugh. "He smells like gym mats and responsibility."

Jessica grinned. "And yet you keep showing up." She grabbed her water bottle, raising an eyebrow. "Admit it, you're only here because you like getting manhandled by my brother." She winked. "For the record, I'm fully supportive. Just don't go making me your maid of honor unless I get first dibs on cake flavors."

I opened my mouth to argue, but Evan's voice rang through the room, commanding attention.

"Let's circle up," he called, his tone casual but commanding. "Tonight, we're reviewing wrist grabs and pressure point escapes. I'll show you how to disarm someone with a knife, then we'll finish with some light sparring. Partners rotate every five minutes—no getting comfortable. No one leaves here without bruised pride or a boost in confidence."

A ripple of laughter ran through the group, and a few of the women smiled at him a little too brightly. I didn't blame them. With his broad shoulders, easy grin, and that calm, steady energy, he was crush material whether you'd known him for five minutes or fifteen years. But Evan was all business now.

"Grab a mat and stretch. If you've got earrings or necklaces, take them off. If you've got long hair—" his gaze flicked briefly in my direction, "—tie it back tight."

Jessica elbowed me. "See? He noticed your hair."

"Jess," I hissed.

"Just saying." She gave me a sly smile, clearly enjoying this way too much.

The warm-up was a blur. Muscle memory kicked in as we ran through stretches and stance drills. Then Evan handed out wrist pads and foam targets, patiently demonstrating each move. When he called for partners, I instinctively looked toward Jessica, but someone else had already scooped her up. Before I could retreat to the edge of the group, Evan stepped forward, holding out a practice pad.

"Want to give it a shot, Han?"

My stomach flipped. "Sure."

He showed me the stance first, gently adjusting my feet. His hands barely touched me, but the warmth of his palm brushing my elbow might as well have been a lightning strike. Still, his tone was all coach.

"Good. Now drive your palm right through the center. Aim like you mean it."

I did.

"Nice," he said, nodding with approval. "You've got more power than you think."

"You say that to all your students?" I asked, trying to sound casual.

He raised an eyebrow. "Only the ones who make me take a step back."

I bit the inside of my cheek to keep from grinning too hard. Maybe he was just being encouraging. Or maybe, just maybe, he noticed me too.

Either way, I couldn't deny it anymore—I was definitely in trouble.

Evan clapped his hands. "Alright, next up: wrist grabs. If someone grabs your arm, you need to break the hold and get out fast. I'll demo, then we'll pair up."

He called over one of the other students, a compact woman named Kara, and showed the technique in slow motion.

"When someone grabs your wrist like this," he said, holding her arm, "rotate toward the thumb, pull away, and step back. It's not about strength. It's about angles and speed."

After the demonstration, the women paired off again. I hesitated, expecting to join someone else this time, but Evan walked over and motioned toward me.

"Want to run it with me first?"

I nodded, trying to mask how my pulse quickened. "Sure," I said, hoping I sounded more confident than I felt.

He stood close, his hand outstretched. "I'm going to grab your wrist. Ready?"

I swallowed, nodding as my heart thudded harder in my chest.

He caught my wrist lightly. "Now break the hold."

I rotated my wrist and yanked back, but my angle was off. I stumbled, stepping forward instead of back, right into him.

Evan caught me without hesitation, steadying me with a hand on my waist. "Whoa," he said, with a flicker of concern in his voice. "You okay?"

"Yeah," I breathed, suddenly hyper-aware of how close we were. His hand was warm through the fabric of my shirt. I could smell the faint, clean scent of soap and whatever detergent he used. It was probably something basic, but it smelled amazing.

I stepped back quickly, cheeks warming. "Sorry. I think I zigged when I was supposed to zag."

He smiled, amused but professional. "That's okay. Here, let me show you again."

He guided my wrist through the motion, his fingers firm but gentle. "When someone grabs you, don't yank straight back. Rotate toward the thumb. It's the weak point. It's all about mechanics."

"I'm more of a music girl," I murmured without thinking.

Evan laughed, a low, surprised sound that lit up his entire face. "Then think of it like rhythm. The right movement at the right moment."

I glanced up at him, smiling despite myself. "Look at you. Turning self-defense into a sonnet."

"Only for you," he said, then blinked and coughed. "I mean, only if it helps."

It was my turn to laugh, though I kept my eyes on the mat. "Right."

He cleared his throat. "Okay. Let's try it again. This time, slow and steady."

I nodded, grateful for the shift in tone, but still feeling like every nerve in my arm remembered exactly where his fingers had been.

Around us, other women practiced, giggling or calling for help. But in that moment, with Evan showing me how to break free from a grip that wasn't entirely unwelcome, I wasn't thinking about the class.

I was thinking about how dangerous it was to fall for my best friend's brother. And how much harder it was not to.

When it was time to rotate through partners, I went through the usual cycle, first sparring with Jessica and then Kara.

Eventually, Evan rotated into my line.

"Ready to make me look bad again?" he asked, offering me a foam training knife.

"You're the one who said I should aim like I mean it," I said, twirling the dull blade in my hand.

"Remind me not to give you good advice anymore."

We moved through the sequence—attack, block, twist, disarm. The rhythm had become second nature now, our movements as synchronized as if we'd been practicing for years. Every time I blocked his strike, my body knew where to go before my mind had to catch up. His hands were steady, his movements controlled, and I matched them beat for beat.

The foam blade sliced through the air, and my hand snapped up to catch it with a fluid motion. Evan's strike came next—strong but controlled, just like all his movements. I blocked, twisting my torso to deflect the blow. He responded with a quick thrust toward my side, which I dodged by stepping back, shifting my weight. The entire exchange felt like a dance, one that had become ingrained in my muscles.

By now, we didn't need to speak. The unspoken communication between us was enough—his eyes would flicker for the slightest moment to signal a change in the sequence, and I'd follow without hesitation.

But somewhere between the third and fourth disarm, our hands locked around the foam blade.

For a heartbeat, neither of us moved.

His fingers brushed mine, a fleeting, electric touch. I could feel the heat of his chest just inches from mine, and the familiar scent of soap and laundry detergent made my breath catch. The weight of the moment settled in, thick and palpable, like the world had paused for us to just…be.

His gaze flickered to mine, and for a moment, the noise of the gym faded—the laughter, the slap of pads, the hum of fluorescent lights above us. It was just the two of us, standing in that small space, the foam blade forgotten in our locked grips.

I swallowed hard, my pulse pounding in my ears. His hazel eyes were intense, the quiet power in his focus enough to make me forget everything but the distance between us.

Then, like a flipped switch, he stepped back, his hand slipping from mine. His breath was steady, but there was a tightness around his mouth that hadn't been there before. He cleared his throat, breaking the moment.

"Nice form," he said, his voice low but steady, masking whatever had just passed between us. "You've come a long way."

"Thanks," I replied, my voice almost a whisper, my chest tight with something I couldn't quite name. Something inside me wanted to add *because of you*, but I didn't.

I couldn't.

Instead, I shifted my weight, adjusting the position of my feet. His gaze had already moved on, scanning the room, but I remained caught in the haze of that brief contact. Around us, the class carried on—laughter, sneakers sliding against the mats, the slap of pads being struck. The rhythm of the room returned, as though the moment had never existed at all.

But it had.

And I wasn't sure how to forget it.

We finished the drill, though my movements felt slower, less confident now. Evan was everywhere, guiding other students, adjusting their stances with the same calm precision he'd used with me. But for a few beats, I lingered in the space he'd left behind.

By the time class ended, I was exhausted. As I wiped sweat from my brow and picked up my bag, I felt Jessica sidle up beside me.

"You okay?" she asked, nudging me with her shoulder.

"Yeah, just tired."

She gave me a look that said *I know better,* but didn't push it. "You're getting good," she said. "Seriously. He's impressed."

"He says that to everyone."

Jessica smirked. "Not like that, he doesn't."

I glanced across the room. Evan was laughing with one of the newer students, his smile easy and warm. But every few seconds his eyes flicked back to me, just enough to make my breath catch. I slung my bag over my shoulder and turned away before I could read too much into it.

And I knew, deep down, that falling for my best friend's brother wasn't just dangerous.

It was inevitable.

Chapter 6: Magic Basics

The rest of the weekend passed in a blur. I kept busy with deep cleaning the cottage, decluttering my closet, and studiously ignoring my phone. Monday flowed quickly, almost too quickly, into Tuesday, and before I could fully process what was happening, I found myself sitting in Jessica's kitchen with a glass of wine.

Evan leaned against the counter, twisting his own glass of merlot in his hand. Jessica sat next to me, close enough for our shoulders to touch. That small contact eased some of my anxiety. I wasn't sure what to expect. Sofia sat across from us. She had requested tea, which Evan already had ready for her before she asked.

Sofia took a sip of her tea and leaned back in the chair, cradling the cup in her hands. She fixed her mousy-brown eyes on me. "How are you feeling, Hannah? I know it's a lot to come to terms with, and it's been a few days."

I nodded, and Jessica gave me a reassuring bump with her shoulder. "It's a lot, that's for sure. Nothing else has happened since then. Thanks to Evan."

He glanced at me with a small frown. "What did I do?"

"You, uh, shielded me. Right?"

"Oh, no. I can only shield people I can see, and I have to be close enough. From what we can tell," he gestured to Sofia, "my range is about a quarter of a mile."

My stomach sank. "And I haven't seen you since the party."

"Right, but you said nothing's happened. So why are you worried?" Jessica asked.

"Because it means it can happen again." I gulped some wine and immediately wished I hadn't as a fit of coughing came over me.

Jessica pounded me on the back, and Evan handed me a glass of water. When I recovered, my eyes still watering, I said, "I hoped if Evan could keep me shielded, I wouldn't have to worry."

"Unfortunately, that's not how magic works," Sofia said. "You need to learn to control it. It's something every witch has to learn. And my job is to teach you. So, we'll start with the basics." She shifted in her seat, placing her mug on the table. "The first thing is to learn how to ground and center."

Jessica groaned. "I'm sure you'll be better at this than I was."

I looked at her, my eyes wide. "Is it difficult?"

"Not for someone like you who regularly does yoga," she said. "I haven't practiced yoga in a long time, and grounding and centering requires similar mindfulness."

Sofia nodded. "That's a very good way to look at it. Now, sit with your feet on the floor and close your eyes."

I did as she said, straightening my back and letting my hands relax in my lap.

"Good. Now, focus on your core, the place where your magic resides," Sofia continued.

"Mine feels like a warm ball in my belly," Jessica added.

"I sense it as a solid spot in my chest," Evan said.

"Each witch's core feels different to them. You will learn how yours feels. See if you can find it. Breath softly."

I allowed my breathing to slow and let my mind turn inward. The familiar meditation exercise calmed my nerves. I tried searching for something inside me that felt like my friends described.

"It's okay if you can't find it this time." Sofia's voice gently broke the silence. "Now, I want you to envision the clean energy of the earth coming up from the ground, through the foundations of the house, through the floor, and into the soles of your feet. This energy flows up into your legs, belly, chest, arms, shoulders, head, and finally exits the top of your head where it spills out around you, forming a cocoon."

I tried to visualize what she said, but it seemed impossible. I couldn't sense any energy coming from the earth, and the only thing flowing through me was the wine I drank too fast. Not only could I not find my center, but I also couldn't use the earth's energy. Some witch I was turning out to be.

"Once you feel the energy completely surrounding you, allow any excess energy to go back into the earth. Then, when you're ready, open your eyes."

I took another deep inhale and opened my eyes. Sofia smiled.

"How do you feel now?" she asked.

"Calm and focused," I said. "But I couldn't find my core or feel the energy."

She nodded. "That's to be expected. This is an exercise I want you to do every day. Eventually, it will be second nature. And soon you will be able to feel both your core and the energy around you."

Jessica shook her head in agreement. "It took a while for me, too. Sometimes it's still hard."

"The other thing you need to do is learn how your magic responds. Keep a record of when you use it and what happened. It will help me to know how to train you."

"Wait, what do you mean 'when' I use it? I don't know how it happened the first time." I shook my head, frustrated.

"Of course, you don't. What I mean is, when it comes out, make a note of it."

"You mean it can just...freeze things at any point it wants?" My chest tightened, and black spots floated in my vision.

"Breathe, Hannah," Evan commanded.

His voice triggered an automatic response due to months of training with him, and I sucked in a deep breath. He always reminded us to breathe because in self-defense, breath powers our moves. Sometimes I would hold my breath during a new exercise, and he would remind me to breathe, like he just did.

Sofia shook her head. "Your magic is uncontrolled right now. It may come out when you don't expect it. Part of the grounding exercise is to keep your mind focused so, hopefully, you will avoid the unintentional use of your power."

"And what is it, the name of it?"

"Suspension magic, dear. It's a rare ability. I've only heard of one other witch in my time who had it, my grandmother's friend."

"Can we ask her how to control it, then? I can't just go around town suspending people."

She smiled ruefully. "I wish we could. She died a few years ago."

"Of course." I slumped in my chair. Jessica nudged my wineglass to me, and I took a sip.

"We currently meet twice a week for practice," Sofia's wave encompassed Jessica and Evan. "Sometimes Jewels joins us, but since her power is solely internal, we haven't managed to figure out how to make her visions come when she wants them to. It's different from using divination tools. Anyway, you will join us and together, we will figure out how you can manage your magic."

"It'll take time, but you'll get there," Jessica said encouragingly.

"And, Evan, do you have your copy of the *Willowbrook Witch History Guide*?"

"Yes, it's upstairs."

"Give it to Hannah before she leaves today, please. Hannah, it's the history book of our island, the true history. Old John could give you a summary, and his story would probably be more interesting than reading the book, but it's important for you to read it over."

I almost spluttered on my wine again. "Old John is a witch?"

Jessica and Evan laughed.

"Could you imagine?" Jessica said.

Sofia shook her head. "No. He's a storyteller, and essentially the Circle's record keeper. Old John doesn't have magic, but he knows of us. He writes the current history for future witches. The Council found it easier to give him a job than to try to keep him quiet."

I giggled then. "That sounds like Old John."

"Yes, well, read the history, and talk to him if you'd like." She glanced at her watch. "It's almost dinnertime, so we'll eat and then start a full lesson."

"On it," Evan said, and picked up his phone. "I'm ordering from Dave's Deli, so let me know what you would like."

"My usual," Jessica and I said in unison.

Evan just rolled his eyes.

"I'll have the garden salad and soup of the day," Sofia said.

Evan called the deli and placed our order. "He said about fifteen minutes. Anyone want to go with me to get it?"

"I'll go," I said.

Jessica wiggled her eyebrows at me. I ducked my head to conceal the blush that I knew tinted my skin, pretending to tie my shoe.

Jessica turned to her brother. "Don't forget the—"

"Cookies," Evan finished for her. "I won't. Come on, Hannah. We need to stop at the grocery store."

Standing, I said, "I don't think I'll want a cookie after my sandwich. I'm usually very full after eating at the deli."

Jessica laughed. "They're for after practice. Trust me, you'll want one then."

Evan gestured to the door. "After you."

We went out the door that led into the backyard and then through the gate to the driveway. He followed me to the passenger side of his truck and opened the door for me.

"Thanks, but you don't have to wait on me."

"Need to make sure you don't slip getting in." He grinned.

I turned and grabbed the handle, stepping onto the running board. I felt his hand at my waist, his fingertips just brushing my hip as he steadied me. It really was a long way up to get into his truck, which must be why my breath caught.

"Thanks," I squeaked out as I settled onto the seat.

"You're welcome." His hazel eyes crinkled at the edges as he smiled at me before shutting the door and going around to the driver's side, where he easily stepped into the truck. Starting the motor, he asked, "How are you really doing with all this magic stuff?"

I shrugged. "Honestly? I'm not sure. It's a lot to take in, and it sounds unbelievable."

He nodded, smoothly maneuvering the vehicle onto the street. "Sometimes I still find it impossible. And then other times, I can't imagine life without my abilities. I think it's something we'll all get used to eventually."

"I suppose," I said, although I didn't really think I would ever get used to magic or being considered a witch.

"Well, we're finally here, after a long and dusty journey across a total of three minutes," Evan quipped, pulling into a parking spot along the curb.

"Such an exhausting trip." I unbuckled my seatbelt and hopped out of the truck before he could come around to help me. "I may need a refreshment after that," I said in my best Southern drawl.

"Let's see what we can do about that." He mimicked my Southern accent, and I laughed.

We entered Stan's and headed to the bakery. I continued to the drink cases while Evan picked up a container of chocolate chip cookies. He joined me just as I pulled out a flavored sparkling water.

"Hmm. I'll take a root beer. And I should probably bring something back for Jessica and Sofia, too. I know Jessica wants an orange Crush. What do you think Sofia would like?"

I shrugged. "I don't really know her, but maybe a ginger ale?"

"Done and done. Let's go."

I followed him to the checkout, intending to get my own drink, but he tugged it from my hand and placed it on the conveyor. "My treat."

"Thank you," I said. I appreciated a man who wanted to take care of me, and yet I refused to be treated like I couldn't take care of myself. So, while he finished running his card, I took the grocery bags. When he went to take the bags from me, I shook my head. "I can carry two bags, Evan."

"Yes, ma'am," he said, giving me a mock salute and holding the door open for me.

I rolled my eyes. "I'm not the boss of you."

"Not yet," he replied with a wink.

What does that mean?

I deposited the bags on the seat of his truck, and we walked the half-block to the deli. This time, he didn't complain when I took one of the bags, but he shook his head in slight disapproval. Once again, he helped me into the truck. A little shiver ran down my spine when his thumb accidentally grazed my bare skin above the waistband of my jeans.

Back at the house he shared with his sister since their parents' death, we gathered the dinner and went into the kitchen.

"Your adventurers have returned," he announced as he entered.

"Fantastic, I'm starving," Jessica said.

"It was a long and arduous journey, filled with many obstacles," I said dramatically. "Mostly, what Sofia would like to drink." I handed her the ginger ale.

"Oh, this is my favorite. Thank you." Sofia beamed at us.

We passed the food around then ate in ravenous silence for a few minutes.

Sofia finished her soup and broke the companionable silence as she drizzled dressing over her garden salad. "Hannah, for tonight's practice, I want you to start off observing. Jessica and Evan, you will work together at first."

Jessica nodded and quickly swallowed a bite of her club sandwich before asking, "What would you like me to do?"

Sofia frowned in thought for a moment before saying, "Lightning bolts. I think you could use more control over how they are formed and where they land."

For the third time that evening, I almost choked. "Lightning bolts?"

"Weather witch, remember?" Jessica tapped her chest. "This will be fun. Ready, brother?"

Evan wiped his fingers with a paper napkin. "Always."

Bemused, I followed them outside. The fall day still held a hint of summer, and now I wondered if it was because Jessica was so happy with Zane. She did say the weather responded to her emotions, after all.

Sofia settled into one of the white wicker patio chairs and gestured for me to sit. As I sat, I adjusted the turquoise pillow behind my back so I could sit straight instead of leaning back comfortably, like Sofia. I twirled a strand of hair around my finger, clamping a hand on my leg when I realized my knee was bouncing from nerves. Jessica and Evan walked to the center of the yard and stood about ten feet apart, facing each other. Evan turned his head toward me and winked before focusing on his sister.

"Okay, Hannah. Now watch. I want you to see if you can sense their magic. Or even see it, other than the physical manifestation of the lightning. Begin." She directed the last word to the others with a slight wave of her hand, like a queen bestowing a favor.

A sudden flash of light hit the ground near Evan. He grinned and shook his pointer finger at Jessica. "Uh-uh. I'm already shielded."

Jessica narrowed her eyes. Another bolt of electricity pulled from blue skies jumped toward Evan, this one larger than the last. I leaned forward in my seat. I almost thought I saw a shimmer around Evan when the lightning struck his shield, but it might have been my imagination or wishful thinking. This time, I saw her flick her fingers just before the lightning appeared. It seemed to get closer to him than the first few strikes. Evan's brown hair rose from static electricity, and he grunted.

"That's a point for you," he said.

"Feeling shocked?" She asked with a feral smile.

"It won't happen again."

With another flick of her fingers, a larger bolt struck out, but Evan must have expanded his shields because it didn't get within three feet of him.

"Okay, enough, you two. You are obviously evenly matched," Sofia called out. "Jessica, did all of your strikes hit where you intended?"

She nodded. "All but the first one."

"And that was the only time you didn't flick your fingers," I blurted out, then covered my mouth with a hand.

"No, it's okay, Hannah. We're in a safe space to learn here. What did you notice?" Sofia asked.

I dropped my hand to my lap. "Well, I saw Jess sort of move her fingers just before a lightning bolt would appear."

Jessica nodded. "It seemed to help direct the energy."

"What else did you see?"

I hesitated but figured it wouldn't be any crazier than freezing dishes in midair. "I thought I saw Evan's shield once. It was just a glimmer, almost like light playing on water."

"Which time was that?" Sofia pressed.

I thought back. "Uh, the second."

"Good! That is when Jessica's power collided with Evan's. He didn't stop her magic with his shield. Instead, his shield absorbed it, for lack of a better word. And when the two powers met, it caused the energy to be visible."

I nodded slowly. "So, it's sort of like when oil and water meet and there's a line, but the two are together."

"Exactly."

"We'll make a proper witch of you yet," Jessica said.

Sofia nodded agreement. "Let's take a break. Is there iced tea?"

"I'll get the cookies," Evan said.

Chapter 7: Catalyst

Once Evan and Jessica returned from the kitchen, they sank into the other patio chairs. The cooling evening air was heavy with the scent of lilacs from the bush next to the back door. I found it strange that the bush bloomed at all times of the year, but figured it had to do with Jessica's mother's love of gardening. Or maybe it was magic? Whatever it was, the scent relaxed me. Jessica handed out tall glasses of iced tea while Evan opened the plastic clamshell of store-bought cookies.

"Here," Evan said, passing me a chocolate chip cookie. "You're going to need the sugar."

I took a sip of the lightly sweetened tea. The first stars were just beginning to twinkle overhead.

"Did you hear about Red Helix coming to the island?" Jessica asked, grabbing a cookie for herself. "The whole island is talking about it."

"Of course, it is," I said. "For the first time, a rock band will be performing in Willowbrook. I'm shocked the mayor agreed."

"Red Helix started in Seattle last year," Jessica said. "They're playing all the local venues to get a following."

"I've heard some of their music," Evan commented. "Catchy stuff."

"I first heard them play at a nightclub," Sofia added.

Evan choked on his cookie. "You heard them *where?*"

"Oh, don't look so scandalized, Evan," Sofia chided with a laugh. "They have some very good songs about inclusivity and environmental conservation. I particularly like the one called 'Losing Green,' which sounds like it's a love song, but it's really about how the green spaces in our cities are being paved over."

Jessica smiled. "And I thought you couldn't surprise me anymore."

"So, we're going, right?" Evan drained the last of his iced tea, then stood and looked at me.

"Absolutely," Jessica replied. "Hannah, you in? I'm sure Jewels will come."

I grinned. "The city finally allows a rock band to play instead of the string quartet? I'm definitely not missing it. And I like some of their songs, too." *Plus, I'll get to see Evan's dance moves.*

"Let's make a plan for Saturday night, then." Jessica stood and stretched. "Now, who's ready for some magic?"

"I'm ready for round two," Evan said.

"Good," Sofia said. "Jessica, you pair up with Hannah this time. I want you to create something small. A little snow flurry or flame. Tiny, mind you. Hannah, your job is to suspend only what Jessica makes. Nothing else. Focus your power so you only affect what you want to affect."

My stomach twisted, and I nodded uncertainly. Recalling the conversation with Jewels and Jessica the night of Zane's party, I muttered under my breath, "I accept I am a witch. I accept I can freeze things."

"What was that?" Sofia asked.

"Nothing. Just thinking."

"Hmm. Well, focus. Let's see what you can do. Evan, be ready with a shield."

He nodded and gave me an encouraging smile.

Jessica and I moved to stand a little away from her back patio. On the opposite side was her garden—a spiral of plants that seemed to bloom and grow at impossible times.

"Ready?" she asked.

"Uh, sure."

"Take a moment to ground and center, first," Sofia said from the safety of the chair on the patio.

I flushed. I told Sofia I didn't think I found my center, but maybe just breathing and calming my nerves would help. I closed my eyes and envisioned magic in my belly. I still had no idea where it really resided, but it seemed as good a place as any. Then I tried to imagine it expanding to fill me. When I felt full to bursting, I pushed. I didn't know what else to call it when I shoved the extra energy from me to the ground. I honestly had no idea if I was doing it right.

When I opened my eyes, Jessica smiled at me. She flicked her hand, and a narrow stream of flame shot skyward.

I flung my hands out. Nothing happened. The fire stream remained steady.

I tried again, more desperately, lifting one hand like a crossing guard, and thought, *Stop.*

Still nothing.

Frowning, I tried again. "Stop," I said out loud. The flame still soared to the sky.

"Enough for now, Jessica," Sofia said.

"What am I doing wrong?" I watched as Jessica's fire dissipated.

"It's your first time." Sofia said calmly. "Did you feel your magic before we started?"

"I think so, but I'm not sure."

"Don't worry. It takes time to connect. Let's try again. It might just take a few times for you to find your way." Sofia smiled.

"Wait, I have an idea." With long strides, Evan went to his sister and whispered something in her ear.

Jessica's grin widened. She turned back to me, mischief sparkling in her eyes. "Let's go, Hannah."

Sighing, I reset my stance and waited for her to do something with her magic. Jessica clenched her fists, then opened one palm toward me. A small fireball flew straight at my head.

With a yelp, I ducked, barely avoiding getting burned. "What the hell, Jess?"

She just smiled like a cat toying with a mouse.

Another fireball shot at me. I dodged again, but I wasn't quite fast enough, or her aim was better, as it singed my sleeve.

"She's attacking me?" I sputtered. "Seriously?"

I narrowed my eyes, waiting for her next move. I watched her hands, and the fingers on her left hand twitched. I started to move, but then I saw the fireball from her right hand. It was a little bigger than the first two and moving faster.

"Knock it off!" I yelled, raising my arms instinctively.

But the impact never came. Slowly, I lowered my arms and stared. The fireball froze only inches from my face. Its heat was palpable, but the flames were unnaturally still.

I glared at Jessica. "Some stunt," I grumbled. Then I noticed she wasn't moving either. My mouth formed a silent oh, and I looked to Evan and Sofia.

Evan clapped. Sofia looked pleased.

"Well done," Sofia said. "Apparently, Evan knew just how to push you."

"I could have been burned!" I shouted.

"Nah, I wouldn't have let that happen," Evan said easily. "My shield skills are faster than that. You were never in real danger."

"Truly?"

"I promise. I won't ever let anything bad happen to you." He sounded determined.

I gave him a weak smile, and my heart gave a slow thump. "What about Jessica?"

"Come over here and let's see how long it takes to wear off." Sofia patted the chair next to her.

I glanced nervously at Jessica but went and sat in the wicker chair, once again adjusting the pillow behind my back. "How long has it been?"

Evan tilted his phone toward me so we could watch the timer. We sat there in silence, watching Jessica and the fireball for any sign of movement.

One minute. Then five.

I began to worry. What if it were permanent? The first time was with dishes that wouldn't be hurt if the effects never wore off.

At seven minutes, I thought I saw Jessica's eyelid flicker, but it could have been a shadow.

At eight minutes, the fireball suddenly continued its path, and Evan waved a nonchalant hand. It stopped again, hovering in midair this time with the flames flickering like fire should.

I stood and went to Jessica, looking at her intently. Then she gasped, took a shaky breath, and focused on me.

"You did it!" she cried, pulling me into a hug and spinning me around.

"Nine minutes, twelve seconds," Evan announced.

"Hmm. I wonder if it will always be the same length. Evan, keep track of that during practice, would you? And get rid of that fireball."

In an instant, the fireball began to move again but then snuffed out, leaving a puff of smoke.

"How did you do that?" I asked. *I would have to get used to that.*

Evan answered, "I released the shield, and Jessica reclaimed her energy. She's unique in that she can pull it back into her or send it to something else, hopefully something useful."

"I can almost always send it to something useful now, depending on the magic, of course," Jessica added.

"Of course," I murmured. I mean, it made perfect sense if one was feeling insane. Which I was.

"How do you feel, Jessica?" Sofia heaved her bulk from the chair, and Jessica went to stand in front of her.

"Fine. Absolutely normal."

"Make magic." Sofia commanded. Was there a hint of worry in her voice?

Jessica flicked her fingers, and light rain sprinkled us. "Do you want more?" Another wicked smile crossed her face.

"Humph. No, that's good enough, thank you. I don't want to walk home soaking wet and have to explain myself to everyone I pass." Turning to me, Sofia said, "Your catalyst for accessing your power is definitely related to the desire for a certain outcome. It appears that it's related to things that will directly affect you. We'll explore that. Next time."

My face must have reflected trepidation because Sofia smiled reassuringly. I never could hide my emotions behind a facade.

"Go eat, all of you. I'll see you next week."

I frowned. "But we just had dinner."

Sofia gave me a wink. "You'll see."

She picked up her rather large pink leather purse and let herself out the garden gate. Just as the latch fell into place, my stomach growled, loud and obnoxious.

Evan laughed and slung an arm around my shoulders. "Come on. We've got leftover lasagna."

My breath hitched. I loved the feel of his arm around me.

"And cookies," Jessica added, picking up the clamshell container. "We always have cookies after practice."

We filed into the kitchen. The signs of their parents were still everywhere, little touches of their parents that would probably always be there. The ceramic cookie jar painted with little blue stars that Diana, their mother, had made when she was in college still sat on the counter. Michael's green coffee mug with the words "World's Best Husband" still hung on the cup tree next to the coffeemaker. I knew their bedroom upstairs was still how they had left it six months ago.

"Coffee," Jessica said, pulling a foil bag out of the cupboard.

"Lasagna," Evan said at the same time, grinning.

"Yes to both," I said with a laugh.

Jessica brewed coffee while Evan reheated plates. She brushed her fingers lightly over her dad's mug before grabbing others for us.

I looked down at the worn kitchen table, tracing a scratch with my finger. Guilt pinched my stomach. I wanted to apologize to her. Here I was, discovering the identity of my father and considering meeting him, perhaps building a relationship with him, while Jessica would never get another chance to talk to her parents.

Evan dropped a plate in front of me, thick with cheesy lasagna. My stomach growled again at the scent of tomato sauce and cheese. I guess guilt didn't surpass magically induced hunger. We ate in silence for a few minutes. By the speed the pasta disappeared from Evan's plate, I could only assume he was as hungry as I was.

"Okay, I see what you mean about being hungry after magic practice, but can someone please explain to me why I'm starving and eating like a hobbit?" I asked, stabbing another bite.

Evan swallowed and said, "It's expended energy. Sort of like physical exercise. You know how you're a little hungry after self-defense class?" When I nodded, he continued, "Magic is the same way. You spent energy, and it needs to be replenished. Jess here can pull energy from living things around her, so she doesn't technically need to eat after a working."

"But," Jessica interjected, "if I pull too much energy from nature, it could be destructive. I could harm a plant, animal, or even person. So, instead, I eat."

"Finished?" Evan took our empty plates to the sink and returned with the cookie container. He handed me another gooey chocolate chip cookie.

"Thanks."

"Okay, now that we're recovering, it's time to spill." Jessica leaned forward and looked at me intently.

"Spill?"

"Did you call your mom?"

Oh. That.

"Not yet. I'm still debating. Do I talk to Jamison first? Get his side of things and then talk to my mom? Or do I confront her?"

Jessica reached over and touched my shoulder. "I know your relationship with your mom is hard. But she had to have a good reason for keeping your father from you. If it were me, I would talk to her." Her voice was quiet, almost wistful.

"Call her," Evan said. "Your dad has waited this long."

I nodded, biting into the cookie and letting the chocolate melt on my tongue, wishing my problems could melt just as easily.

Chapter 8: Mother Dearest

"**C**harlotte Stewart."

My mother's perfunctory greeting when she answered the phone made me think she must be busy. This might not go my way.

"Hi, Mom."

"Hannah? Is everything okay? It's Wednesday."

I always called her on Sundays. I would give her any updates, which weren't many, and she would tell me about her latest book club meeting. The calls never lasted longer than ten minutes.

"I know. I'm fine. Well, mostly. I'm not hurt." I rushed to reassure her. Despite our strained relationship, I knew my mother loved me.

"What's wrong? I have a meeting in a few minutes. No, the other report." She directed the last sentence to someone in her office.

"I'm on break so I need to get back soon, too. Can I come see you soon? I need to talk to you."

"Can we schedule a call? Yes, that's the one. Call Tom and tell him I'm on the way."

"Mom, I really need this to be in person."

"Fine. Schedule." I heard her snap her fingers. "Looks like I'm free Friday evening, for once. My dinner appointment had to reschedule. We can meet at the restaurant. Seven?"

By "the restaurant" I knew she meant Bateau, an upscale French restaurant in midtown she preferred, especially for meeting clients. Most likely, her canceled dinner appointment was supposed to be there, and she didn't want to cancel the reservation. I agreed and quickly said goodbye. The day after tomorrow would hopefully bring answers.

My mother never wanted to talk about my dad. I don't think she realized how painful it was to be one of the few kids in class who didn't even know who their dad was.

The first time I asked about him, I was eight. The school had a Father's Day celebration, and Jessica's dad sat with both of us for lunch, including me in each event and even dancing with me during one of the songs. "Where's my dad?" I had asked my mom when I got home that afternoon.

My mother had barely glanced up from her laptop, her tone clipped, impersonal. "He made his choice. And now we move on."

I figured out the truth when I was twelve—not in some dramatic revelation, but in the quiet moments, the empty ones. The way my mother never asked about my day. How she filled her life with work and social events, always just busy enough to keep me at arm's length. I noticed she never said, "I love you," unless someone else was around to hear it.

She never wanted to be a mother. She just tolerated it.

I shook my head to clear my thoughts from my reverie. I had to go back to work. I hurried across the street from the park and into Over the Moon Books and Coffee. Old John was sitting at his usual table with the rest of the Crony Crew. Jessica had her back to the door as she pulled smoothie ingredients out of the fridge.

"Be right with you!" She called without looking.

"It's me," I said as I slid behind the counter and took a quick glance at the rest of the room.

"Oh. Hi! I'm glad you're here." She smiled at me then efficiently added fruit, milk, and protein powder to the blender.

A small group of young moms sat on the couches in the corner, their children playing with the toys in front of them. A brief yearning bloomed inside my heart, but I quickly smashed it down. Besides the Crony Crew and the group of mothers, the place was empty.

"Where's the after-school rush? It's three."

"Mmm, I think there's a game today. Hold on." Jessica pressed the button on the blender. "Did you have a nice break?" She asked when it quit.

"Yes. I called my mom."

"Really? And? Wait, let me get this out." She dumped the smoothie into a cup, smashed a lid on top, and stuck a straw in. "Hazel," she called, leaving the smoothie on the pickup counter. One of the mothers came over to claim it. "Okay, now. Tell me." She leaned on hip against the back counter and crossed her arms.

I shrugged and straightened the stack of cups next to the register. "There's nothing to tell. I called her and she worked me into her schedule where she had a cancelation."

"Seriously? That woman, who gave birth to you and raised you, by the way, can't be bothered to make extra time for you?"

The air temperature in the room rose a little with her words. Prickles of sweat broke out on my neck, and I fanned my face with one hand.

"Crap," she muttered. I watched as she took a deep breath. "Sometimes I still forget when I get angry. It's always the anger that gets me."

"Your," I looked around to make sure no one had moved closer to us then lowered my voice even further, "magic?"

Jessica laughed. "Yup. The weather, the air, the plants, all affected. Anyway, how do you feel? Aren't you angry?"

"About my mom? No. This is how it's always been since she landed this job. I'm used to it. Besides, if Jamison can't wait a couple more days for a response, then I don't want him in my life." My own words stung, but I didn't take them back. I meant every one.

"I'm here for you, Hannah. You know that, right?"

"Even if this is hard for you?"

"Hard for me? What do you mean?"

I looked at the scuffed toe of my right boot and shifted my weight a little so I could rub it on my other boot. "Well, it's just that, my father shows up and you've lost your parents. It seems a little unfair, especially considering how great your parents were."

She grabbed both of my hands in hers. "Hannah, look at me." She waited until I raised my eyes to meet hers. "My parents were great. They were the best parents I could ask for. But you getting to know your dad has nothing to do with that. You're still my best friend, and I will support you."

Tears stung my eyes, and I blinked rapidly. "Thank you," I whispered.

Just then, the bell over the door chimed. Jessica released my hands and turned to greet the customer while I turned my back to the counter and pretended to clean the prep area until I thought I could interact with people without crying.

About an hour before closing, a bunch of high schoolers came in, rowdy in their excitement. So, there was a game. I think maybe football? I didn't follow sports that closely. Okay, I didn't follow sports at all. One guy was giving a girl a piggyback ride as they entered.

They seemed orderly enough as they placed their orders, telling Jessica thank you and saying they wouldn't stay too long. I eyed my friend as I made mochas and Lotuses and Red Bulls. I wondered if she realized how much even the kids of this town respected her. She always did her best to stay on the fringes of community, but they valued her.

Once the last kid had paid, Jessica moved to help me get the drinks out, taking over the espresso machine while I focused on the cold drinks. After a few years of working together, we had a system. Jessica expertly pulled shots and steamed the milk, creating mochas and lattes. I scooped ice into cups and poured the energy drinks. Bottles of flavorings moved between us in a dance, each of us calling out the name of the syrup we needed and reaching to take it without looking. As soon as the last drink was served, we both automatically moved on to the closing tasks of wiping tables and stacking chairs before sweeping. Jessica would count the register last in case we had a late arrival.

The bell rang again, and I quietly groaned. Please, not another group. I glanced over my shoulder to see Zane striding in.

"Hey," he said. "Looks like business is good." He leaned over the counter and gave Jessica a quick kiss on the cheek.

"Football game. Looks like our team won." Jessica made a shooing motion to get Zane to step to one side so she could sweep in front of the counter.

"Well, I am here to walk you both home. When you're ready, of course."

"We can manage," I said. "Well, I can, anyway. Since I'm in the opposite direction from Jessica."

"Nope." Zane shook his head. "The visiting team hasn't quite cleared out yet and some of the spectators are celebrating at Ironwood. Evan had a class tonight, and I'm under strict orders."

"Zane and Evan are both a little overprotective since that incident." Jessica almost rolled her eyes at her boyfriend.

"I don't blame them," I replied. "A couple of drunks from the city corner you and you wonder why the men in your life are protective." I gave her a mock glare before smiling at Zane. "I'd be happy for an escort home."

"No Jewels?" Zane looked around, trying to spot our 80s dressing friend.

"It's her day off." Jessica nudged him again, and he moved to stand a few more feet away from where she was sweeping.

The teenagers filed out with a chorus of "thank you" and "goodbye." I hoped they were all going home, and that the girls had escorts like we did. Even as a teenager, I didn't attend the games, preferring to stay in the library or at home with a book. I had heard of afterparties, but surely, they were going home. It was a Wednesday, after all.

Jessica locked the door behind the last of them, flipped most of the lights off, and turned the open sign off. "Zane, can you take out the trash while I pull the register? We're mostly finished, otherwise."

"Aye, aye, captain." He saluted her, and this time she did roll her eyes but smiled.

"What else needs cleaning, Hannah?"

"Just the coffee machine. I've got it."

Fifteen minutes later, we were ready to leave. I grabbed my purse from behind the counter and followed Jessica out of Over the Moon. She locked the doors, and we stepped onto a hushed Main Street. The park across the way glowed invitingly in the setting sun. It surprised me to see it so empty already.

"Really, I think I'm fine," I said to Zane.

"No can do, little lady." He slung an arm around Jessica and then me. "I've got to make sure my girls are safe," he said with an old west accent.

"Okay, cowboy." I shrugged his arm off. "Let's go then."

Zane and Jessica talked about the next issue of the *Willowbrook Chronicle*, set to come out that weekend. I walked slightly behind them, tuning their conversation out. How would I approach my mom about this? Start off during the appetizer or wait until dessert? Maybe if I wait until she drank glass or two of wine, I had a better chance of getting some answers out of her. She always got chatty when she had wine. I knew she never drank with clients for that reason. But since it was just me, maybe if I ordered a bottle of wine…although, the wine at Bateau cost more than I made in tips in a week. But it might be worth it.

All too soon, we were at my little cottage I shared with Jewels. The lights were on, and I wondered if Jewels had attempted to cook dinner. She was still learning but would occasionally try something we had made together before.

"Thank you for walking me home."

"Of course. I'm adopting Jessica's sense that friends are family, so I would be a poor relative if I didn't make sure you arrived safely."

The formality of his words reminded me that he came from money.

"See you tomorrow." Jessica hugged me.

"Good night."

They waited to leave until I was safely inside.

The smells wafting from the kitchen were delicious. "No way," I muttered, walking through the small living room and the archway that separated the kitchen from the rest of the house.

"Hi!" Jewels said brightly. She was sitting at the table painting her fingernails a bright shade of green that was almost painful to look at. "Dinner is in the oven, keeping warm. I'll eat as soon as this hand is dry." She wiggled her fingers at me then blew on her nails.

"What did you make? It smells divine."

She giggled as I opened the oven and saw two foil pans. "I can't cook like this. Takeout from Rosita's. Enchiladas. Chicken for you, beef for me. But we can trade if you want."

"No, chicken sounds great. Thank you." I pulled the pans out and removed the lids.

"Wine?" Jewels asked.

I remembered what I thought about my mom on the way home. "Uh, not tonight. I'll just have water."

"Make it two, please."

I filled two glasses with ice water and moved everything to the table.

"Dry yet?" I asked, stabbing my fork into the enchilada.

She peered at her nails. "Almost. How was your day?"

"It was good. I have a meeting with my mom on Friday."

"Oh? I'm still willing to be backup. I could hang out someplace nearby. Where are you meeting her?"

"Her favorite French restaurant. I'm okay, though. I'll ask Jessica if I can borrow her car and take the ferry over. That will at least save me cab fare."

"Let me know if you change your mind. I'm always up for adventures."

Laughing, I said, "Oh, I know that. Listen, I've been meaning to ask you something." I dragged my fork though the refried beans before setting it down. "When you first started having visions, you said you felt like you might be crazy, right? You went to group counseling, and that's where Jessica met you. Was she also there because she felt insane? I'm sure it was from grief, but still."

Jewels took a long drink of water before answering. "First of all, you are not crazy. Yes, I thought I might have been. My parents told me I was unstable. The group counseling isn't what it seems to be. I mean, it's definitely therapeutic for those who aren't baby witches."

"I don't understand."

"When powers manifest in Mundanes, often they don't have anyone close to them who can explain it. Jessica didn't. Neither did I. So, we feel like we're losing touch with reality. It is insane to think I could have visions of the future. I thought I was dreaming or imagining the dreams. Or making things up without realizing it, especially when my parents suggested that was the case. I started going to that therapy group under protest. My parents said I either went to counseling to get my head on straight or I went to a live-in facility."

"That's terrible!" I couldn't imagine. My mother was distant, but at least she never threatened to have me committed.

"Yeah, so I went to therapy hoping I could figure out what was wrong with me and somehow stop it. Much the same reason Jess went. Turns out, that group exists solely to find new witches in our area who don't have mentors. Once a person accepts their powers, they are told the truth by a mentor and start training."

"But Sofia lives here." I tried to wrap my mind around a therapy group that also acted like a witch-to-be screening service.

"Yes. And her circumstances with Jessica must be special because I never saw Sofia at therapy. That's a story you'll have to ask them. But the bottom line is you are perfectly sane. You're just a witch who needs to learn how to control your powers." She took another bite of her enchilada then talked around it. "Speaking of, how did practice go? You were asleep when I got home yesterday."

I felt comforted knowing that my nervousness about this was normal. As we finished our dinners, I told her about the fireballs. She burst out laughing when I said Evan actually asked his sister—my best friend, by the way—to aim fireballs at me instead of near me.

"Gee, thanks," I grumbled.

"I'm sorry. It just seems like such an Evan thing to do, don't you think? He's a bit of prankster."

"I suppose," I admitted.

My phone dinged, and I dug it out of the bottom of my purse. A message from Evan appeared on the screen. **Glad you made it home. Tomorrow, I'll walk you myself.**

Chapter 9: Butterflies

"You look fantastic," Jewels said, coming around the counter at Over the Moon to hug me.

"Thanks. I figured dinner with my mother warranted more effort."

I had chosen my outfit carefully—black wide-leg trousers with a subtle sheen, a tailored dark-red blouse that tucked in cleanly, and a structured black jacket that made me stand straighter. Underneath, I wore a soft silk camisole in muted silver, like a whisper of moonlight only I could feel. I kept the jewelry minimal: small silver hoops, my grandmother's watch, and a ring Jessica had given me with a smooth hematite stone. Even my makeup was a touch sharper with defined eyes, matte lips, and high cheekbones. Altogether, the look felt like armor: polished, impenetrable, and deliberate.

"Call if you need anything. I mean it. And I'll be at your house until you get there." Jess handed me her keys.

"You don't have to do that, Jess." I twisted her car keys in my hand. "I'm sure it will be fine."

"Fine or not, we want to know how it went."

Jewels nodded emphatically. "Yes, and we will have ice cream waiting."

My chest tightened. These women were literally the best friends anyone could ask for. "Thank you. I'll text when I'm on the way back."

"Okay, go. Do your errand, then see your mom. We'll stop by Stan's for supplies after we lock up." Jessica hugged me.

"Remember, it's okay to get up and leave if you don't want to be there anymore. You don't have to ask permission," Jewels said, hugging me again.

I nodded. It was easy for her to say. My mother's career came about because she was ultra organized and controlling. Nothing seemed to happen without her permission.

I slid into the driver's seat of Jessica's car and started the engine. I gave my friends one last wave before backing out of the driveway. The ferry left in ten minutes, which was plenty of time to get through Willowbrook and onto the pier.

The wood for the pier was still pale and new-looking after being replaced that summer. I now knew that Jessica had caused the freak storm that destroyed it, making it impossible to leave the island for a couple of months unless you had a boat. Some of the fishermen went to the city a few times a week for supplies for the entire town. Despite its sad state afterward, the storm didn't destroy Jessica's community garden. Thankfully, a lot of the vegetables were hardy enough to withstand the high winds and, combined with donations from Stan's Grocer, people's pantries, and the supplies the fishermen brought in, Willowbrook had enough to eat until we replaced the pier. Community meals became the norm, and sometimes I missed them. I wondered briefly if we could make that a regular thing. It brought everyone together, and I got to know some people better.

A snort escaped me as I remembered Jessica going home every night exhausted from being around so many people all the time. She was truly an introvert.

A deck worker guided me onto the ferry and into the very short line of cars heading to the city. Most people walked or took public transportation, but occasionally there was a need to drive. Like tonight. I did not want to be stuck waiting for a bus back to the dock when I wanted to go home.

I turned off the car and put the emergency brake on, per the regulations, then stepped out of the car. The fresh ocean air blew on a gentle breeze, and it was still warm from the fall day. I wondered if the unseasonably agreeable weather was Jessica's doing and decided I didn't really want to know. This was all too much.

Stepping to the railing, I looked out over the water, enjoying the setting sun's display. Glancing at my watch, I noted it was only six now. I would probably get to the restaurant fifteen minutes early, but that was better than being late. My mother would be exactly on time, sitting at the table at seven o'clock on the dot. I hoped most of the rush-hour traffic finished before I got there, especially after the last time I was in the city. The ferry dock was in the middle of downtown.

The ferry jerked a little as it left the pier, and I grabbed the railing to steady myself. As the ferry accelerated, the wind picked up. I turned my face to the sun and into the wind, closing my eyes. This would be the last peaceful moment before finally knowing the truth about my father. I hoped I would learn the truth, anyway.

I opened my eyes and gazed over the water, watching the boat's wake and how the sun made the tips of the waves look gold. Seabirds wheeled overhead, their raucous cries barely heard over the boat's engine. A sense of peace settled over me despite the impeding conversation. The water always did that to me, ever since I was small and my mother took me to the beach to relax.

"I'll take it," I whispered to myself. "I'll take every beautiful moment in life."

Twenty minutes later, a blast of the ferry's horn announced our arrival, and I got back in the car. I was the last car on, so I was also the last car off, but there were only four in front of me. In no time at all, I was in the midst of downtown, navigating the narrow streets and heading up the hill to midtown.

My friends didn't know the reason for leaving much earlier than I needed to. I told them I had a personal errand to run, and that was true. This felt like something I had to do alone, a quest just for me that only I could complete.

Tucked between a hair salon and a bookstore, the tattoo parlor was the kind of place that would be missed unless you knew where to look. And I did. I'd been thinking about it for days—ever since I was told I was a witch. Something in me had shifted then, like a new version of myself had stretched its wings and tried to take flight.

Inside, the shop was warm yet brightly lit, nothing like the sterile place I'd half-expected. Plants in the windows released scents of eucalyptus and basil into the air, and mellow acoustic guitar music played from a speaker in the corner.

"You sure about the butterfly?" asked the artist. Remy had gentle eyes, tattoos up both arms, and silver rings on every finger.

I nodded. "Yeah, it's kind of a symbol for me. Of transformation and hope. And holding still even when everything's moving."

Remy smiled but didn't press me. "Shoulder, right?"

"Left shoulder." I shrugged out of my jacket and tugged the sleeve of my blouse up. "I want to be able to see it when I look in the mirror but also keep it hidden if needed."

"Do you have something else under that? The shirt will be in the way."

I nodded. "I'm wearing a camisole."

"Perfect. Let me get the stencil ready. You can sit there." She nodded to a padded chair with wide armrests.

As Remy prepared the stencil, I sat quietly, watching her efficient movements. My heart thudded, but not from fear. It thumped with the certainty that I was stepping into something permanent. Not just ink in skin, but a quiet promise to myself.

Once Remy applied the stencil to the back of my shoulder, I looked in the full-length mirror on the wall and told her the placement was perfect. When the needle buzzed to life, I clenched my fists for a moment then relaxed. It stung, but it was a sharp, clean kind of pain. Grounding, almost.

"You're doing great," Remy murmured, wiping my skin gently. "Just a little more."

The butterfly took shape in delicate black lines and turquoise blue, with the faintest shimmer of silver ink that caught the light like moonlight on water. It looked like it could flutter off my shoulder at any moment.

When it was done, I stared at my reflection. The butterfly sat next to my bra strap, wings open, poised in mid-flight.

"It's perfect," I whispered.

I didn't cry, but I felt something shift, like a gear clicking into place.

"Here, I'll cover it, so the ink doesn't get on your nice clothes. You'll want to remove the bandage tomorrow." As she applied the clear barrier to my skin, she told me how to take care of my new tattoo.

When she finished, I pulled my blouse and jacket back on, my skin tugging gently as I moved. It didn't hurt much, just a reminder. I thanked Remy and paid her, then stepped outside.

The breeze was cool and smelled like fallen leaves and city smog. The golden light of early evening stretched long shadows across the sidewalk. I hesitated for a moment, letting the warmth of the ink settle into my skin and soul. Then I slid behind the wheel of Jessica's car, started the engine, and maneuvered through the streets.

Chapter 10: Dinner Conversation

I knew the way to Bateau by heart, having been there many times to meet my mother. Traffic was average, with no jams or major slowdowns, so I was there when I figured I would be.

Bateau stood nestled in the crook of midtown's finer streets, its discreet gold signage and stone exterior making it blend in with the high-end boutiques and minimalist art galleries nearby. Inside, soft lighting spilled from alabaster sconces along slate-colored walls. Glass panels and polished wood divided the space into intimate alcoves, and the soft hum of conversation rose and fell like tidewater. The smell of lemon-oil polish and truffle butter hung in the air, and a pianist played gentle jazz in a corner, just loud enough to keep things from being too quiet.

The Maître d' took one look at me and smiled as if he'd been expecting me, which he probably had. My mother never made dinner plans without ensuring every detail was confirmed twice.

I saw my reflection in the dark window near our table as I approached. I looked older. Not like my mother, but like someone who could sit across from her without flinching.

A server brought the wine list, and I selected a mid-priced merlot. I hoped it was good. If not, my mother would choose a different one. In short order, I had a glass of wine in front of me and took a few sips to steady my nerves, allowing the flavors of black cherry and cedar to swirl on my tongue.

I mulled over how to broach the subject of Jamison with my mother, and my gaze drifted over the table. Crisp white linens formed a backdrop for plates rimmed in gold, and a single white camellia floated in a square glass vase at the center of the table. Bateau always gave the illusion that time paused for you inside, while the rest of the world bustled outside unseen.

Right on cue, my mother arrived at exactly seven o'clock, as if summoned by an unseen bell.

Charlotte Stewart wore a steel-gray sheath dress that clung without being tight, the kind of designer fit that whispered power instead of shouting it. A soft wool cape in charcoal hung from her shoulders, the hem fluttering as she walked. Her heels were sharp and soundless, her pale hair twisted into a sleek French knot, and her lipstick was the color of fine burgundy—calculated to match the wine, no doubt. A silver pendant lay flat against her chest, subtle but deliberate.

"Hello, Hannah. I see you've started without me," she said, sliding into the seat as the server poured her glass of wine.

"Just wine, mother. I haven't looked at the menu yet."

She nodded and took a small sip from her glass. "Hmm. Not bad. A decent choice."

That small acknowledgment released some of the tension in my shoulders. Perhaps this wouldn't be terrible after all.

"We can eat before talking, if you don't mind? I had a long day and didn't stop for lunch."

"Sure, that's fine." I picked up the menu and tried not to wince at the prices.

"Don't bother looking at that." To the server, she said, "We'll have the Chef's Experience. And bring us some of the soft breadsticks, not the crunchy ones. For dessert, we will have Tallow Cake, with the muscatel, of course. That's fine with you?" She looked at me and continued when I nodded. "And coffee."

"Certainly," the server replied without flinching at my mother's demanding tone.

"Thank you," I said, trying to soften the situation.

He gave me a deep nod that was almost a bow and departed.

"I'm paying," my mother said almost offhandedly.

"Thank you," I said. Then, gently clearing my throat, I asked, "So you had a busy day at work?" I wanted to lead into the main topic for tonight, and hoped she was in a good mood despite her client canceling on her, leaving the dinner spot open for me.

She waved her hand dismissively. "Oh, the usual. Creating advertising campaigns for clients who do not really know what they want yet they seem to have an opinion about everything I do. I finally landed the TredLite account, though."

"Congratulations. That's wonderful."

"Yes, after three years. It's about time. You wear sneakers, right?"

"Um, yes. Not all the time, though. Why?"

"What size are you? Still a seven? I want you to try a pair of their new shoes and tell me what you think. Be honest. I need to know where you wear them, for how long, how your feet feel. Everything."

"Yes, size seven." It wasn't the first time she used me for market research.

"I'll have them sent over. How is your job? Still a waitress?" Her tone indicated how she felt about her daughter being in the service industry.

"Yes, I'm still a *barista*." I slightly emphasized the word. "I also started teaching preschool part-time."

"Oh? I didn't know you had goals of becoming a teacher."

"I don't know if I want to be a teacher. I don't need special credentials to teach preschool," I hurried to explain. "But I really like children and watching them learn new things. The way their little faces light up when they finally make a letter is very satisfying."

"Well. I see. That's very nice."

I could tell she didn't really see. She didn't understand why I loved serving and helping others. Oh, she helped others, too, but her motivations were fame and money while mine was peace in my soul.

The server placed our salad plates on the table.

"Ah, that was fast."

"We know your preferences, madame. Can I bring you anything else at this time?"

"No, thank you."

He nodded and melted into the background.

"This looks delicious," I said.

"It always is." My mother took a delicate bite.

We continued small talk throughout the meal as servers deposited and swept away plates, replacing them with new ones. They whisked away salad, steak, pasta, and vegetable compote as we finished each course in a succession that seemed to be almost a dance. We managed to keep to topics about general news, avoided politics, and only mentioned the weather once.

When the server came for our final dinner plates and brought the dessert and coffee, I knew it was almost time to broach the subject of my visit.

My mother took a bite of the decadent fluffy cake and a sip of coffee, then said, "Well? What is so important that you had to see me?"

I straightened in my chair. I didn't see any way this would be easy, for either of us. "I had a message from someone the other day. Jamison Stewart." I watched her closely.

She carefully set her fork down, dabbed at the corners of her mouth with the cloth napkin, put her hands in her lap, then went very still. She pressed her lips together, and her face paled.

"Your father," she finally said.

"He claims to be. You just confirmed it."

"What did he say?"

"He said he knew me when I was a baby but hasn't seen me since I was three years old."

"True."

"He wants to meet me."

Her eyes flashed. "I forbid it, Hannah."

"Mom," I said gently. "I'm an adult now. You can't tell me what to do like when I was a kid."

"Then what is the point of this dinner?" She demanded.

I took a deep breath and let it out in a rush as I said, "I want to know why he hasn't been around since I was a toddler. What happened? Why did he leave?"

"I told him to." Her matter-of-fact tone took me off guard.

"What?"

"I told him to leave," she repeated. "We lived on Willowbrook Island. You were actually born there. He agreed to leave and move to the city. And, as you know, I moved here when I got the job with this agency. By then, you were eighteen, so you decided to stay in Willowbrook."

"But why did you ask him to leave?"

"I won't talk about that."

Knowing she could be more stubborn than a mule, I took a different tactic. "Do you know where he lives now?"

She tilted her head as she looked at me. "He stayed here in the city for a while, tried to get me back. When I refused and the divorce was final, he moved further inland. I think he hoped to catch glimpses of you from time to time."

"It must have been painful for you when I stayed on the island," I murmured. I knew that hurt often disguised itself as anger, and my mother was furious when I announced my decision to live in Willowbrook. There was something about the place that drew me, and now I knew. I had been born there, and magic lived there. Maybe it called to me.

"Yes, well, as you said, you're an adult." She looked over my shoulder at something in the distance, refusing to meet my eyes.

"Mom," I said, trying to ease the strain between us. "I didn't know."

She looked at me then, steel in her gaze. "Would it have made a difference?"

I thought for a moment. "Probably not. I love living there. Mom, why didn't you let Jamison see me? I think I would have liked to know my father."

"I have my reasons. Good ones. But—"

"But you won't tell me," I finished for her.

Her expression and tone finally softened. "I'm not ready to relive that part of my life. It wasn't an easy decision. I loved Jamison very much."

Tears prickled the corners of my eyes. "Would it bother you if I met him? Maybe got to know him?"

"You're an adult," she repeated, but this time there was a note of acceptance. "For the record, I am against you meeting him. I don't think it's a good idea. So be careful." She picked up her fork and resumed eating her dessert.

It was obvious she wouldn't say anything more on the matter, but her warning made me more curious about my father. Did he have magic, and she knew and disapproved of it? Or was there another secret?

Chapter 11: Pressure

The drive and ferry ride home gave me plenty of time to wonder about my mother's resistance to telling me anything about my father. I grudgingly allowed that her history with him was her business to disclose or not, but I wished she had said more.

I texted Jessica and Jewels when I got on the ferry. **On the boat. Not much info.**

I hoped that would deter them from asking too many questions, even though I knew they'd want details anyway.

As the ferry pulled away from the city, I stepped onto the deck and pulled my jacket tighter against the evening chill. The night air was cooler now, the wind brisk, carrying the scent of salt and seaweed. Behind me, the city glittered across the dark water, its windows gleaming like distant stars. Ahead, Willowbrook Island waited, its profile dark but comforting, with only a few scattered, golden porch lights visible along the shoreline.

By the time the ferry docked, the world felt quieter, the wood of the newly repaired pier glowing softly under the boat lights. My low-heeled black boots made a soft *thunk* on the planks as I walked back to the car. The familiar island road welcomed me home, lined with trees that stretched overhead, their branches whispering faintly in the breeze. Somewhere in the distance, a dog barked; the air smelled of damp leaves and faint wood smoke.

When I reached my cottage, I parked Jessica's car on the street out front so she could easily pick it up later. I sat for a moment in the driver's seat, hands resting on the wheel, taking a long breath. My shoulders ached from the tension of the night, but here—finally—was home.

When I stepped out of the car, the cool air wrapped around me, smelling of fallen leaves and sea air. A soft light shone in the windows, and when I pushed open the front door, the scent of chocolate and caramel hit me immediately.

Inside, my friends sprawled on the sofa, sporting messy ponytails and faces covered in green goo. Jessica had her feet tucked under her, a pint of ice cream in her hand, while Jewels stretched out with a blanket over her legs and her sketchbook balanced on her knees, drawing a beach scene.

Jessica looked up first, grinning as her face mask crinkled at the edges. "You're home. Come sit. We saved you some ice cream."

I burst out laughing. "What are you doing?"

Jewels patted the spot between them on the couch. "Facials. And we want *all* the details."

Warmth spread through my chest, soft and grounding. These were my people. My armor tonight might have been clothes, but here—here was where I could take it off.

I settled into the chair facing the sofa, and Jessica immediately pulled my hair into a high ponytail while Jewels used a makeup remover wipe to clean my face. Then she scooped some of the green goo from a small jar and smoothed it over my skin. It tingled, but not unpleasantly.

"What's in this?" It smelled fruity.

"Green tea and mango. It's fantastic for rejuvenating your skin."

"Will it help with wrinkles?" I asked.

"Hannah Marie Stewart, you do not have wrinkles!" Jessica exclaimed.

"I saw some by my eyes," I protested.

"Those are smile lines. We all have them," Jewels said. "There, I'll set a timer for you. Once it goes off, go wash your face using warm water. Not hot, just warm," she stressed.

A timer went off, and Jessica said, "That's ours."

They disappeared into the bathroom. A few minutes later, they reappeared, their faces shining and smooth.

"Once your time is up, we'll get the ice cream, then we want to know everything," Jessica said.

"In the meantime, though, has anyone seen Donna lately? She visited her cousin in Arizona, and I thought she said she would be back by now." Jewels asked.

"I haven't seen her," I said.

"Donna and I have a truce now, and I doubt we'll ever be friends again, so it's not like she would let me know her plans. But I hope she's okay," Jessica said.

I nodded in agreement. "She's not the easiest person to get along with, but I don't want anything to happen to her."

"I don't have a difficulty with Donna," Jewels said. "She's actually quite nice."

Both Jessica and I stared at her.

"What?"

"I've never heard the words 'Donna' and 'nice' in the same sentence unless it was about her clothing," I said.

Jewels shrugged. "Maybe it's because I'm new to town. I don't have the history with her that you do."

"Possibly," Jessica said thoughtfully. "I do wish things were different. Oh, well. How much time does she have left?" She gestured at me.

Jewels checked her phone. "Two minutes."

"Okay, so Hannah, we've got a selection. Cookie dough, of course, Sunburst Berry, fudge brownie, mint chocolate chip, and Reece's. You get first pick."

"We also got regular vanilla, chocolate sauce, and sprinkles, in case you want to create your own. Oh, and peanuts, bananas, cherries, and whipped cream in case you want a banana split."

"Did you leave any ice cream for the rest of the town?"

Jessica and Jewels grinned.

"We would have bought the store if we thought it would make things easier for you," Jessica said.

"Thank you. I had dessert with my mom, but a banana split sounds wonderful. The French cake I had was tiny, even though I'm sure it was expensive."

"You got it." Just then, Jewels's timer went off. "Okay, go wash your face, and we'll get the ingredients ready."

I obeyed and had to admit that once the green goop was off my face, my skin felt smoother and hydrated.

"Thank you both for doing all of this," I said as I entered the small kitchen. "I don't think I could do this without you."

They hugged me at the same time.

Jewels said, "I can imagine. I was mostly alone when my powers emerged."

Jessica nodded. "I was too at the beginning. We're happy you're not alone. Now, let's build these things."

With that, we each created a banana split according to our preferences. No nuts for me, but extra cherries. Jess ignored the cherries, added nuts and extra whipped cream. Jewels's banana split was just banana, ice cream, and chocolate sauce. We carried our desserts to the living room.

"Alright. What happened with your mom?" Jessica asked as soon as we sat down.

"Not much." I recapped the brief conversation.

Jessica frowned. "I can't believe she actually tried to forbid you from seeing him."

"It's just her way," I said.

"And she really didn't tell you anything else?" Jewels pressed.

I shook my head. "Nope. She refused to tell me why she made him leave or why she kept me from him. Or maybe she kept him from me? Either way, she won't talk about it."

"Then the only way you'll find out is to ask him," Jewels said.

I pursed my lips. "I don't know. I mean, I'm twenty-eight. He's had ten years of my being an adult to reach out. And he's just now doing it?"

"Maybe he has a good reason?" Jewels suggested.

"Maybe. I'll think about it."

Jessica dropped her spoon in her bowl with a clatter. "If it were me, I would want to talk to him. Maybe it's not his fault he stayed away for so long. But he's family."

I could almost see the grief building up in her. Her lips tightened, and her breath came quickly.

"I thought," I started, with a sigh, "that he might be a criminal. Maybe he's been in jail or something."

Jewels started shaking her head before I finished. "No way. That's not it."

Jessica peered at her. "Did you see something?"

"See something?" I asked. "Oh, like a vision?" It would be a while before I caught on to all the magical influences in my life.

"No," Jewels said slowly. "I just feel it in my gut. That's not it. I think you should ask him."

I looked at each of my friends in turn. This was a big decision. While I appreciated my friends' input, I needed time alone to decide. I wanted to think about things. "Maybe. I'll think about it," I finally said. "I've been fine without him for this long. What's a few more days?"

I knew I was avoiding making a decision. But so what? I wouldn't get pushed into something before I was ready. I'd face it when I *chose* to, not just because everyone else thought I should. If that meant dragging my feet a little longer, then fine. I'd do it on my own terms. But deep down, I wasn't sure I was ready to face something that had been missing for so long. Waiting felt easier. Safer.

The silence stretched out a little too long, and the weight of their expectant looks pressed on me. They wanted me to act, to decide, to move forward. But I wasn't sure I could.

I ran a hand over my hair, glancing away. "I just—" I stopped myself before I said too much. My head was spinning. How could I explain that the idea of meeting

Jamison felt like opening a door I wasn't sure I was ready to walk through? "I just need a little more time. That's all."

"Well, I should go," Jessica said, standing abruptly. "Hannah, are you good to open tomorrow? I want to stop by Becca's and drop off some receipts. She gets to the office at nine. Jewels is already opening, but Saturday mornings can get busy."

"Sure, no problem." I stood, pulled her car keys out of my pocket and handed them to her, my chest tight with something I couldn't name. "Are you okay? You seem irritated."

"I'm fine." Her voice was sharp, but she wouldn't meet my eyes. "Let's make a plan for the concert tomorrow. Okay?"

I nodded, but her quick exit left a small knot in my stomach.

Plopping into the chair, I looked at Jewels. "She's upset with me, isn't she? Because I don't know if I want to meet Jamison or not."

Jewels studied the green nail polish on her right hand, flicking at the edges of one nail with her left thumb. "I don't know if she's upset, necessarily. I think she may be having some waves of grief. It can't be easy to watch your best friend refuse to have a relationship with a parent when both of your parents are dead. Give her some time. She'll come around."

"I hope so." I sighed.

Jewels patted my hand lightly before she collected the dishes and carried them to the kitchen. The soft clink of plates and the low hum of the dishwasher filled the silence, steady and rhythmic. I stayed where I was for a moment, the warmth of the room pressing in on me as I tried to shake the heaviness in my chest. With a long sigh, I decided I'd had enough for one day. I pushed myself up, the worn cushions of the chair creaking beneath me, and shuffled to my bedroom. The sheets felt cold and slightly crisp against my skin as I collapsed into bed, the faint scent of lavender from the pillowcase mixing with the lingering taste of coffee on my tongue. I didn't even bother to brush my teeth. I just needed to sleep.

Chapter 12: The Question

Saturday morning came with a sharp, almost blinding light streaming through the curtains. The sun sliced through the space, casting long, golden beams across the floor. I groaned softly, squinting at the light, but the day was already awake. I threw on a loose gray sweater and some jeans, my body stiff from the restless sleep. As I walked into the kitchen, the smell of fresh coffee hit me—warm and earthy, swirling through the air and grounding me.

"This is good," Jewels said with a soft smile when she saw me, her voice a little teasing. She gestured toward the bright sky outside the window, where the light painted the world in vibrant colors. "If Jessica was upset, the weather would not be this nice." She paused, her fingers lightly tapping on the edge of her coffee cup. "Oatmeal?"

"No, thanks." I shook my head. "I think I'll get a croissant at work later. I'm not that hungry right now."

Jewels chuckled, the sound warm and familiar. "I must be growing. I'm hungry all the time."

I raised my eyebrows at her, the faint creak of floorboards beneath me as I shifted my weight. The mug in my hands felt comforting, the heat seeping into my palms. "Evan explained that using magic is like exercising. Are you using more magic lately?"

Jewels paused, her fingers tapping against the edge of her coffee cup thoughtfully. The sound a soft rhythm, like a heartbeat. "I don't think so," she said after a moment, voice drifting as she stared into her cup. "But that's something to consider. Thanks."

I glanced at the clock on the stove. "I'm going to go start opening," I said, the words feeling final, like I had made a decision without even realizing it.

"It's only 6:15," Jewels protested, her voice faint with surprise.

"I know." I nodded, my fingers brushing the doorframe as I moved toward it. The cool metal of the door handle felt familiar against my skin. "But I want to walk and think."

Jewels nodded, the soft rustle of her sweater as she turned back to the counter the only sound as she resumed her morning routine. "Okay. I'll see you in a bit."

I cast her a grateful look and grabbed my favorite black leather jacket from the hook by the door, the smooth texture of the worn leather instantly familiar against my fingers. We would probably go straight to the concert after work, so I wanted to be prepared.

Popping my earbuds in, I adjusted the volume enough to feel the gently thrum of the bass from the new album by Loveless, the music settling around me like a second skin. The notes wrapped me in a cocoon of sound as I stepped outside, the crisp morning air biting at my cheeks. I breathed in, the smell of damp earth lingering in the cool breeze. This part of the island contained cozy cottages, like mine, with weather-beaten shingles and white picket fences. Some homes had front porches adorned with wicker chairs, where residents sat on warm evenings, sipping iced tea and chatting.

As I walked slowly from my cottage, the neighborhood was just waking up. Mrs. Stevensen tugged her bathrobe tighter before waving at me and calling to her dog, Minnie to "hurry up." I couldn't hear her over my music, but I knew that's what she said since that seemed to be the code for "do your business." I smiled and waved back, quickening my pace slightly so Mrs. Stevensen didn't have a chance to stop me to talk.

I didn't think about anything in particular, but I enjoyed the space to just be without anyone asking me questions or telling me what they thought. I expected to decide quietly, without fanfare. Knowing that not making a choice about meeting Jamison was still making a choice, I promised myself to enjoy tonight, then contact him tomorrow, one way or another. He deserved a response, even if I denied his request to meet.

Arriving at Over the Moon, I unlocked the door with a satisfying click and stepped inside, the floorboards creaking slightly under my weight. The space was quiet and cool, with the morning light filtering through the windows, casting long shadows across the polished wooden floor. After I locked the door behind me, I took a moment to inhale the calm atmosphere, the familiar scent of books and coffee beans mingling in the still air.

We didn't open until seven, so I began my routine. The chairs were still upside down on the tables, their metal legs cold against my fingertips as I set them down one by one with a soft scrape that echoed in the room. The wood of the tables felt smooth but slightly cold under my palms as I moved them into place. After stowing my purse and jacket in the back, I turned my attention to the bookshelves, straightening the books and arranging them just so, the scent of paper and dust rising gently as I moved the spines. Pulling the toy bins from the shelves, I set them on the carpet, the faint rustle of plastic as I shifted them into a more accessible position. I found that having the toys more visible made the kids realize it was okay to play with them, their excitement tangible whenever they saw them.

Jessica and Jewels had cleaned well the night before, so there wasn't much for me to do. I double-checked that the bean hopper was full, the rich, earthy aroma of fresh coffee beans filling the air as I twisted the lid back on. I also made sure we had enough cups and lids on the counter to last for the morning, the slight weight of the lids pushing against my fingers as I stacked them neatly.

In the back room, I opened the safe and pulled the cash tray out, making sure I locked the safe again, the metallic sound of the latch snapping shut echoing in the quiet room. I placed the tray in the register, the slight rattle of coins accompanying my movements, then glanced at the receipt tape level. After that, there wasn't much else I could do besides wait for seven o'clock to arrive, the quiet ticking of the clock a steady reminder that the day was inching forward.

I decided a caramel mocha sounded good, so I made one. Jessica, being a bit of a coffee addict herself, allowed us all the drinks we wanted. Usually, it was only one or two, but it was a nice perk. Tamping the ground coffee into the portafilter and watching the dark liquid drip into the waiting glass, then frothing the milk, adding caramel, and putting it all together soothed my nerves. The familiar motions gave me a sense of stability that I had missed with everything going on lately. I sat on the sofa with my drink and sipped slowly, allowing my mind to wander.

At 6:45, Jewels came in, wearing an old Guns N' Roses t-shirt over acid-wash jeans, and flipped the lights on. The sudden brightness in the space made me squint. I hadn't realized my eyes had become used to the soft diffused light coming from the windows.

"Did you make me one?" She asked. I began to stand, and she waved me to stay. "I'm kidding! I have time to make my own. It looks like you already took care of everything."

"You and Jessica did a very thorough job of closing last night," I replied.

"It was unexpectedly slow."

Once she had her coffee, she came to sit beside me. "We have five minutes," she said.

I sighed. "I know. Maybe today won't be too bad?"

She laughed. "Are you kidding? With a concert in the park? We're going to be busy, but probably not until the end of the day."

"At least we close earlier on Saturdays."

"Cheers to that."

We knocked our cups together and sat in silence for a few minutes.

"Okay, let's do this," she said. The clock on the wall behind the counter read 6:59.

I groaned and stood, stretching my back. Jewels went to turn the open sign on and unlock the door.

"I think I needed more sleep," I complained as I went to the register to prepare for the first customer.

The Crony Crew were the first ones in, as usual.

Old John was a wiry man in his seventies with a sun-leathered face, deep smile lines, and a shock of thick white hair combed neatly back. His pale blue eyes were sharp and always seemed to twinkle with mischief, even when he was silent. He wore a faded flannel shirt, suspenders, and old work boots that had seen decades of wear.

Thomas Mason was heavier and broad-shouldered, with a thick gray beard and a slow, thoughtful way of speaking. He had once been a soldier, and the pinky and ring fingers were missing from his left hand. A tattoo of an anchor was faintly visible on his right forearm. He wore a navy wool sweater over a collared shirt, his cap always tilted slightly back on his balding head.

Frank Thatcher was the youngest of the trio, in his early sixties, with salt-and-pepper hair and a trimmed mustache. A retired schoolteacher, he had a tidy, deliberate manner — glasses perched on the end of his nose, sleeves neatly rolled, always reading the local paper or jotting notes in a little leather-bound notebook.

After they ordered their usual coffees with cream and sugar, they sat at their table. I don't think I would ever be able to think of the round table in the center of the room as anything besides their table. They were there every morning. It only took minutes for Jewels and I to pour the coffee into three large cups and add the cream and sugar to their specific tastes: more sugar than cream for Old John, more cream than sugar for Thomas, and more sugar and cream than coffee for Frank.

Once I had delivered their cups to the table, the three men leaned back comfortably, their familiar banter already starting up. I could hear the low rumble of their voices drifting to the counter where Jewels and I stood.

Frank flipped open the latest issue of the *Willowbrook Chronicle* and laid it on the table. "Did you see this?" He tapped the paper with his finger. "They're talking about adding another ferry run on the weekends. About time, I say."

"Hmph. About time?" Old John snorted. "You remember what happened the last time they tried that? Half the crew quit after two months."

Thomas chuckled. "Only because they were all related. You can't run a ferry schedule when half the staff are cousins who won't work Sundays."

Jewels glanced at me with a grin. "Sounds like island politics again."

Frank nodded sagely. "Everything's politics on an island this small."

Old John winked at us. "And the real question is, when are you girls going to add whiskey to that coffee? Mornings would be a lot more interesting."

I laughed and leaned on the counter. "Not a chance, John. We're barely keeping you all civilized as it is."

"She's right, John," Thomas said with mock seriousness. "We can barely handle you sober."

Old John raised his coffee cup as if he were making a toast. "Fair enough."

After the Crony Crew, we didn't have any customers for a while.

"Why don't you get your breakfast?" Jewels suggested.

My stomach clenched at the mention of food. "That's a good idea. I think I can eat now."

Taking a croissant from the case, I warmed it up in the microwave for a moment before slathering it with strawberry jam. I started for the back room when the bell over the door chimed. I glanced at it, worried it would be a large group, only to see Evan striding in.

The dark gray fitted t-shirt clung lightly to his broad shoulders, the short sleeves revealing the tan lines on his muscled arms. His faded jeans had faint smudges at the knees probably from some early morning repair job, and his work boots thudded solidly on the wooden floor. His brown hair—always a little tousled—looked freshly windblown, and that somehow made it worse. Better? Both.

I felt a quick flutter in my chest as his hazel eyes landed on me and a grin spread across his face. He made directly for me. I suddenly became aware of how messy my own hair probably looked, and how jam definitely smeared my thumb. I straightened instinctively, but my pulse betrayed me, ticking faster under my skin.

"Mmm, that looks good." He reached a finger toward my breakfast.

"Hey," I protested, moving my plate out of reach. My voice came out a little too high. "Get your own."

"I will, thanks."

"Uh, no you won't," Jewels interjected. "But I'll get it for you. You know Jessica doesn't like you behind the counter."

"That's why I do it." He smirked.

I looked down, focusing way too hard on my croissant.

"Well, she's not here. So, you want a croissant with jam?"

"Yes, please," Evan said to Jewels.

"Hannah, here's your hazelnut latte," Jewels said.

"Oh, thanks. You didn't have to do that."

She shrugged. "I figured you'd want something to wash down the jam."

Evan interjected before I could respond. "Hannah, will you wait? I have something to ask you."

"Okay." I tried not to sound like my heart was doing little flips. It wasn't unusual for Evan to want to talk to me; we had practically grown up together. But lately, it had felt different.

"Do you want coffee, too?" Jewels asked him.

"Not just yet, thanks."

Jewels handed him a plate, and Evan followed me to the back. His footsteps were close behind me, with the faint scent of sawdust and clean soap trailing with him.

In one corner, Jessica had placed a small table with mismatched chairs for us to use during breaks, so we were out of sight of the customers. I sat down quickly, trying to act casual as I pulled apart my croissant, the jam sticky and sweet on my fingers.

Evan settled across from me, his long legs stretching out easily. His knee brushed mine for a second, shooting a jolt of warmth up my spine.

I licked the smear of jam from my thumb, feeling his eyes on me.

"Are you going to actually eat that?" I asked him, forcing a light tone, even though my stomach had knotted up.

"Eventually." His grin softened, and his eyes crinkled at the corners in a way that made my chest tighten further. "I wanted to ask you something."

"Sure," I replied. I tucked a loose strand of hair behind my ear, wishing my face didn't feel so warm.

"It's about tonight," he started. His hazel eyes never left mine.

I swallowed, nerves prickling along my skin.

"We're most likely going to the concert as a group."

"We haven't really talked about it," I managed, hoping I sounded normal.

"I know." He leaned in slightly, elbows resting on the table, and my pulse spiked. "But that's the most likely scenario. I mean, Zane and Jess went to the movie in the park together as a date, but he arranged that ahead of time."

"True." I gave a small laugh even though I had no idea where he was going with this. My heart pounded, stupidly hopeful.

"So, that's what I want to do." He looked at me expectantly.

I furrowed my brow. "You want to arrange a date?"

Why was he asking me about it? Did he want advice on how to set the evening up for whomever he asked? Or was he letting me know he wouldn't be part of the group that night because he didn't want to tell his sister?

"Exactly," he nodded, watching me intently. "What do you think?"

"What do I think about you arranging a date? Um, that's great."

He grinned. "Great. I'll tell Jess so she doesn't bother us. And I'll be back here at closing with dinner."

"Wait, what?" My brain finally caught up to what he said. "You mean a date with me? You're asking me on a date?"

He frowned. "Yes, that's what I said."

A nervous, incredulous laugh bubbled out of me. "No, it isn't. You never actually asked me."

"Oh." He gave an almost sheepish smile, scratching the back of his neck. "Well, I meant to. I'm not doing very well here, am I?"

I shook my head, grinning. The warmth flooding through me was almost too much to contain.

Clearing his throat, he straightened and said formally, "Miss Hannah Stewart, will you please attend the concert with me as my date?"

I thought I might float out of my seat. "Why, yes, I will. I think that will be fun."

The relief on his face was almost comical and entirely endearing. "Okay. I'll pick you up when the shop closes."

"With dinner," I reminded him.

He smiled, and my heart did a little flutter. "Yes, with dinner."

"I heard there is going to be a popcorn stand tonight."

"I can take a hint." He stood and gave me a playful bow. "My lady shall have popcorn for the show. I have a class now, but I'll see you tonight."

"See you tonight."

I waited until the door shut behind him before doing a little dance in my seat.

Chapter 13: Floating

I finished the last bite of my croissant, brushing the crumbs from my fingers, before heading back to the main room of the coffee shop, an extra bounce in my step. The comforting scent of roasted espresso beans filled the air, mingling with the faint traces of cinnamon and vanilla from the pastries in the display case. Jessica and Jewels stood behind the counter, chatting, their laughter an easy, familiar sound.

"Just in time," Jewels called, waving me over. "We're talking about tonight."

A thrill of excitement bubbled up inside me. "I have a date," I announced, unable to keep the grin from my face.

Jessica's eyes widened, her fingers tightening around the cup she held. "A what?" she almost yelped.

"Finally!" Jewels exclaimed, clapping her hands together. "I knew it. It's about time."

Jessica blinked rapidly, still processing. "With who?" She finally asked.

I hesitated for half a second, the sudden shift in the air catching me off guard. "With Evan, actually." I rushed to add, "Is that okay? I won't go if you're not okay with it."

The words sounded wrong the moment they left my mouth. I knew Jessica was protective of me, but this felt different. Her face shifted from shock to something more complicated. A hint of sharpness flickered across her features, almost too fast for me to catch.

Jessica's face shifted from shock to something softer. "Are you kidding? That's great!"

Jewels nodded in agreement, crossing her arms with a knowing smirk. "And now we know not to bother you."

She winked. "I thought he looked nervous when he was in here."

"Hold up." Jessica held up a hand. "He just asked you?"

I nodded, starting to feel uneasy. "He didn't tell you?"

"I haven't seen him since this morning at home." She pulled out her phone, frowning. "He was just here?"

"Yes," I said. "He said he would tell you."

Jewels held up her hands as if refereeing. "He left a few minutes before Jessica arrived. And since his dojo isn't too far away, and he has that long stride, she probably didn't even see him."

"I'm sure he would have said something," Jessica said doubtfully. Just then, her phone chimed, and she looked at the screen. "Oh, there it is. 'I asked Hannah to go with me to the concert tonight. Just the two of us.' How should I respond? With the typical 'don't hurt my best friend' or as a little sister teasing her brother?"

"A little bit of both?" I suggested.

Jessica thought for a moment then typed, speaking as she went. "'She's too good for you. And if you hurt her, I'll tell everyone what happened at camp when you were in fourth grade.'"

"What happened at camp?" Jewels and I asked simultaneously.

Jessica grinned. "Oh no. I'll only tell if he breaks Hannah's heart. And I'll be sure to tell the whole town."

Her phone dinged again, and she giggled as she read the message. "'I would never hurt her. And if you tell people about fourth grade, I'll tell them about your sixth-grade incident.' We really do have too much dirt on each other for our own good." She turned to me. "Now, how much detail do you plan on giving me about your date?"

I hesitated. Talking to my best friend about dating her brother felt... weird. Before I could answer, the bell over the door chimed, and we all turned to look.

"Donna, hello!" Jewels called. "We were wondering where you've been."

I exhaled, grateful for the distraction.

"I extended my trip by a few days. It's good to know I was missed," Donna replied primly, setting down her laptop bag with a little more force than necessary.

"Well, what would you like?" Jewels asked brightly. "The special is a pumpkin spice latte."

"That sounds good, actually. I have some emails to catch up on." Donna pulled her laptop out and irritably blew a breath up to get her bangs out of her eyes.

"I'll have it ready in a minute," Jewels promised, her movements smooth and practiced as she prepared the drink.

I noticed Jessica discreetly stepping to the side, her eyes still locked on her phone, not meeting Donna's. Donna and Jessica had a history, and despite their efforts to move past it, I could always feel the weight of it whenever they were in the same room. Donna's cool demeanor was the perfect foil to Jessica's ever-tightening control.

As Jewels made Donna's order, the door swung open again, and a large group of people poured in, all clamoring for coffee and snacks. I groaned. So much for a quiet morning.

I worked quickly, placing drink after drink on the pickup counter, barely noticing that Donna hadn't retrieved hers. It wasn't until I had stacked several drinks beside hers that I realized she still hadn't moved.

"Donna!" I called over the din.

I kept making drinks and setting them out, while Jess retrieved pastries from the case and made smoothies. More time passed, and Donna's drink still sat there. I finally looked up to see her with her back to the counter, headphones on.

"Of course," I grumbled. I wished I could just teleport the coffee to her, but of course that was impossible. That wasn't how my magic worked.

Then, to my horror, Donna's cup lifted from the counter and drifted toward her.

"Oh, shit," I said.

Jessica, returning from delivering a tray of bagels, turned just in time to see the floating cup. She darted forward, intercepting it smoothly and taking it to Donna when she saw the name written on the side of the cup. The cup steamed a little when she set it down, and I assumed Jess had used some of her fire magic to reheat it since it had sat for a while. She looked at me, frowning.

"I'm sorry," I mouthed at her.

As she walked by me to return to the blender and the next smoothie, she said, "We will talk about this later with Sofia."

I wanted to ask Jessica if this meant my magic had changed from freezing to moving objects. Or was it a new addition? I shook my head to clear the thoughts; I didn't have time to think about this right now.

I pasted on a smile to give to each customer as they retrieved their order. After another half-hour of a constant influx of people, I reached for the next cup with the order and name written on the side only to find my hand closing on empty air.

"That's it finally," said Jewels, wiping her brow as if she were sweating. "Where did they all come from?"

"I think they're here from the city to see Red Helix," Jessica said. Then, looking at me, she continued in a quieter voice, "What the hell was that?"

"I don't know," I whispered back. "I was worried about taking too long to get Donna her drink. It sat there for a long time before I realized she had headphones on and couldn't hear me call her name. And then it just...happened."

"What did I miss?" Jewels asked.

I glanced at her but didn't have a chance to answer.

"So, you decided to float it over to her?" Jessica demanded.

"No!" It came out louder than I intended, and a few customers looked our way. I lowered my voice again. "I just thought that I needed to get it to her, and it did its own thing."

"Oh, shit," Jewels said.

"Really? What did you think, exactly? What were the words going through your head?"

My heart raced as I answered in barely a whisper, "I wished I could teleport it to her."

"You what?" Jessica shrieked. All eyes were on us now. Jessica rolled her head to release the tension in her neck, then turned to the room with a charming smile. "Sorry about that. Girl talk." Looking back at me, she hissed, "Don't ever think anything like that again in my shop."

"I won't. I promise," I said in a hushed voice.

Jessica grabbed her purse. "I need some air. I'll be back." She stamped out of the shop, not quite slamming the door behind her.

My throat tightened, and I willed myself to get control before I cried. I couldn't leave Jewels here alone. Besides, the light coming through the suddenly dimmed, and the Crony Crew looked outside and murmured to each other. I didn't want to run into Jessica accidentally and make the weather worse.

"It's okay," Jewels said. "She just needs to blow off some steam. Probably literally." She frowned in the direction Jessica had gone. "It will be fine." She patted my shoulder and went to bus a table.

I didn't believe her. I had never seen Jessica so angry, certainly never at me.

Old John stood and came to the counter. "Hey, Hannah. Can I get a refill to go? Jessica seemed unhappy when she left, and I don't like the look of the clouds coming in."

Clearing my throat, I croaked out, "Sure." Then I pasted on a smile as I refilled his gray travel mug.

The other two members of the Crony Crew shuffled out the door after him.

When Jessica returned, she walked directly over to me and said, "Sofia wants us all at my house tomorrow." Then she stomped away without even looking at me.

I decided it wasn't such a bad thing that we wouldn't be attending the concert together. At least I wouldn't have to spend a couple of hours pretending everything's fine while Jessica acted like I'm a stranger.

As customers started drifting outside, casting curious looks at us, Jewels, bless her, tried to lighten the mood.

"Well, this is fun. Three friends working together in what is supposed to be harmony. Instead, we have enough awkwardness to qualify as performance art."

I glanced at Jessica to gauge her reaction only to see her shake her head and turn away to clear off a table. As she returned to the counter to drop the cleaning rag in the sink, Jewels tried again.

"Smile, people. Remember, we're the charming local weirdos, not a live-action soap opera."

The silence between Jessica and me had its own gravity, pulling everything joyful down with it. We started cleaning to close early, and the remaining few customers trickled out. At 5:00, Jessica locked the door behind the last customer, flipping the sign to closed.

Jewels stood in the middle of the room with her arms crossed and looking annoyed. "Okay, time out! I'm officially invoking the United Nations Treaty of Don't Make Me Choose Sides. You two want to act like bitter enemies? Fine. But you're both still supposed to be my friends."

Jessica heaved a sigh. "Jewels, it's not about you."

"I know that," Jewels retorted. "Look, you're both brilliant, stubborn, and slightly terrifying. It's like watching two angry cats argue over who knocked the plant off the shelf."

Jessica's lips twitched as if she wanted to smile. "You're comparing me to a cat?"

Jewels grinned. "Only in the best way. Regal. Proud. Occasionally knocks stuff over for attention."

Her comment almost pulled a smile from my lips. And then I looked at Jessica again. Her green eyes flicked toward me, and she frowned.

"You know," she blurted, her voice low and flat, "some people don't get surprise visits from long-lost parents. Just saying."

I blinked. "What?"

"Nothing," she muttered, turning away, her jaw tight as she wiped an already-clean countertop.

I looked down, scuffing the toe of my shoe on the floor. "Jess, I—"

She didn't even let me finish. "Figure it out," she said coldly.

I don't remember ever feeling so abandoned, not even when my mom refused to talk to me for a month after I moved back to Willowbrook. At least I'd expected that. Bracing for my mom's silence was almost a tradition at this point.

Jessica had always been there. We met in preschool and have been practically glued together ever since. Birthday parties, scraped knees, first crushes. Even attending high school on the mainland hadn't changed that, and we talked every night.

But one flash of magic I didn't understand and couldn't control and suddenly she won't talk to me?

Fine. Screw her.

Chapter 14: Shifting Moods

I was the first one out the door once we finished cleaning, which didn't take long since we stayed focused on our jobs and there wasn't any of the usual banter. Evan waited for me, leaning against the side of the building, hands in the pockets of his jeans. His black leather jacket was open at the front, revealing a pristine white t-shirt, and a black baseball cap shadowed his face. He grinned when he saw me, and I tried to smile back. Jewels came out behind me, followed by Jessica, who locked the door.

"I hope you have a good time tonight," Jewels offered.

"Thanks," I said with forced brightness. "You too."

Jessica didn't say anything, just strode off toward the park. Evan looked between us, his smile fading slightly, and I remembered what he said the night of Zane's party when my powers first manifested. I knew he probably could have sensed the tension between us, even without magic. Thankfully, he waited until Jewels also crossed the street before he said anything.

"So what happened today?"

I took a steadying breath. "I actually don't want to talk about it right now."

"Does it have anything to do with the text I got from Sofia saying we're meeting tomorrow?"

"Unfortunately, yes. But can we please just have a good time tonight? I really need the distraction, and I want to enjoy the evening with you." I flashed a genuine smile at him.

"Of course," Evan said, holding his hand out to me.

The gesture surprised me a little, but I took his hand. His warm fingers, calloused from work, folded around mine. The tension within me eased slightly as we walked.

"Wait a minute, didn't you say you would bring dinner?" I asked.

A mischievous grin spread across his face. "So I did. And I did."

"I don't see anything."

"Look." He pointed across the street to the sidewalk in front of the park.

A bistro table sat there, complete with a red and white checkered tablecloth, a candle in a jar, and covered plates.

"Fancy," I said approvingly.

"I got Bolognese from Benny's. I hope that's okay."

"Are you kidding? I love it." I did not know Evan's playful, sporty demeanor hid a romantic heart.

We crossed the street, and he pulled out a chair for me to sit, then sat across from me. From under the table, he produced a bottle of Sangiovese wine.

"Benny said this wine pairs with his Bolognese like a dream," Evan said.

"Then it must be true." I held my glass out to him.

"Well, actually, he said, 'this wine, it is.'" Evan kissed his fingers with a mwah sound.

His imitation made me giggle, the sound slipping out before I could catch it. I hadn't realized how nervous I'd been until that laugh loosened something in my chest. "Let's give it a try, then." I said.

Evan smiled again, his eyes softening as he gazed at me. I cast a glance down, feeling the heat rush to my cheeks. *Get it together, Hannah. It's not your first date ever.*

I took a sip of wine. "Mm, that is good."

With a flourish, he removed the covers from our plates, letting the aroma of Benny's sauce waft between us.

"Oh, I almost forgot." He reached into his pocket and pulled out his phone. A moment later, the soft strains of rich Italian music played.

"We could have just gone to Benny's, you know," I said, glancing around. A few passersby had slowed as they admired the setup. At his pained expression, I hurriedly added, "This is lovely, but it seems like a lot of work."

Relief crossed Evan's features as he responded, "It's not, actually. Zane helped me set it up. He said something about how girls like grand gestures."

"You didn't listen to everything he said, did you?"

"Nope. I heard grand gestures, and this is what we ended up with." His grin pulled an answering smile to my lips.

"I appreciate it. But for future reference, I love simple, too."

"I'll remember that. Cheers."

We clinked glasses and dug into the food.

The Bolognese was amazing, of course—Benny never missed—but the company made it something else entirely. As we ate, the gray clouds that had hung over Willowbrook most of the afternoon finally gave way. The sun slipped out as if it had been waiting for the right moment, casting everything in warm gold.

Evan tilted his face upward. "There we go. Jessica probably just met up with Zane."

I sighed, my mood dampening a little. "I wasn't sure we'd see the sun this evening."

"Maybe the sun couldn't resist showing off when it heard you laugh."

I looked at him, stunned for a second, but he kept twirling pasta around his fork like he hadn't just said something that made my heart skip.

Between bites, Evan told me about Zane nearly knocking over a whole wine display at the shop, and I told him about the time Jessica and I tried to recreate Benny's sauce and set off the fire alarm.

"I'm just saying," I said through a laugh, "if your sauce is starting to *smoke*, you're probably doing something wrong."

"You sound like someone who needs cooking redemption," Evan teased. "We should cook together sometime."

I gave him a look. "Is this your way of getting me to make dinner?"

"Only if it comes with fire insurance."

We laughed, and for a while, the buzz of conversation and the music from the park faded away. It was just us, this little table, and the soft flicker of candlelight.

"I hope we can find a good place," I said eventually, glancing toward the growing crowd in the park across the street. Blankets and lawn chairs had already staked out territory like a miniature land rush.

"I have that covered, too."

"Oh?"

"Yep. I'm tall and strong. We're going to push our way to the stage."

Laughing, I reached for my wine. "Please tell me you're kidding."

"I am. But since it's standing only, I'm sure we can find a spot. And if you can't see, I'll just put you on my shoulders."

"You will not!" I protested. "I don't need to see the band to hear them."

"Fair point." Evan pushed back his chair and stood.

"What do we do with all this?" I pointed at the table.

"I don't think anyone will bother it, and Benny promised to send one of his busboys to take the dishes. My truck is parked over there, so after the concert, I will load the table and chairs and take them back home."

I looked at him suspiciously. "Are they from your garden?"

His aghast expression could have meant yes or no, but he put my mind at ease when he said, "They're from the garage. Mom liked to have garden tea parties from time to time and needed extra tables. Come on." He grabbed my hand and tugged me in the direction of the stage that the road crew had set up earlier that day. "The table will be fine."

We walked hand in hand into the park, weaving through clumps of people. It felt good, even natural. The scents of popcorn, beer, and fried foods floated in the air, and the heat from the day hadn't dissipated yet. The light jacket I brought would be enough to keep me warm once the sun fully set. I thought it a perfect evening for an outdoor concert.

"Where did all these people come from?" I asked. A lot of the faces were unknown to me.

"If I lived in the city and heard of a free concert in the park on an island that's only fifteen minutes away by ferry, I'd be here, too." He grimaced. "I'll be keeping my shields up tonight, for sure."

"Shields?"

"Magical shields," he explained. "With so many people, the emotions are wild. Sofia has helped me learn how to block the noise. I can also choose to only sense certain people." He winked at me.

I shifted uncomfortably. "I'm not sure I like you knowing what I feel all the time."

"Don't worry. I don't intrude. Promise."

I wasn't sure that helped much, but I trusted Evan. It must be difficult to feel others' emotions constantly, so I wondered if he had his shields up more than not, but I didn't want to ask.

Evan led me through the swelling crowd, weaving between picnic blankets, folding chairs, and clusters of people juggling snacks and glow sticks. The air was thick with the scent of kettle corn and summer sweat, and every few steps, someone brushed past me, their arm or bag grazing mine.

We edged closer to the stage, the murmur of the crowd swelling into scattered laughter and chatter. Someone behind us shouted for their friend, and a kid darted across our path chasing a rogue balloon.

By the time we stopped, we were close enough to see the words on the T-shirts of the stage crew. One read, *"Why yes, I am a rock star."*

"This seems like a good spot," Evan announced, shifting to shield me slightly from a group of teens nudging past.

I turned in a slow circle as if assessing the area, but I couldn't see much beyond shoulders, hats, and a partial view of the stage. Being short at an outdoor concert was basically nature's way of saying *good luck*.

Still, I smiled. "I agree."

"Good. Would you like something to drink? Are you ready for popcorn?"

"No popcorn yet, but maybe some water?" The wine sat heavily in my stomach, and I did not want to be completely silly with Evan on our first date.

"Okay, save our spot. I'll be right back."

I watched Evan until I could no longer see his brown hair over the heads of the crowd. It didn't take long. Being short definitely had disadvantages. I looked around. Maybe if I saw Jessica, I could talk to her for a minute. I didn't quite understand why she was so angry about my magical mishap this morning. A nagging thought made me wonder if something else was going on with her.

Jewels's infectious laugh had me turning my head. I spotted her in a cluster of women that did not include Jessica, but it did include Donna, of all people. And Donna was grinning at whatever had Jewels laughing. Jewels must have felt my gaze because she glanced up and waved. I returned the gesture, and she smiled and went back to her conversation.

A few minutes later, Evan reappeared at my side and offered one of the two bottles of water he held.

"Thank you."

"Let me know if you need anything else. I don't want you to miss a moment of the concert."

"Don't you like Red Helix?"

He took a swig of water and replaced the cap. "I do, but I want this night to be perfect for you."

His words echoed my earlier thought, and I smiled, leaning into his side a little. Being with him allowed me to forget temporarily that Jess and I were fighting. Another thought had me tilting my head to peer up at him with narrowed eyes.

"Are you manipulating my emotions?" I asked in a low voice so only he could hear.

He glanced down at me, his eyebrows raised in surprise. "Can you tell?"

"So you are." It came out more as an accusation than a question.

He shrugged and looked sheepish. "Not manipulating, exactly. Sometimes, I'm able to push my feelings toward other people. It's a new thing. I can't make someone feel something they don't want to, but I can increase feelings they are already feeling. Does that make sense?"

I frowned. I couldn't decide if I appreciated his efforts to make our date pleasant or if it irritated me that he would assume to make an adjustment to my emotions.

"I wasn't trying to upset you. I'm trying to do the opposite, in fact," he offered.

I took a deep breath, held it for a moment, then blew it out. I smiled slightly as I said, "I know. I appreciate it. I think I can manage to have a good time with you, enjoy tonight, and be upset all at the same time. I can hold more than one emotion at a time without exploding."

"Okay, then. I'll back it off. My apologies," Evan said with a smile and bumped my shoulder with his.

"You're not offended?" I had already angered one Barnes, and I wasn't eager to offend a second.

"Not at all. I should have asked first."

A silence descended between us, and I didn't know what to say to break the awkwardness. Thankfully, it didn't last long as the stage lights suddenly dimmed and came up moments later with the band in place.

Chapter 15: The Concert

The crowd roared. The opening chords of Red Helix's song, "Almost Gone," blared through the speakers, and I clapped. I didn't know all of their music, but I knew this song. As they played, Evan's foot tapped the side of mine, and I took a sideways half-step away to keep my balance. I leaned into his side briefly, then bumped him with my shoulder. I looked up at him with a smirk, and he adjusted his stance slightly then moved. Looking down at his feet, I saw him tapping one heel out then do a little shuffle with his other foot while tapping heel-toe.

Shocked that Evan knew how to dance, I looked at him. "What was that?"

He did it again, a little slower, and I tried to copy him. He paused, then started over, moving one step at a time so I could mimic the steps.

"One more time," I said.

This time, I could almost do it with him, both of us grinning.

The music stopped, and the band introduced themselves and did the obligatory, "How are we doing, Willowbrook" bit before launching into another song.

Evan's hand brushed mine. When I looked at him, he pointed to his feet, and we did his dance step in sync. He nodded at me with approval. Then we swayed to the music. The band switched songs, and this one was another upbeat one, not too fast.

I nudged his arm to get his attention and did a side shuffle dance step of my own. He gestured to do it again, so I did, and he managed to follow the move for the first few counts before tripping on his own feet. Laughing, I caught his arms before he could accidentally trample me. We reset our positions, and he followed my movements a little better this time. Like me, on the fourth time through, he could do it with me without any issues.

I swear my face was going to split from how much I was smiling and laughing. The last time I felt this happy was before Evan and Jessica's parents' car accident.

He bumped my side gently and pointed at his feet, then mine. I understood at once and nodded. He did a countdown on his fingers, and we did his little tapping dance move followed directly by my shuffle.

"This is great! Our dance needs a name!" He shouted to be heard over the din.

I leaned toward him, stretching on tiptoes so he could hear me. "We need one more move first."

He nodded agreement, and we spent the next song or two making up another tap-shuffle dance step that could pair with the others. I focused on the steps and suddenly realized I didn't even know what songs the band had played when they started in on "Losing Green." By then, we had a three-part dance move we could both do without error.

Now, the lead singer of Red Helix said they would take a short break and come back with more music. The lessening of noise allowed Evan and me to talk without shouting.

"Have you ever made up a dance before?" He asked.

"No. Have you?"

He shook his head. "I know a few moves and some specific dances, like the waltz. My parents loved to dance and wanted to make sure we could be in polite society without looking like fools. So, they taught us a few dances. We all used to practice in the kitchen." The corners of his mouth turned down, and I knew he was remembering many evenings with his whole family.

Wanting to lighten the mood again, I asked, "So, what shall we call our dance?"

"Hmm. How about the Haven?"

"The Haven?"

"Yeah, it's a combination of Hannah and Evan." He smiled that mischievous smile again that was doing odd things to my head.

"Are people really going to say, 'Let's do the Haven' like they say, 'Let's do the cha-cha'?" I thought for a moment. "Oh, what about the Haven Shuffle?"

"Hmm." He pursed his lips and rolled his eyes up to look at the sky. Finally, he said, "I like it! We'll have to show the others if we see them."

At the mention of our friends, my stomach sank a bit.

"You know what? I think it's popcorn time," Evan announced.

"Oh, yes. That sounds great." I turned to see what direction the booth was in.

Evan took the hat off his head and placed it on mine.

I laughed and tried to put the hat back on his head. Of course, I couldn't reach, so instead I shoved it into his chest.

"Nope. It's so I can find you later." This time, he placed his hat gently on my head, gave me a peck on the cheek, then said, "I will be right back with popcorn. Anything else?"

My cheeks had heated, and my thoughts were feeling a little incoherent, so I just replied, "Sounds great."

As before, it didn't take very long before he returned.

"Do you have a special power or something to get in the front of the lines?" I asked when he handed me the warm bag of buttery goodness.

"Nope. I just time things well."

The band came back on stage then, to another roar from the crowd. This time, Evan and I paid more attention to the music, but we still occasionally bumped shoulders and did the Haven Shuffle. When the music ended and the band thanked the crowd, Evan took my hand again.

"I don't want to get separated from you," he said. "It's my turn to walk you home, as promised."

Willowbrook's park wasn't very large, and everyone had either walked from their homes or the ferry, so it was slow going to make it to the street.

"Let's get the table," I said. "And then you can drive me home instead of walking, if you'd like." My cheeks heated again, and I put my free hand on one side of my face and then the other, trying to cool them. But it wasn't from outside heat.

"Or, since the streets are packed, I can walk you home and come back for my truck. It would probably be faster. Although," he let the word hang for a second, "if we drive then I can keep you for longer." With that smile on his face again, he tugged me in the direction of the table.

Once there, he picked up the now-empty wrought-iron table with ease. I grabbed one of the chairs and followed him to his truck.

"What are you doing?" He asked.

"I'm not helpless," I replied. "Or weak."

"I know. I didn't mean that. It's just that I figured I would do all the heavy lifting tonight."

"You are. This chair isn't very heavy at all. No heavier than the ones in the coffee shop."

When I turned to go back for the other chair, he grasped my arm gently, steered me to the passenger side, and opened the door for me.

"Wait here. I'll get the chair."

He said it with such concern and sweetness that I didn't want to protest. I climbed into the truck and settled in the seat. With a pointed look, he locked the door before closing it. I watched as his long strides ate up the short distance to the lonely chair and back. Once the chair was in the back, he used the key fob to unlock the doors and slid into the driver's seat. Evan peered up the street.

"It's still pretty crowded. How about we go the other way, around the outskirts of town? At least that way there is less risk of accidentally hitting a concert goer who had a few too many."

"And we can see the moon over the water," I added by way of agreement.

"Ah, a romantic at heart, are you?"

"It seems so are you."

"Touché."

He started the engine and turned the wheel to point the truck away from the main part of town and the ferry. Main Street ran from the ferry dock to the other side of the island where it ended at Ocean Avenue, which followed the outside of Willowbrook in a huge loop, broken only by roads branching toward the center like a spider's web. The water was visible from Ocean Avenue the entire way around. It was a frequent favorite of mine especially when I went jogging. At any point when I got tired or bored, I could veer off on one of the branching streets and cut my way back through town instead of running the entire loop.

The moon was not quite full, but the light shimmered off the water anyway, making it look like the stars themselves had taken to earth.

"Did you have a good time?" Evan asked softly.

"I did, thank you. It was the most fun I've had in a long time."

"For me, too." Reaching over, he clasped my hand, intertwining his fingers with mine.

I settled more into the seat, allowing the heat of the leather to seep into my skin. *Is this what contentment feels like?* I wondered.

The companionable silence lasted until he pulled up in front of the cottage.

"Is Jewels here already?" He asked.

I looked at my house. The porch light was on, as well as the lamp in the living room. "Hard to tell. We usually leave at least one light on inside when we leave. Her bedroom is in the back, so I can't see if her light is on or not from the street."

In one smooth motion, Evan slid out of the truck. I reached for the door handle, but the locks clicked down with a definitive *thunk.*

I blinked in surprise and looked at him through the window. He grinned, pure mischief on his face, then waggled his eyebrows before strolling around the front like he had all the time in the world. With exaggerated ceremony, he clicked the fob and opened the passenger door.

"Was that necessary?" I asked, amused.

"Absolutely," he said, offering his hand. "Adds to the drama."

I took it, and he helped me down, then gave me a playful spin out of the way so he could shut the door without letting go of me. Still holding hands, we made our way to the porch. When we reached the top step, he turned to face me.

"Thank you, Hannah, for agreeing to go out with me tonight."

"I'm glad I figured out your question earlier today," I teased.

After I had said yes to going out tonight, his nervousness about asking me disappeared, and he transformed into the confident guy I've always known, complete with silliness and some fancy footwork.

He moved a little closer and used one finger to tip the hat up so it wasn't quite so low on my brow.

"Oh, I forgot your hat," I exclaimed, raising one hand to take it off.

"Shh," Evan whispered, taking my free hand in his and leaning closer to me. His head angled slightly.

My breath caught as I realized he was going to kiss me. Unconsciously, my lips parted. Desire flickered in his eyes before he closed the distance, and our lips met.

Evan's mouth was soft on mine, undemanding. I tasted the lingering buttery salt from the popcorn mingled with the warmth of red wine and something earthy and unmistakably him. I tilted my head up a little and my back arched slightly, trying to push my body closer to his, wanting more. Evan broke the kiss off, leaning his forehead against mine.

"Oh, Hannah," he breathed. "I'm sorry it took me this long to truly see you."

I didn't trust my voice, so instead I pulled my hands free of his and wrapped my arms around his waist. He tucked my head against his chest.

"I can sleep at Jessica's tonight," Jewels's voice called.

I sprang away from Evan, feeling oddly guilty, and saw my roommate standing at the end of the small walkway leading from the sidewalk to the porch.

Evan laughed, and the sound made the butterflies flutter in my stomach. "No, but thank you for the offer. I'll take you up on it later." He plucked his hat off my head and touched my cheek reassuringly. "I will see you tomorrow, Hannah. Good night, ladies."

"Good night, indeed," Jewels quipped as Evan walked past her to his truck. Looking back at me, she said, "No need to ask you how it went."

I turned to unlock the door. "It was the best night ever."

Chapter 16: Friends

When the next morning came with light streaming through a crack in the curtains to tease my closed eyelids, I groaned and pulled a pillow over my head. Reality could wait. I wanted to stay in my dreams, where Evan and I had one amazing date after another. Of course, I couldn't remember details, only the happy feelings that remained.

A knock at my door made me groan again.

"Hannah? Are you awake?"

"Why do you keep interrupting the good parts?" I grumbled at Jewels through the closed door.

"It's almost nine. Sofia wants us at Jessica's in an hour, remember? I thought you might want some breakfast and coffee first."

Reality came crashing back. As usual, Jewels didn't take offense at my grumpiness. Sometimes I wondered if she even noticed the mood.

"Okay, thank you. I'm coming." I waited until I heard her footsteps receding to the kitchen before throwing back the comforter and swinging my legs over the side of the bed. I glanced at my phone, hoping for a text from Jessica. The only notification I had was a text from my mom.

Shoes delayed. Will update when I have an ETA.

I rolled my eyes. Testing her client's new sneakers was not even on my radar anymore. I didn't care if they showed up or not.

The amazing events of last night had pushed both the message from Jamison and today's meeting with Sofia from my mind. I almost convinced myself that the entire debacle with Donna's coffee had been a nightmare.

I didn't know what to expect this morning, so I opted to prepare as if I were meeting my mother. I took a shower and carefully dressed in my favorite jeans, a blue sweater that brought out my eyes and made me feel beautiful. Putting my red in a loose bun at the nape of my neck, I allowed a few tendrils to escape and curl around my face. I applied minimal makeup, just enough to look put together, but not so much that it would smear if I cried. When I at last walked into the kitchen, Jewels was finishing her breakfast of oatmeal and toast.

"There's plenty of coffee," she said between bites.

I smiled in thanks and prepared my own breakfast. Oatmeal and toast were among the few things Jewels could make without burning something, but it sounded good this morning. Plus, it was quick, and we needed to leave soon if we were going to be on time.

When Jewels stood to take her dishes to the sink, I finally got up the nerve to ask her, "Do you know what's going to happen today?"

"Your powers expanded suddenly. It usually takes a while for that to happen, at least from what I heard. I think Sofia just wants the details, so she knows how to adjust your training." She shrugged as if it weren't a big deal.

"Then why was Jessica so mad? It's not like I could control it."

Jewels's expression became guarded. "You'll have to ask her."

"You know something."

"Being a friend in the middle of two friends who are not quite agreeing is very difficult. I won't say anything to either of you about what you each tell me. But you can talk to me if you want."

I blew out a breath. "Fine. I'll wait and see what she says today."

Jewels nodded and left, presumably to get her shoes.

Alone, I quickly finished my meal and deposited my dishes in the sink before leaving to find my own shoes, opting for comfortable black flats. Jewels and I met in the living room and walked to Jessica's together.

Technically, it was Jessica and Evan's house, although with how serious Jessica and Zane were getting, I had a feeling Evan would move out soon. Their house wasn't too far; nothing in Willowbrook was far.

The air held a crisp note of autumn that wasn't there yesterday, and some of the leaves were more yellow than before. I made a mental note to go to the city for anything I might need over the winter. I preferred to keep to the island when the waters of the bay were choppy from winter tides and winds.

All too soon, we were at Jessica's house. I briefly closed my eyes to steel myself before following Jewels through the gate and into the backyard. The others were already there, Sofia sitting in one of the bistro chairs, Evan leaning casually against the railing of the steps leading up to the kitchen door, and Jessica pacing in the middle of the yard barefoot. Evan flashed me a smile when I glanced at him. I tried to smile back, but it probably came off more as a grimace.

"Good, you're here," Sofia said. "Have a seat. Jessica, come over here."

I sat next to Sofia, and thankfully, Jewels sat next to me. I don't know if she just picked the closest chair or if she was trying to keep space between Jessica and me, but either way, I appreciated it. Jessica didn't sit. Instead, she stood behind the last remaining chair with her arms folded.

Sofia glanced around at all of us. "Here's how this will go. Jessica, since you already called me and told your side, I want to hear from Hannah. I do not want any interruptions while she is talking. I do not want any outbursts when she finishes. I get to speak first. Understood?" She waited until we all nodded our agreement. "Oh, and Evan? No projecting, but keep tabs on what everyone is feeling. Okay, then. Hannah, dear, tell us what happened yesterday."

The kindness in her voice made me think this was less an inquisition and more of a support group. Jewels gave me an encouraging nod.

I started slowly, describing the quiet morning followed by the mad rush and how I didn't want Donna to have any reason to be angry with Jessica. "I knew it had been quite a while since Donna ordered her drink, but she was sitting with her back to the counter with headphones on, so she didn't hear me call and it wasn't like I could get her attention. And with the number of people in there, I didn't think I could take the time to walk it over just then. I wished..." I paused, worried it would sound ridiculous. "I wished I could teleport it to her, and it lifted from the counter and began floating over."

"Is that it?" Sofia prompted.

I looked down at the concrete. An ant was crawling in a crack, and my eyes tracked its movement while I said, "And then Jessica saw it and picked it up out of the air and took it to Donna."

"I want to be sure I understand. You were feeling overwhelmed about the amount of orders and worried about how Donna would act to Jessica?" When I nodded, she said, "Interesting. Jewels, anything to add? You were there."

"I didn't really see anything except for how upset Jessica got. It was only after, when they were taking, that I knew what happened."

Sofia asked, "And how did Jessica react?"

I saw Jewels hesitate. Wait. Were we here because Jessica screwed up, not because of what I did?

"Well, she was upset. Angry, even. She left the shop, and the sky darkened a little bit. But then it cleared, and it was lovely for the evening."

Sofia nodded. "It was a lovely evening. I enjoyed the concert. Did all of you go?" She cast her shrewd gaze on me.

"We went. Separately," Jessica snapped.

"Explain," Sofia said.

"Jewels, Zane, and I went together, but Evan and Hannah went as a date." Bitterness seeped from her voice.

"Hold on," I said. "Are you mad because I went on a date with your brother? You seemed perfectly fine with it when I told you. Happy for me, even."

"I was happy for you. And that's not why I'm mad."

"Then why?"

"Have you contacted your dad yet?"

My mouth dropped open. "You mean, Jamison, the man who hasn't seen me since I was a baby? No, I haven't decided whether or not I want to meet him. Are you telling me you're mad because I haven't responded to him? How is that any of your business?"

"If my dad came back right now, I wouldn't hesitate to see him!" An icy wind blew around us, whipping her hair across her face. She brushed it away angrily.

"Well, you loved your dad. I didn't even know the name of mine!"

"You don't get it." Jessica turned and headed to the garden.

I gave Evan a questioning look.

"Let her go," he said. "She'll either come back when she's more reasonable, or I'll get her when we're ready." It wasn't until he spoke that I realized he had been silent until now.

Sofia harrumphed. "That girl still needs to figure some things out. Her control is much better, but she needs to do more work. In the meantime, let's talk about you, Hannah. It's not often that a new witch's powers expand in so short a time. Jessica is the strongest witch that I know of right now. She's the strongest witch in several generations, in fact. But even she had a slow progression of the increase in her powers."

"Does that mean something is wrong?" I asked.

"Oh, absolutely not, my dear. I think it means you have a very strong desire to protect yourself and those you love. When we did the exercises the other day, the only time you could stop the fire Jessica threw at you was when it directly endangered you. Yesterday, you subconsciously found a way to solve a problem that otherwise might have negatively affected your best friend, whom you care for deeply."

"So, her catalyst is the same for both powers," Evan said.

"Correct. But now that we know she has a new power, we can work on training that as well."

I heaved a sigh, and the tightness in my chest eased just a little. "So, I'm not in trouble?"

"Oh, my dear girl," Sofia chuckled. "If Jessica didn't get in trouble when she destroyed the pier with her temper tantrum," she held up a hand to forestall Evan's protest, "and it was a temper tantrum regardless of why, then you are not in trouble for unintentionally discovering a new power by trying to protect your friend."

"How do I keep things from happening when I don't want them to?"

"That was Jessica's question, too," Evan put in. "You can talk to her when she calms down some, but I think part of the answer in your case is to try not thinking about magical solutions to everyday problems. So far, when you've accidentally used your magic, it was a reaction to something else. The plates, the coffee. Maybe try being aware of the stray thoughts that pop into your head. Perhaps that will help."

I nodded. What he said made sense. It sounded impossible too, but I was willing to try.

"We will not practice today. I merely wanted to find out what happened and get some of this out in the open. Hannah, I'll tell Jessica this too, but you two need to mend this rift."

"I know," I muttered miserably.

Sofia stood, patted the pockets of her red swing dress as if looking for something, then reached up and found her glasses on her head. "I'll be going now. I have a bridge game soon, and I refuse to let Gladys spike the punch with that cheap rum she prefers. Only the top shelf for me."

As she left, Jewels said, "That woman keeps surprising me. Well, I'm going to go too. I heard Willow Wears is having a sale and I'm hoping for some feathers or tie-dye." She actually skipped out of the gate, and I heard her prancing steps down the driveway.

"I feel like I should tell her Willow Wears is too upscale for tie-dye," I said.

Evan pushed himself off the railing where he had been leaning this whole time. "Nah, she'll be happy just shopping. And who knows? Maybe she'll find something to suit her 80s style."

I stood, uncomfortable to be still sitting, and craned my neck up to look at him. "Evan," I started slowly. "Can I ask you something? As a friend?"

Something flickered in his expression, but he nodded. "Sure, but let's walk," he said, casting a glance to the garden.

He tilted his head toward the garden gate, and I followed him out to the street. Without needing to say it, we turned away from the center of town, onto the quieter side streets where old maples arched overhead, casting cool shadows on the sidewalk.

We walked close enough to feel each other's presence but not quite touching. The space between us felt different now. Before, it had been easy and comfortable. Now it buzzed with something cooler and more formal. I told myself I appreciated it as I needed space to think. But in truth, it left me feeling uncertain, like I'd knocked something loose and didn't know how to put it back.

He didn't press me to speak, which I also appreciated. That was Evan, steady, quiet, and reliable.

I took a breath, keeping my eyes ahead. Finally, I blurted, "What do you think? Should I agree to meet my dad?"

He slowed, but didn't stop. Out of the corner of my eye, I saw his posture shift slightly, just enough to notice.

"Hannah," he said carefully. "Tell me more of the story. Jess said you talked to your mom, but she didn't tell me what happened."

"My mother didn't tell me much. She said she made Jamison leave but refused to tell me why. That's it, really. I was wondering if he might be a criminal since he waited ten years after I turned eighteen to contact me. That would make sense, right?"

"Maybe. There might be other reasons, too. Like maybe he had a hard time tracking you down."

"It's a possibility."

"Everyone has a digital profile these days. Have you looked him up?"

"No," I said slowly. "I looked at his Facebook profile after he messaged me but that was it."

"So maybe start there."

"That's a good idea. But Evan?"

"Hmm?"

"How do you feel about it? About me maybe meeting him? Jess is so upset that I'm not sure. And I completely understand. It must be painful for her to see me suddenly getting a dad when she's lost hers."

He stopped walking abruptly, turning to stare at a rosebush in someone's yard. His arms stayed crossed, and his body angled away from me. I waited, letting him gather his thoughts.

When he spoke, his tone was neutral. "I think Jess has her own stuff going on. But that's her story, not yours."

I turned toward him, trying to read his face. "That's not really an answer."

He shifted his weight, still not looking at me. "You said you wanted the friend version, so…" He shrugged. "From a friend's perspective, yeah, it's good you're cautious."

"And do you think I should meet him?"

"I think this is a unique situation. You don't know if this man has good intentions or not. What does he think he's going to gain by contacting you now? What prompted him to reach out now instead of ten or even five years ago?"

"I haven't thought about any of that yet."

"As far as how I feel, if you're asking if it hurts me to see you gain a father after mine is gone, the answer is no. I'm happy for you. You might have some closure now or some answers about your past, and while it might be hard to discover, it's important. But the choice is yours. Not mine, or Jessica's, or anyone else's."

"That's very mature of you," I blurted, hating how awkward it sounded.

His mouth lifted in a smirk that didn't quite reach his eyes. "I've been known for maturity from time to time. I am the big brother, after all."

I gave him a little shove with my elbow, trying to recapture the easiness. "That's not what I meant."

"I know." He looked back at the street. "Jessica...she's feeling too much right now. Once she has time to think, I'm sure she'll come around."

"I hope so. I miss her." I quickly added, "Don't get me wrong, Jewels has been great. I see her more than Jessica these days since we live together, and she's been answering all of my random magical questions. As much as she can, anyway. But Jess and I have been best friends for years. This is really hard." My throat caught on the last words, and I looked away from Evan.

He nodded, and for a second I thought he might reach for my hand, but he didn't. He kept his hands tucked in his pockets.

I glanced up at him. "I told myself I'd decide today. Whether to meet Jamison."

"You want to walk some more?"

"I think I need to. You can go back if you want."

"Okay," he said quickly. "Yeah, I'll go."

I blinked at him, surprised. "Oh. Okay."

He took a small step back with a polite smile. "Let me know what you decide. I'll see you around."

I watched him walk away, but he paused after a few steps and turned to look at me.

"Hannah, I want you to be safe. Above all else, that's what I want."

He said it the same way he tells in self-defense class to me mindful of our surroundings.

"Thank you," I mumbled.

He nodded, and soon his long strides took him to the end of the street, and he turned the corner toward his house.

For the first time, I felt like I couldn't read him at all. Maybe I should have said something more. Maybe he should have. Either way, neither of us did.

Chapter 17: Retail Therapy

J ewels must've still been at Willow Wears because the cottage was silent by the time I made it home. Flopping on the couch, I pulled out my phone and opened the browser.

Jamison Stewart, I typed.

Pages of results appeared on the screen. The top few were men in Texas or Vermont. Throwing myself into the search, I shifted through pages of results, letting the rhythm of scrolling and clicking drown out any lingering thoughts of Evan. I told myself I wasn't going to avoid him. I just had more pressing concerns. Like figuring out whether my father was a criminal.

"Okay," I muttered. "How about 'Jamison Stewart, Washington?'"

That was better. There were still ten pages or more of results, but the first page narrowed it down to Washington and Oregon. I tapped on the first one. Not him. Nor was the next, or the next. I went through three pages of results before they started getting desperate and showing me obituaries or other names, such as Bob Jamison. My father didn't have an online presence.

I thumbed back to the Meta messaging app. Jamison's last message was still on top. From there, I went to his profile and then the about page. He joined Facebook in 2023. His profile was just a year old.

"So, where have you been all this time, Jamison?"

The lack of an internet presence supported my theory that he was a criminal. Either he had been in jail and not allowed to access the internet, or he kept a low profile so he can't be found. What other explanation was there?

I went back to the messaging app. Slowly, I typed out my reply, rearranged a phrase, and hit send.

I don't know where you've been or why you are just now asking to see me. My mother must have had a good reason for leaving you. She doesn't do anything without a reason. I've done well without you so far and see no reason to introduce you into my life now.

I hit send and dropped my phone on the couch. Leaning back, I closed my eyes. I let my thoughts drift aimlessly. The last few weeks' events drained me. I almost wanted to take a vacation somewhere, but I knew leaving wouldn't solve anything.

I pulled my phone back into my lap and opened my texts, automatically scrolling to Jessica's name. The last message between us was still unread—mine. Just a simple apology that had gone unanswered. I missed her. Missed the easy way she grounded me with her practical logic and the way her laughter could knock loose whatever weight I was carrying. We hadn't spoken since the disagreement, and even though I kept telling myself she needed space, I hated the silence. Things never used to be this complicated between us.

A notification from my phone alerted me to a new message. I opened my eyes and looked at the screen.

Please, Hannah. Let me explain. If I can't satisfy your questions in twenty minutes, you will never hear from me again.

I didn't respond. I dropped the phone and decided it could stay on the cushion until tonight. I grabbed my purse and went to see if I could catch up with Jewels at the clothing sale. I found her with an armload of clothes in colorful fabrics, trying to pick up an equally loud hat off the shelf with one hand without dropping her prizes.

"Here, let me help," I said, rushing over and taking the clothes from her.

"Hannah! Thanks. This sale is amazing. Look at this hat."

I obliged, taking in the plum felt of the form with a lemon-yellow fluffy plume sticking out of the beet-colored band.

"That's something, alright," I finally managed to say. "Where would you wear it?"

"To work, or the bank, or wherever! It's gorgeous. I found this." She tugged a blouse the color of summer sunlight out of my hands. "And this hat will set it off wonderfully."

I couldn't deny her individual fashion sense. We could always find her in a crowd.

"Okay, I think I'm done. I'm going to check out, and then I'll help you."

I followed Jewels to the counter where Sandy West calmly rang customers up, making sure to properly fold and bag their purchases and even chatting while doing it. She always made sure that everyone felt important when they walked into her store. Once Sandy had safely bagged Jewels's treasures, Jewels followed me around, offering me advice. Her chatter distracted me just enough from my worries that I relaxed.

I fingered a white T-back, knee-length dress with teal and jade vertical stripes.

"Ooh, get that one," Jewels said. "You would look stunning in it."

"Do you think?"

"Absolutely. Evan would love to see you in it." Jewels winked at me.

I made a noncommittal sound. After our conversation today, I wasn't sure if his interest extended to the romantic anymore. I hoped so. Maybe this dress would help with that. I lifted it off the rack, and Jewels took it from me.

"So you can have your hands free," she said.

I ran my fingers down a soft, coral-colored boho-chic dress with a subtle pattern of cream-colored flowers and a crocheted collar. I held it up to my shoulders and turned to Jewels.

"What do you think?" I asked.

She studied me for a moment. "It's not your usual style, but I think it would look great with leggings and your black riding boots. Get it." She took it from me and draped it over her arm with the dress. "Does anything else catch your eye?"

I looked around the boutique and wandered over to the wall of accessories where Jewels had found her hat. A dove-gray cashmere scarf practically begged to go home with me. Gloves and a hat nearby created a complete matching set. I sighed. I didn't know if I could justify the expense of cashmere, but I was expecting a bonus from the preschool soon. For a while, they had trouble finding someone to fill the position, so they offered a signing bonus after three months. If I got this set, it would be my last splurge for a while.

"What the heck," I muttered.

"Exactly," Jewels nodded.

Surprised that she heard me over the other shoppers and ambient music, I said louder, "I mean, after the last few days, I deserve a treat."

"Agreed." Jewels deftly put the cashmere set in the stack on her arm. "Anything else?"

Laughing, I said, "I don't think my wallet can take any more." I took my selections from her and waited my turn to check out.

"I'm so glad you came," Jewels said. "I love shopping, and it's always better with friends."

"I'm glad, too. I needed something to take my mind off things, and this was definitely it."

"Want to get lunch at Dave's?"

"Sure. That sounds good."

Dave's Diner was packed with people, but we squeezed onto two stools at the counter, shoving our shopping bags beneath our feet. After ordering our usual sandwiches and fries, I listened as Jewels chatted about her purchases.

"And then, I thought a white chicken would be just the thing to go with the green dress. I could perch it on my shoulder," Jewels declared.

My eyebrows knitted together as I frowned. "I'm sorry, what? A chicken?"

Jewels giggled. "I knew you were zoning out. At least that got your attention. What's on your mind?"

Sighing, I slumped in my chair. "I'm sorry. I told Jamison I didn't want to see him. And now I'm wondering if it's the right decision. Jessica seems to think I should at least hear him out, and Evan said it's up to me but to be careful. And there is zero information about him online, which makes me think he's a criminal. My mom isn't telling me why she left him. It's a complete puzzle, and I'm at the center. What do you think?"

Jewels toyed with her napkin. "Well, I can understand Jessica's view since she still sometimes struggles with the loss of her parents. I can also understand Evan's, as he's a protector and doesn't want you to get hurt. I'm sure your mom has her reasons, and maybe this situation is painful for her."

"Okay, maybe. I could see that. But what do you think?"

Tracing her finger through water droplets on the counter and not looking at me, Jewels said, "I don't know. My parents kicked me out when I started having visions. They aren't exactly supportive. I suppose if my dad messaged me asking to explain himself, I'd be curious enough to at least hear him out. Letting him talk doesn't mean we suddenly have a relationship again, so I don't see how it could hurt any worse than being told they don't want me anymore."

The agony in her voice made my throat ache. I pulled her into a one-armed hug against my side. "I wish they didn't do that to you," I said.

"Yeah, me too." She wiped at her cheek and then said, "Looks like all of us have daddy issues, just different ones."

I chuffed. "Seriously. It's so sad that it's almost funny."

Our food arrived then, and I think we were both grateful for the distraction. I picked at my fries, not really eating, as I thought about what she said. Jewels nudged my knee with hers.

"Hey, eat up. We still have to lug our purchases home, you know. And I may need help carrying mine."

The change in topic pulled me from my reverie, and I managed to eat half of my sandwich before asking for a box.

"Oh no! Now we'll have to carry that, too." Jewels put the back of her hand to her forehead in a dramatic pretend faint.

"I'm sure we'll make it." I laughed.

"I am so glad Over the Moon is closed on Sundays so we can shop. It's super convenient that the other stores are closed on Mondays. Maybe we should stop by the salon on the way home and see what new hair products Rita has."

I remembered thinking I needed eye cream and quickly agreed. As we walked, Jewels gave me a little bump with her shoulder, which instantly had me thinking of dancing with Evan at the concert.

"So, you and Evan are finally together, huh?"

I shrugged, keeping my gaze on the street ahead.

"Oh, come on. It's obvious you've had a thing for him for a while. He finally figured it out, too. So? Tell me. How is it?"

"I don't know if there's really a 'thing' between us at all."

Jewels stopped in her tracks. "Wait—what? After the concert? After the way he looks at you?"

I shifted the bags in my hands, pretending to be preoccupied. "We only had one date," I said lightly.

"And it seemed to go well," Jewels insisted. "So, what's the problem?"

"Well, I sort of put him in the friend zone today."

Jewels stopped walking and turned to face me, shock clear on her face. "You did what? Why would you do that?"

"I didn't mean to!" I protested. "I wanted his advice about my dad, but I wanted it from a friend's perspective, not from a romantic view."

"So, you basically told him you only wanted to be friends? Hannah!"

I shook my head. "It wasn't like that. I asked him if I could ask him a question as a friend."

Jewels hit her forehead with her palm, smacking me with a shopping bag in the process. "Hannah, how do you think he's going to take that? Evan is all heart. He's either in or out, and you just asked him to step out."

Suddenly, I had difficulty breathing, and my mouth felt dry. "Do you really think he took it that way?"

She shook her head slightly and bit her lip before responding. "I don't know. I don't know him as well as you do, but he definitely seems like the all-or-nothing type." Then she brightened. "I'm probably wrong. Don't worry about it. Come on."

She started walking again, and I trudged behind her, worry filling me. I needed to talk to Evan again as soon as possible.

We left The Beauty Den about twenty minutes later, Jewels armed with new pink hair color and strawberry-scented lotion, and I had found an eye cream that promised to reduce fine lines and wrinkles.

"I don't think you need that stuff," Jewels said as she held the door open with one foot.

I squeezed past her, juggling the shopping bags. "Have you seen these lines?" I widened my eyes at her since my hands were full.

"They're laugh lines. Ask Evan about them. He stares at your eyes often enough."

I groaned. "Thanks for reminding me that I friend-zoned him."

"Do a little shopping today, ladies?"

Evan's husky voice from behind us sent shivers down my spine.

"Here, let me help."

Before I could react, he lifted the bags from one of my hands, then turned and did the same for Jewels.

"Thanks!" Jewels said brightly. "Speak of the devil," she muttered when she stepped beside me.

I glared at her, then turned to Evan. "I didn't plan on shopping, but it seemed like a good idea."

"Retail therapy, huh?" Evan grinned. "Jess does that sometimes, but mostly she just works in the garden."

"That's probably healthier for the bank account," I said.

"Oh, I just remembered that we wanted to get some cheese to go with the crackers and olives tonight," Jewels suddenly said. "I'll stop at Stan's."

I opened my mouth to remind her we got the cheese yesterday, but Jewels continued.

"Can you take my stuff home?" She lifted her other bags toward me.

I narrowed my eyes at her, and she winked in response. Traitor.

"I've got it," Evan said.

I tried to ignore the way the muscles in his arms tightened as he took the bags from Jewels.

"You're a dear." Jewels quickly crossed the street and headed in the opposite direction.

"Yes, thanks. I think my arms might have fallen off by the time I made it home," I told him.

"No problem. I'm heading over to Old John's house to repair his back steps, so it's on the way."

Biting my lip, I frantically searched for something to say to reassure him I still wanted to explore the possibility of a romantic relationship.

"Last night was fun, huh?" I finally managed.

"Yes, it was."

I glanced at him and saw a small smile playing on his lips.

"Have you shown anyone else the Haven Shuffle?" He asked.

"No. Things have been a bit busy."

"Well, maybe we can get together and practice sometime before we show the others." He grinned then and gestured at the sidewalk leading up to my cottage. "After you."

I opened the door, and he followed me into the living room. I deposited the few bags I was carrying on the sofa, and he did the same.

"This is the second time you've walked me home today, Evan Barnes," I said, trying to put a teasing note in my voice.

"It's becoming a habit, Hannah Stewart," he replied in a soft tone.

"I don't mind."

"Good."

Evan leaned in a little, and I thought he would kiss me, but then he bent and picked up my phone from the sofa. I let out a small sigh of disappointment.

"Did you decide about your dad?"

"Yes. I told him I didn't want to see him."

"I take it he responded, so you left your phone here during retail therapy."

I nodded. "I just needed space."

"I understand."

For several heartbeats, we stood there looking at each other. I wanted to tell him I desired more than just friendship from him, but I wasn't sure where to start. Just as I took a breath to attempt some kind of apology, he shifted his stance and turned to the door.

"Well, I'd better get going. Old John is expecting me."

"Oh, right. Thanks again," I said. Ugh, I sounded like I was thanking a salesperson.

His mouth tightened in a line that wasn't quite a frown before he waved and shut the door behind him. I watched out the window as he sauntered back down the street, his long, easy strides eating up the distance. I could have stopped him, said something—anything—to make it clear I wasn't actually pushing him away.

But I didn't.

Flopping onto the overstuffed chair, I leaned my head back and closed my eyes.

"Stupid, stupid, stupid," I muttered.

Jewels found me like that when she came home, carrying yet another shopping bag, this one from Stan's Grocery Store.

"Hannah?"

I didn't bother raising my head. "I blew it."

"You think? I doubt Evan would have carried my bags home if you hadn't been there. He wanted to see you again. What happened?"

"We talked about general things, and then I thanked him as if he were a bellhop."

"All you had to do was tell him you couldn't wait to go out again. It didn't have to be a long conversation."

"I know. I couldn't get the words out. I tried hinting at it by bringing up the concert, and for a moment, it seemed like he was going to ask me on another date. But then he asked about my father, and it basically ended the entire conversation."

"Hannah!" Jewels gave my shoulder a little shove. "Evan is straight-up, remember? You can't just make hints and expect him to act on them."

I waved a hand. "I just didn't say what I meant to."

Jewels sat beside me. "So, say it next time."

I exhaled slowly. "I don't think there will be a next time."

Jewels scoffed. "Of course there will be."

I wasn't so sure. Avoiding things was one of my strong suits. I wasn't sure I knew how to stop.

I glanced at my phone again, half-hoping Jessica had texted me. Still nothing. It was ridiculous how much that silence stung. We'd always been able to talk through anything before, even the hard stuff. But this time, it was like a wall had gone up between us, and neither of us knew how to climb over it. I wanted to tell her everything, about

Evan, about Jamison, about how lost I felt. But I didn't even know where to begin anymore.

I shrugged. "That's that, then." Heaving myself off the chair, I began sorting our shopping.

Jewels stared at me. "You're giving up?"

"I'll still see Evan a lot. He comes into Over the Moon almost every day, and we have magic lessons. It's not like I won't talk to him again or something. But obviously I'm not good at dating. So, yeah, I'm giving up."

For now, I added silently.

Chapter 18: O is for Owl

The next morning was one of the days I worked at the preschool. When Jessica hired Jewels, it opened my schedule up a bit since Jewels could open the store. So, three days a week, Jewels opened the store by herself, and I did activities and crafts with three-to-five-year-olds before heading to Over the Moon just in time for the midday rush.

I mulled over the small selection in my closet, finally selecting jeans and a nutmeg-colored t-shirt. Both of my chosen jobs could be somewhat messy, so I tended to wear clothing that I could easily wash or even replace. I glanced longingly at the soft coral dress I had bought at Willow Wears and wondered if I'd ever get a chance to wear it. With a sigh, I firmly closed both the closet door and that train of thought and moved on with my morning.

The preschool was conveniently located next to the small elementary school. The middle and high schools were near to each other, just a few blocks over. Idly, I wondered if the original city planners had intentionally clustered all the schools like this or if it was simply a matter of available land on the island.

I stepped into the preschool's familiar red brick building, the faint scent of finger paints and disinfectant mingling in the air. After greeting Marissa at the front desk, I walked the short hallway to my classroom, the soles of my sneakers squeaking slightly against the worn linoleum.

The room was cheerful and bright, with a large round table in the center surrounded by ten pint-sized chairs and one adult-sized one for me. Colorful posters of shapes and letters lined the walls, and a sunny rug with the alphabet in bright block letters took up one corner, inviting small bodies to sit and learn. Cubbies waited by the door, and my desk—always just a little cluttered—sat next to them. The room buzzed with the quiet promise of activity.

Today, the theme was O for Owl, so I set about gathering supplies for the craft and queuing up songs on the computer. As I worked, I thought back to my own childhood. I vaguely remembered coming to this school when I was little. I didn't remember much, mostly just flashes of red brick and the creak of the swing set. Miss Helen remembered me, though. She still taught in the other classroom.

A knock on my door caused me to look up from the stack of colorful paper I was sorting.

"Hi, Miss Helen," I greeted her.

"It's just Helen now, remember? I don't teach you anymore," she replied with a warm smile as she stepped inside. Her silver-streaked hair pulled back in a no-nonsense bun somehow made her kind eyes and warm smile stand out even more.

I grinned. "It's habit. All the kids call you Miss Helen."

Her kind chuckle broadened my smile. "Well, then I shall call you Miss Hannah. I'm just checking to see if you need any help this morning."

"No, I think I've got it."

"You're a natural. I'm so glad you applied."

"Me too."

"See you at recess." Helen strode from the room, her back still ramrod straight.

Soon after, the children began trickling into the room. The air filled with the noise of tiny feet stomping, backpacks unzipping, and jackets being flung on the floor despite the cubbies. The slightly chaotic scramble of getting them settled took all my focus. Once they settled on the alphabet rug, I started the lesson. One child in particular, Owen, had energy to spare. He kept interrupting me as we practiced the 'o' sound.

"O is for Owen!" He shouted, puffing his chest proudly.

"Your name does start with O, but today we're doing owls. Now, who can tell me what color owls are?"

"Brown, like my hair. I could be an owl. Owen Owl." He flapped his arms enthusiastically, nearly smacking the girl next to him.

"Yes, some owls are brown. What other colors?"

Owen had tousled hair that never seemed to lay flat, freckles sprinkled across his cheeks, and a spark of constant movement in his limbs, as if his thoughts came faster than his body could keep up. He was five going on whirlwind.

Anna, the girl he almost hit, shifted away from Owen as she raised her hand. "Some owls are white," she whispered.

"Very good. And what do owls like to—"

"Whooo! I'm an owl!" Owen flapped his arms, almost hitting Anna.

"Owen, please settle down. Does anyone know what owls like to eat?"

The kids groaned and shrieked with varying guesses, from cookies to carrots. Then Maya, a dark-haired girl with bright blue eyes, raised her hand and waved it in the air.

"Yes, Maya?"

"They eat mice."

I nodded. "Yes, they eat mice. They might even eat bugs and fish and frogs." I paused as the kids made sounds of disgust. "Okay, it's time to read a story. Remember, voices off so everyone can hear and stay seated crisscross."

I took a deep breath and hoped Owen would be interested enough in the story that he wouldn't cause any more disruptions. He was always one of the more rambunctious kids, but today he seemed particularly excited. I read *The Knight Owl*, and Owen stayed unusually quiet, eyes wide, and only fidgeted during the last page.

"Let's go to the table, and we can make our craft. Owen, how about you sit by me?"

He hopped up and ran to the table, flapping his arms and hooting dramatically before plopping down beside me. I showed them the craft we would make—an O with wings, a beak, and eyes to make it look like an owl—then showed them step-by-step. Owen, as one of the older boys, knew how to use scissors without help, so I kept one eye on him as I walked around and helped some of the other kids cut their pieces.

I watched as they smeared glue on the paper and attached their cut-out Os to a larger piece of paper, then placed their owl parts, managing to make their projects look more or less like an owl. Owen stuck his owl's beak upside down and laughed, totally delighted with himself. I never forced them to make their craft look just like mine, as I knew they were learning the skills and needed to feel accomplished.

As the kids glued and chatted, a soft joy settled over me. This was one of the few places where I felt completely present. I had a role, a rhythm, and tiny humans who looked up at me like I held the world in my hands.

When it appeared that most of the children were almost done with their craft, I glanced at the clock.

"If you're finished with your craft, please put the lids on your glue and throw your paper scraps away."

Clean up always took a while, and by the time the first few kids had their area clean and their owls in their cubbies, the stragglers were ready to put their things away. Finally, all the children were ready for the next part of our day.

"Recess time," I called out. "It's sunny and warm today, so you don't need jackets unless you want them. Please line up at the door."

They were still learning how to make a line, so it looked more like a zigzag, and I patiently reminded them to stand behind the person in front of them and closer to the wall. Owen excitedly bounced on his toes.

"Remember to walk in the hall and keep your voices down in case Miss Helen's class is still working. Let's go."

I pushed open the door and led them into the hall. There was a door at the end opposite the office that went outside to the playground. The air smelled of grass and distant salt from the ocean.

As soon as the kids made it out the door, they let out whoops of joy and raced to the structure. I smiled and leaned against the sun-warmed brick, watching my charges. Owen was a blur of motion, running up and down the stairs and around the yard, flapping his arms and hooting. After a little while, I pulled out my phone to check the time.

When I looked back up, my breath caught in my throat.

Owen was balancing on top of the monkey bars, holding his arms out.

"Look, Miss Hannah! I'm an owl!"

Terror surged through me. "Owen, no!"

I couldn't reach him in time. Everything blurred. Things seemed to both slow down and speed up as I thrust myself forward. My pulse roared in my ears. My hands automatically reached up as if I could catch the little boy from twenty feet away.

"No!" I shouted again as Owen bent his knees to prepare for jumping.

Then time stopped.

Or rather, everyone in the schoolyard stopped. The laughter, the squeak of the swing set, all of it froze. The moment held still in perfect, terrifying silence.

Except for me. I didn't hesitate. I scrambled up the metal bars, heart pounding, and reached Owen. He stood frozen mid-motion, mouth open in joy, completely unaware of what he had been about to do. I wrapped my arms around him and pulled him down onto the platform.

I didn't know how long I had. Jessica remained frozen for almost ten minutes, but that was just one person. Did the number of people in the vicinity make a difference? I had no idea, and I wasn't going to waste time finding out.

Panic threatened to rise in my chest, but I forced myself to breathe. I had to be fast.

Once Owen was safe, I sprinted down the metal steps and headed back to my spot by the door.

Then the door opened.

Helen's form was silhouetted against the dim hallway. Her back was to the door as she instructed her classroom.

No, no, no.

Twisting around, I saw the faintest flicker of movement from the nearest child.

Hurry up, I thought.

Helen turned toward the opening. In a panic, I waved my hands at the students and said, "Resume," in as commanding a tone I could muster, willing the world to move again.

With a sudden burst, the playground resumed its cacophony of sound and movement.

"Sorry we're a little late," Helen said as her classroom joined mine on the playground. "We had a glue mishap."

"Oh." I tried to control my panting. "Is everything okay?"

I looked back at my students. Owen still stood where I left him, looking at the top of the monkey bars with a puzzled expression.

"Just fine. We learned that glue is not lip balm."

I forced a laugh, but it came out too high. *Did she notice? No.*

She turned to help a child with her shoelace. I watched Owen slowly make his way down the stairs and over to me, his freckled face scrunched in confusion.

"Miss Hannah?" he mumbled.

"Yes, Owen?" I crouched down so I was eye-level to him, still shaking. "Are you feeling okay?"

"I think I have a headache."

He still had a dazed expression, and I'm sure he wondered how he got down from where he was. I didn't know how much someone frozen by my magic would see or remember. Making a mental note to ask Jessica what she remembered from our training session, I said, "Go see Marissa in the office. You can lie down until snack time."

He nodded, and I opened the door for him, watching as he trudged down the hall.

I obviously needed to learn how to control my powers, and quickly.

Chapter 19: Lectures

That afternoon, I walked into Over the Moon to see Jessica and Jewels on their hands and knees, sopping up a sticky purple mess that spread across the floor behind the counter.

"What happened?" I asked, quickly getting another towel and bucket. I knelt down next to Jessica and wiped the floor, dunking the rag into the bucket of water and ringing it out.

"The blender burst," Jewels said with a pointed look at Jessica.

Jessica glared at her, then sat back on her heels and sighed. "My fault," she said. "Apparently, irritation and huckleberry shakes don't mix well."

"Your magic did this?" I whispered back. My shoulders slumped as I realized I wasn't the only one still learning control.

She nodded sharply, but I caught a shimmer of tears in her eyes. "I'm irritated with myself about fighting with you." She swiped at the floor, smearing the goop more.

Jewels nudged Jessica's hands away and deftly scooped the remaining clumps into her rag, dropping the whole thing into her bucket.

"I'm sorry," I murmured.

Jessica looked up. "You're sorry?"

"I didn't think about how my situation would make you feel. I should've supported you more."

She let out a breath. "I was being a brat."

"No, you weren't." I shook my head.

Jessica snorted. "I was jealous. Stupidly jealous that you have a dad who wants to know you. And I don't have anyone. I thought I was past this part of the grieving process, but then you have this chance that I'll never get. And it hurt. So, I lashed out."

My throat tightened, and I reached over to grasp her hand. "That doesn't make you a brat. It makes you human."

Jessica squeezed my hand once. "It wasn't fair to you."

"No, but I get it. I'd feel the same if the situation were reversed."

She winced but then gave me a sad smile. "I missed you."

"I missed you, too." I took a deep breath and released her hand. "I told Jamison I wasn't interested in seeing him."

She looked at me sharply. "Why not?"

"Because I didn't grow up needing a dad. I had yours."

"Oh, Hannah." Tears streaked down her cheeks. "I should have realized that it wasn't just mine and Evan's loss."

I shook my head. "No, it's okay. He was your dad. But he sort of stood in for mine when I needed someone." I smiled gently. "Jamison is trying too late to be a father."

"I suppose," she said slowly, "that I can understand that."

"Well, this mess isn't going to clean itself," Jewels broke in.

I glanced at her and saw her surreptitiously wipe her cheek on her sleeve.

"Why didn't one of us end up with cleaning magic?" Jessica said.

We all laughed, and instantly the room felt brighter. The weight on my chest lifted, and I knew things would be okay.

We finished wiping the floor, then I mopped any remaining stickiness while Jewels took the buckets and rags in the back to clean. Jessica made another huckleberry shake for Kara, one of our self-defense classmates, who was very understanding about the mishap.

"One time, when I went to make a pie, I didn't vent the top and the whole thing exploded all over the oven. Apple pieces everywhere!" Kara laughed as Jessica handed her the milkshake. "My mama never asked me to make the pie for Thanksgiving again. See you in class."

A few teenagers trickled in after that, but the shop was relatively quiet. I took the opportunity to whisper to Jessica, "When you were frozen, did you see what was going on around you?"

She gave me a puzzled frown and whispered back, "Not really. Why?"

"What did you see?"

Jessica frowned at me and shook her head slightly, her eyes darting to the three teenage girls browsing the bookshelves. "We'll talk about this later."

Later turned out to be when we were cleaning after closing. Jewels merrily hummed as she wiped tables, moving with a lightness that suggested she didn't have a care in the world. Meanwhile, Jessica and I followed behind, stacking chairs, the quiet weight of the conversation hanging between us.

Jessica broke the silence first. "So, about your question earlier," she started. "I didn't see anything until just before I could move. And then it was hazy, sort of dreamlike. Why do you ask?"

I shifted uncomfortably, gripping the back of a chair tighter than necessary. Jessica's powers manifested last spring, so she wasn't exactly an expert. But she seemed to know so much more than I did. And she was my best friend. If I couldn't tell her, who could I tell? Finally, I took a deep breath and dove in.

"At the school today, there was a little boy—Owen—who was pretending to be an owl. During recess…" I hesitated, pressing my lips together before continuing. "He climbed on top of the play structure, and it looked like he was going to jump. I panicked, and before I knew it, the entire class froze."

Jessica stopped stacking chairs, her gaze snapping to mine. "And then?"

Glancing up, I saw Jewels had paused in her cleaning to listen, her eyebrows raised in curiosity.

"I ran up, grabbed him, and set him on the platform. And when everyone unfroze, he looked confused then said he had a headache." I swallowed. "He seemed fine after he rested for a little while, though."

"Maybe he didn't see anything, and it was moving him that was the problem," Jessica suggested. "No one touched or moved me when you froze me last week, right?"

I shook my head.

"So, how would you feel if one second you were, say, standing on the sidewalk and the next you were in the middle of the street?"

"Definitely confused," I admitted.

"It's possible he didn't have a headache. Maybe he didn't know how to make sense of what happened," Jewels offered. "Did anyone see you?"

I wasn't going to admit that part, but since she asked... "No, but almost. Helen and her class came out, but I said 'resume,' and everything went back to normal."

Jessica grabbed my arm. "Wait. You said 'resume' and reversed your magic?" she asked sharply.

I nodded. "But I don't know if it was that or just that time was up. You were frozen for almost ten minutes, but you're just one person, and I have ten kids in my class."

"It makes sense. Magic has limitations, after all," Jewels said. "Well, maybe not yours." She flapped her dish rag at Jessica.

Jessica scoffed. "My power has limitations, too. It's just less limited."

"Brag much?" Jewels teased.

"I'm not—"

"She's kidding!" I interrupted before Jessica could argue.

Jewels grinned. "Everyone knows how powerful you are. But back to Hannah. All I'm saying is it makes sense. Ten minutes for one person, one minute for ten people. Balance, you know?"

"I guess." I shrugged.

"Well, I would say you should tell Sofia at our next lesson, but that won't be necessary," Jessica said.

"Why not?" I motioned for Jewels to keep cleaning and picked up another chair.

"I have a feeling she'll be seeing you tonight. She seems to know when her charges are causing chaos."

"Oh, so now you're clairvoyant as well as a nature witch?" Jewels taunted.

Jessica stuck her tongue out at her. "It's happened to me a time or two. Sofia showing up, not the visions. I'll leave that to you."

A knock on the window caused all of us to look. Sofia waved at us through the glass.

"Speak of the devil," muttered Jessica as she went to let Sofia in.

Sofia entered with the air of someone who already knew the conversation. "Hello, girls. I figured it would be easier to talk to all of you here rather than calling a meeting," Sofia said as she settled into one of the plush chairs by the bookshelves. "Go ahead and keep working, but tell me what happened as you do so."

"Jewels and I will take care of the counter. You can sweep so you can chat," Jessica said.

I went to the back to get the broom then started sweeping as I told Sofia everything that happened at the preschool.

"You are very lucky that Helen didn't see you," Sofia said when I finished. "She is a Mundane and a firm believer that magic is evil. The Council works very hard to keep her from knowing anything that really goes on in Willowbrook."

I grimaced. Good to know. And it meant I would have to be more careful while at the preschool.

"What about Owen and his headache?"

Jessica interrupted and told Sofia her theory.

"Yes, that's definitely a possibility," Sofia said. "We will have to test that and your magical reversal at our next lesson. And work on your new teleportation abilities."

She stood, rubbing at her knees. "For now, try to remember that it apparently takes both a gesture and some sort of word that involves 'stop' or 'no' to activate your magic. Don't do them together unless you mean to."

"Yes, Sofia," I said.

Satisfied, she nodded. I followed her to the door and locked it behind her. Leaning against it, I heaved a sigh.

Jewels turned to me with a mischievous grin. "Now, it's not all bad! At least your magic won't destroy the boat dock."

"Hey! I helped with the repairs. And I made up for it with the garden." Jessica glared, throwing a wet rag at her.

Jewels batted it away. "I'm just trying to make her feel better."

Jessica rolled her eyes, but then she came and wrapped an arm around my shoulders. "For what it's worth, I'm a little jealous. Truly. Your magic being out of control is tame compared to mine."

"And don't worry," Jewels piped up with a nod. "Every new witch has to go through the process of learning, and it's different for everyone. Magic triggers are personal."

"But it all seems to be connected to emotions." Jessica pursed her lips in thought.

"True. I think that's because we're human." Then Jewels grinned. "Now, how are you going to get Evan back?"

"What? Wait. What do you mean? Don't tell me you two are already fighting." Jessica groaned.

I shook my head. "No, we're not fighting."

"She friend-zoned him."

"You what? Hannah!"

"Not on purpose!" I clenched my hands around the hem of my shirt so I didn't accidentally suspend my friends.

Jessica sighed dramatically. "Okay. We're going out. Margaritas and tacos at Rosita's? I need to know what happened."

We agreed and walked the short distance, claiming a table in the back. I refused to give any details until after we had drinks in front of us. When I finally told Jessica what happened, she snorted then choked on her margarita.

She regained control and finally said, "So that's why he's been acting weird at home."

"What do you mean?" I scooped salsa with a chip, enjoying the spice.

Jessica leaned forward on her elbows. "I mean, he's been scattered. Evan is usually very thoughtful and efficient. I suppose it's a result of his empathy. But he made coffee this morning without actually putting coffee in the filter, and last night he put dinner in the oven but didn't start it. When I asked him what was wrong, he said he was fine, but I know my brother."

My heart stuttered. "So, he doesn't just want to be friends?" I inwardly groaned at the hopeful note in my voice.

Jewels playfully slapped my arm. "Are you that dense? Even I could see it when I first got here."

Jessica shook her head ruefully. "Hannah, you've been my best friend for forever. For a while, he looked at you like another little sister. But that was years ago. He may act like he doesn't care for you that way, but that's just because he doesn't want to hurt our friendship. I love both of you, and you two dating - or more - won't change that."

I sighed and leaned back in the bench seat. "I'll have to talk to him."

"Tonight, Hannah." Jewels looked meaningfully at me as she chewed her bottom lip. "Your magic might depend on it."

Chapter 20: Self-Defense

I almost didn't go to class on Thursday night. When I told Jewels I might go home right after work, she raised her eyebrows.

"Don't be a coward, Hannah," she finally said.

"I'm not!" I protested. "I'm just tired."

"And avoiding Evan. Listen, I saw a glimpse of something the other night. He's tied to your control over your magic. I'm not sure how. I just know that something bad will happen if you two don't resolve this weirdness between you."

Walking by with a stack of receipts, Jessica heard Jewels's comment.

"Oh no. The last thing Willowbrook needs is another misunderstanding causing destruction."

"Do you really think I'm that powerful?" I asked.

She shrugged. "Anything is possible. I didn't think my magic was strong enough to ruin the town, but it almost did."

"Exactly. So, you need to talk to Evan and clear this up, one way or another," Jewels said.

"What did you see?" Jessica asked.

Jewels frowned, her eyebrows furrowing as she thought. "It was very vague, which is unusual." When I tilted my head questioningly, she clarified, "I usually have perfectly clear visions, even though I only see what will happen if I'll be there to actually see it. But this one was more like an impression, almost as if I were seeing things under water or through fog. All I know is that Evan wasn't there, and you were very upset."

"Maybe it has to do with my dad," I suggested. There was no way I would admit that my feelings for Evan were strong enough that my control over any part of my life would suffer.

"Perhaps, but I don't think so." Jewels gave me a small, encouraging smile. "So go to class tonight and make sure."

I agreed, but the queasiness in my stomach told me it was a bad idea.

***

I stepped into the dojo, wiping the cold sweat from my palms on my jeans, and took a few deep breaths. *I can do this.*

Evan stood on the mat, still working with some younger students. Crossing the floor to the small locker room to change clothes, my shoulders tingled as his eyes tracked me, but I refused to look at him. On the short walk here from Over the Moon, I tried to think of how to open the conversation and came up with exactly nothing. I sucked at dating.

As I tugged off my jeans and ribbed t-shirt and pulled on black leggings and a black tank top, I heard Evan dismissing the class. Hopefully, the other ladies had arrived. I didn't want to be alone with him right now, at least not until I could gauge his mood. Although, with his empathetic magic, he probably already knew how nervous I felt. Closing the locker, I stepped out into the main room.

Children and their parents were still milling around, chatting. Evan stood facing away from the door, speaking with one of the dads. As soon as I entered, his eyes locked on me. A pleasant little shiver made its way down my spine, and I turned away from him on the pretense of pulling my dark brown hair up into a ponytail. The intensity of his gaze unnerved me. I kept my back to him as I did some light stretching, pulling one arm across my body, then the other. The babble of voices slowly died down until it was silent.

That's weird.

Evan's women's self-defense classes were well-attended. He offered various levels depending on age, agility, and skill. The Thursday night ones were for women ages twenty to forty who were moderately active, and they were always full. Evan didn't date much, but that didn't stop the eligible ladies of Willowbrook from trying to capture his attention. I pivoted to face the room.

Evan stood in the center of the mat, his feet slightly apart and his arms folded across his broad chest. He watched me, his hazel eyes holding a weight I couldn't quite name. I swallowed hard, then padded soundlessly onto the mat with my bare feet.

I glanced toward the door as I asked, "Where is everyone else?"

"I canceled class." His voice was calm, but his tone carried something deeper.

My stomach twisted. "Oh. Well, I guess I'll go then. I didn't know you were canceling today."

Before I could turn away, he stepped forward, his hand closing gently around my wrist. Not forceful, not demanding. Just asking me to stay.

"Hannah, wait."

I exhaled slowly and met his gaze. "What is this, Evan?"

He didn't let go. "I needed to talk to you. And I figured this was the only way to make sure you wouldn't run."

I sighed. "I wasn't running."

He arched an eyebrow. "Weren't you?"

The worst part was that he wasn't wrong.

Evan was quiet for a moment, searching my face. Then, in a deliberate movement, he stepped back, releasing me. "You want to get started?"

I blinked. "You still want to train?"

He shrugged. "You came here. Might as well."

I hesitated, then nodded. "Alright."

We moved into our stances, circling each other. He let me take the first move. I sank into a squat and shifted my hips, preparing to move my legs behind his so I could throw him off balance. Before I could complete the move, he sidestepped smoothly and swept one foot underneath mine, toppling me to the floor and letting me go. I rolled onto my shoulder, just like he taught, and stood up, spinning toward him.

I caught the flicker of a smile on his lips, just a ghost of amusement, like old times. The tension between us eased a little.

I met his gaze, breathless. "Holding back?"

He smirked. "Wouldn't dream of it."

Then he feinted left, and before I knew it, I stumbled. Instead of throwing me outright, he held me steady, giving me just enough time to correct.

We kept moving, falling into a familiar rhythm. I could feel his focus, his careful awareness of my movements. I should have been watching for my moment to strike, but instead, I was distracted by how right this felt.

The last time we trained like this, there had been no hesitation, no walls between us. But now, everything was different.

He must have sensed my distraction, because in one swift motion, he closed the distance, hands catching my waist. I gasped as he lifted me slightly off the mat, throwing me just enough that I stumbled when my feet landed. I whirled, attempting to come behind him and get him in a chokehold.

In a lightning move, his hands reached for my shoulders as if he planned to grab me. I leaned back, shifting my weight to duck, but he immediately changed tactics and stepped to me, both arms coming around my waist. This time, he yanked me against his body so my stomach pressed against his. I felt the hard planes of his body through the thin layers of cotton separating us.

Focus, Hannah, I told myself.

Using the natural pull of gravity, I once again started to sink down to break his hold. Before I could, he shifted, lifting me off the ground. I hissed in frustration. Evan hadn't taught us how to get out of a hold like this yet. He winked at me as he waited for my next move. I put my hands against his shoulders and pushed, twisting my hips at the same time in an effort to force him to release me.

He grinned as he tightened his grip. I gasped, then sucked in half a breath, all I could manage with my lungs in a vise. Realizing he had won, I tapped twice on his shoulder. Evan chuckled and let go. Unprepared for the sudden drop, I fell to the floor in an undignified heap. He returned to his original stance with his arms folded and watched me.

I stared up at him, my heart pounding for reasons that had nothing to do with the fight. "Does this count as our second date?"

"We're just friends, remember?" Evan said, stepping forward to offer me his hand.

Flinching, I took his hand and stood. At that moment, I wished I had empathic powers. I would have given almost anything to know what he was feeling.

"Are we still just friends?" I asked quietly.

Even if he didn't want a romantic relationship with me, I wanted him to still be my friend. The whole reason I've been hesitant to show my feelings for him was because I didn't want to ruin my friendship with him, or with Jessica.

Evan's expression shifted—something vulnerable flickering in his eyes. He exhaled through his nose, running a hand through his hair. "That's not how things work, Hannah. I can't be both things."

"Why not?"

He hesitated. "Because I don't know how."

"Jessica once told me your parents were best friends before they fell in love. That they had a wonderful marriage."

He smiled, just barely. "That was them. Not me."

I tilted my head. "When was your last relationship, anyway? High school?" Frustrated, I paced away from him.

"I've dated. Not that it's any of your business."

"Dated. Dating is not a relationship."

He blinked, surprised. "Why does that matter?"

"So how do you know if you can or can't be both things?" I turned to glare at him. "You're acting like you know this won't work when you haven't even tried."

He blinked rapidly several times and rubbed the back of his neck with one hand. "I guess," he said slowly, "I don't. Not really. You're right. I haven't had an actual relationship for a few years, and that obviously didn't work out. But I didn't realize we were in a relationship, either. I thought we were just dating and figuring it out."

"So did I," I conceded, my voice barely above a whisper. "After all, one amazing date doesn't mean we're together. I just know that sometimes boyfriends will give different advice than a friend."

A long pause stretched between us.

"Oh, Hannah." This time when he said my name, it came out almost as a sigh. His shoulders slumped, and he looked deflated. "I'm sorry. I misunderstood. When you asked me for advice as a friend, I used my empathy to feel what you felt. It was all confusion and nerves and uncertainty. I thought you were telling me you didn't want this." He gestured between us.

"Of course, I was confused and nervous! I was thinking about my dad." Exasperated, I turned and started for the locker room. "I'm going home."

He grabbed my hand before I could take more than two steps. Damn his long legs.

"Hannah, wait. I said I am sorry, and I mean it." His soft voice held a pleading note. "Can we go somewhere else and talk?"

I shook my head. "I don't want to talk anymore right now. I just need to think."

He let me go and stepped back, nodding slowly. "Okay. Can I see you later?"

"Yeah, but not until I figure some things out."

He gave a small nod and turned, heading to his office. I tried to pretend I didn't see the way his jaw clenched as

I spoke. This was not the way I wanted this conversation to go.

I didn't bother changing clothes, just grabbed my bag and put my shoes back on before striding out of the dojo.

Chapter 21: Out of Thin Air

I strode several yards down the sidewalk before pausing long enough to put my earbuds in. Hitting play on the music app, I tried to drown out the thoughts swirling in my head. I felt pretty proud of myself for remembering not to use my hands and voice at the same time during my confrontation with Evan.

"Although he deserves to be a human popsicle for a few minutes," I muttered under my breath.

He wanted to accuse me of running, yet he was the one who didn't want to try to be friends and, well, whatever else it was we might be. He acted like I was the one pulling away, but wasn't he doing the same thing?

The frustration burned in my chest, hot and heavy, but I pushed it aside as I neared the park. A group of boys played soccer, their voices ringing out as they darted after the ball. I slowed, watching them. They were probably part of the parks and recreation team since they looked to be only nine or ten years old, not old enough for school teams. A man, probably the coach, stood nearby watching and calling out encouragement.

One boy scored a goal, and the rest of the team cheered. The coach went over and scooped him up in a hug, and I could only assume it was his father.

My heart twinged, and something twisted inside me. Would I ever have a moment like that? My husband coaching our son's soccer team? Before I could shove the idea away, my mind conjured an image of a little boy with messy brown curls and curious hazel eyes. Evan's eyes.

I groaned, shaking my head. I cannot think like this right now.

Before I could fully banish the thought, the current song in my earbuds—one by Red Helix—faded out, leaving an opening for other noises. I heard the guttural roar of a car engine coming from the ferry landing. I turned around, already knowing what I'd see. It would be some tourist from the city in a fancy sports car thinking our sleepy little town made the perfect racetrack. I pulled out one earbud in order to hear so I wouldn't get run over when I crossed the street.

Sure enough, a red BMW drifted around the corner, its tires skimming dangerously close to the curb before straightening out.

A sharp shout from the field caught my attention. I turned just in time to see the soccer ball bounce away from the game, rolling into the middle of the road. One of the boys jogged toward it. To my horror, he reached the edge of the sidewalk and stepped off just as the car picked up speed and shot forward.

I knew I couldn't get to him, and his coach stood even further away than I did.

He was at the curb, his foot lifted.

My heart pounded, and bile rose in my throat. The BMW's tires screeched as the driver slammed on the brakes. Too late.

No, no, no, no.

The soccer ball abruptly vanished. A fraction of a second later, it reappeared in the boy's hands. The car came to an abrupt halt just past where the ball had been.

My lungs burned, and I drew in a shaky breath.

A lanky man of about my age got out of the BMW. "You okay, kid?" he called.

The boy stared at the ball in his hands.

"Levi, come on!" Another boy shouted.

The boy with the ball—Levi—didn't move. Did I accidentally suspend him? My breath became shallow. Someone would definitely notice a child frozen in place.

"Did you see that?" Levi called back.

My heart restarted at his voice. I didn't lose control of my suspension magic.

"Yeah! The car's tire made the ball bounce back to you. So cool! Now, come on. Let's play."

Levi turned and wandered back to his team, dropping the ball in front of him and dribbling it with his feet as he went.

The coach, however, wasn't so easily distracted. He stormed across the grass, his face dark with anger. "Hey, you!"

I turned, my stomach lurching again. But the coach pointed his finger at the driver.

"I know the city teaches reading! Didn't you see the speed limit?"

The young man raised his hands. "Woah! Hold up. Nothing happened. The kid's fine."

"He could have been killed, you idiot! I'm getting the sheriff. You stay right there."

As the two men argued, I slowly realized what had happened. I used my teleportation magic to move the ball so the boy wouldn't run into the street and get hit by a car. I had lost control again.

"Can you watch him? Hello? Miss?"

I blinked. The coach was talking to me. "Oh, sure." Pulled out of my inaction, I moved swiftly to stand in front of the BMW.

"Seriously?" the driver protested.

"Locals stick together." I said with a shrug.

The coach jogged across the street to the tiny police station, leaving me alone with the idiot driver.

The driver let out an exaggerated sigh and leaned against his car. "Great. So, I have to wait here until Officer Small Town writes me a ticket?"

I ignored him, my mind racing. What if someone had noticed? Levi's friends distracted him enough that he didn't question the ball's sudden redirection, but what if he figured it out later? What if someone had filmed it? What if—

"Hannah? Hey, what happened? Do you need help?"

The familiar voice pulled me from my thoughts. I looked over my shoulder to see Evan jogging toward me, concern etched into his features.

The driver groaned. "Oh, fantastic. Another local coming to scold me."

Evan barely spared him a glance before locking his gaze on me. "Are you okay?"

I nodded. My pulse still pounded from the adrenaline, but Evan's presence steadied me. "I'm good. This guy, however, is about to meet Linden." I nodded to the driver, who rolled his eyes before sitting sideways in his car, his Converse-clad feet on the pavement. "He decided to speed through town and almost hit a kid."

Evan exhaled through his nose. "And you're holding him for the sheriff?"

I shrugged. "I saw the whole thing. The coach is in the station now." Turning so my back was to the car, I lowered my voice. "And, Evan, I used my magic."

To his credit, he didn't react beyond tilting his head. "How?"

I glanced toward the park where the soccer practice had resumed as if nothing had happened then back at Evan. "I teleported the ball so the kid wouldn't run into the street."

Evan ran a hand through his hair. "That's good, right? You saved him."

"I did, but what if someone noticed? I didn't think. I just did it."

He placed a hand on my shoulder, warm and solid. "Hannah, sometimes that's what magic is supposed to be. It's not always about control in the way you think it is. Sometimes it's about instinct and trusting yourself. Like in the dojo during training. You don't always think through the moves anymore; you just do them."

It made sense, and I wanted to believe him, but after hearing the story of Jessica's storm and what could happen when magic got out of control, the fear of my own power overwhelmed my confidence. Before I could respond, the coach returned with the sheriff, a large man in his fifties with sharp eyes. The driver sighed and rubbed his temples.

Evan gave my shoulder a reassuring squeeze before stepping back. "Let's get through this first, then we can talk."

I nodded, exhaling. Maybe Evan was right, and I needed to trust my instincts. But did that include how I felt about him?

And what about Jamison?

The sheriff asked for my statement, and I made sure to speak very carefully and not say anything about the ball's sudden redirection.

"Okay, but you said the ball was in the street, correct?" Sheriff Linden asked.

I nodded, unable to deny it with the coach and driver both there.

"Then how did it get back to Levi?" He looked up from his notebook and studied me, waiting for my answer.

"I, uh, I'm not sure. I was focused on the car." *Please, please believe me.*

Sheriff Linden narrowed his eyes slightly but nodded. He turned to the BMW's driver. "Sounds like you get a ticket, son, and a driving ban on the island."

The guy scoffed, glaring. "What? Oh, come on! Nothing happened."

"Nothing happened this time. We don't risk it here in Willowbrook. From now on, if you want to visit, you have to leave your car in the city, or it will be impounded at the dock upon arrival." Linden checked his watch. "The next ferry leaves in ten minutes, and you better be on it." He handed the man a ticket.

"Two-hundred bucks? For a little speeding? This place is ridiculous."

"Get back in your car and leave before I double it." The sheriff drew up to his full height.

Evan took a few steps and flanked the driver, situating himself between me and the car.

The young man looked back and forth between them for a moment before raising his hands in surrender and getting into his car.

"Slow, now," Linden reminded him.

The driver started his car and slowly pulled away, executing a turn at the next intersection. We all watched as he headed to the ferry landing.

"Well, that's that," said Linden, stowing his notebook in a pocket. "Where are you two headed?"

"Home," I said.

"The coffee shop," Evan said.

"Well, take care then." He gave me a wink and sauntered across the street to the station.

"Don't worry about good ol' Dennis Linden," Evan said, mimicking the sheriff's Texan drawl.

I gave him a startled glance. "What do you mean?"

He nodded his head toward the sheriff. "He's on our side. He's Mundane, but because he's the law keeper, he knows enough to help us stay off the radar, so to speak."

I frowned, concern flaring through me. "So, he knows about me?"

He shrugged. "Sofia probably told him. Even if someone said the ball somehow moved from the street to Levi, the sheriff would put it down to unreliable witnesses and move on."

"Good to know," I said flatly. Did everyone in this town know about magic except for me until I had it?

"Do you want to talk about this?" Evan gestured at the park and street.

I shook my head. "Not right now. Too much is happening too fast. I need to go home where there wouldn't be a possibility of accidental magic in public."

He frowned slightly but didn't argue. Instead, he shoved his hands in his pockets and walked beside me for a few paces, his usual easygoing, confident energy replaced with something less certain.

"Alright. I get it," he muttered.

I sighed, rubbing a hand over my forehead. "It's not that I don't want to talk to you, Evan. I just need a minute to process." I glanced at him, offering a small, tired smile. "Is that okay?"

His expression eased, and he nodded. "Yeah, of course." He hesitated and added, "Just don't shut me out."

"I won't," I promised.

He studied me for a moment longer, as if making sure I really meant it, then gave a small nod. "Okay. I'll see you later."

"Yeah. Later."

He turned toward the coffee shop, and I kept walking, my mind still buzzing.

Then my phone rang.

I pulled it out, expecting it to be a call from Jessica or my mother.

But it wasn't either of them.

I didn't recognize the number.

Chapter 22: Lessons

"Hello?"

"Hannah, dear. Do you have a minute?"

I took a relieved breath when I heard her voice. "Hi, Sofia. What's up?"

"I am just calling to let you know I am adding an extra training tomorrow at Jessica's house. Seven o'clock." Her motherly voice was nothing like my own mother's. My mom was all business all the time, even with me. Sofia's tone was always kind and understanding, even when she scolded. "Are you available?"

"An extra day?" I asked. I shouldn't find this surprising; I barely knew what I was doing.

"Yes, I sense something is off. And Susan did a reading today. She said something big is going to happen, like when Jessica caused the storm."

I noted a worried edge in Sofia's voice. She seemed unflappable to me. What could cause her to worry?

"I'll be there."

"Of course you will. See you then." She disconnected the call.

I walked in the door of my little cottage to find Jewels sitting on the couch flipping through an art magazine. She looked up.

"Sofia call you?"

"Yep," I said.

"She called me too. I think she sounds worried. She usually just calls one of us and tells us to let the others know." Jewels closed the magazine and paced to the kitchen. "Wine?" She called over her shoulder.

"Most definitely," I replied. I dreaded telling her about my encounter with Evan. "Oh, no." I dropped onto the sofa.

"What happened? How was class? Wait, you're home early." Jewels returned, carrying two glasses of white wine.

"Evan will be there tomorrow, won't he." It came out like a statement instead of a question.

"I'm sure he will be. He's the only other one besides Sofia who can shield others' magic. What happened?" She repeated, handing me a glass.

"I don't really want to talk about it." I took a long sip of wine, letting the light fruity flavors slide down my throat and willing it to do its relaxing trick.

"That good, huh?"

"Let's just say we had a misunderstanding. And it did not bode well for me being in the dojo."

Jewels furrowed her brow. "He didn't hurt you, did he?"

I gave a wry snort. "No, not exactly. He just took his training to a new level, and I was ill-equipped to keep up."

"That's not cool. He shouldn't take his frustration out on you."

"He didn't do anything that he wouldn't usually do in class, except he didn't demonstrate the hold after he used it. Although it wasn't like I gave him time to teach."

"Jess will be furious when she finds out. She loves her brother, but she doesn't tolerate anyone hurting her friends."

"It wasn't like that. We talked a little. Apparently, he thought I didn't want to date him."

"And did you set the record straight?" Jewels asked over the rim of her glass.

I froze, the wine halfway to my lips. Shakily, I lowered the glass and set it on the coffee table. "Actually, no. I just left."

Jewels gasped. "Why didn't you tell him you wanted to resume where you left off the night of the concert?"

"I don't know. I just…panicked, I guess. And then this thing happened with the car and the soccer ball, and he was there, and it felt so good and—"

"What thing with a car and soccer ball?" Jewels interrupted.

I picked up my glass and took another sip before telling her.

"So, the knight in shining armor came to rescue you." She smirked.

"I didn't need rescuing," I protested.

"And yet, he was there when you needed someone."

I nodded, staring into my wine.

"And you liked him being there," she continued.

"Yes," I mumbled.

"So, tell him!"

"I can't." I stood and paced the small room. "Not now. Not yet. With my magic out of control and doing random things, I can't just start a relationship."

"Why not? I think now is the perfect time. It will be one less thing that is uncertain in your world." Jewels stood and stepped in front of me, grabbing me by the shoulders. "He could be your anchor in all this."

"Maybe. But what if he rejects me? He doesn't like drama, and that's all that is happening in my life right now."

"He won't. I know." She winked.

I sighed. "I just need to get through tomorrow's lesson. I'm going to bed." I took my glass to the sink and poured out the rest of the wine. I felt exhausted on several levels and knew I needed energy for tomorrow. It was my day to open the shop, and it would most likely be a long night of magical training. Before I closed my bedroom door, I called out, "Jewels? Don't tell Jessica what happened with Evan tonight, okay?"

"I won't. But I think you should."

"I will. After training." Closing my door, I stripped and fell into bed, pulling the soft comforter over my head. I willed my body to relax one muscle at a time, starting with my feet. By the time I got to my neck, I drifted off to sleep.

The clanging of my alarm woke me, and, groaning, I slapped my phone until the noise stopped. Flopping over, I stared at the ceiling, which was just beginning to lighten from the early sun.

"Why did I agree to opening shifts?" I mumbled as I staggered out of bed and into the bathroom.

After a hot shower, I felt a little more human. I combed my hair out, wincing at the tangles. I guess that's what I get for not doing my evening routine before bed. Despite the slow start to my morning, I was still ready by my usual time, and I quietly shut the door to the cottage on my way out so I didn't wake Jewels. She had the closing shift today. Lucky girl.

I walked the few blocks to Over the Moon, returning smiles and waves to the few people I saw. It was the off-season, so only a few tourists remained on the island, and they typically slept in. They would visit the coffee shop soon enough, though. Arriving, I unlocked the door, entered, and relocked it behind me. I flipped on one of the banks of lights and went to the counter, stowing my purse underneath. The automatic rhythm of opening soothed my nerves and created a calm despite feeling lost in a sea of emotions.

Jessica came in as I placed bagels, cookies, and other pastries in the case.

"Good morning," she sang out.

"Morning. Someone is cheerful," I commented.

She tilted her head and smiled. "Today is a good day."

"And how was your night?" I prodded. She rewarded me with a grin.

"Really good. Yours?"

Shrugging, I turned away so she wouldn't see my facial expression. "Same as usual. Class, then home."

I felt cold air stir through the room.

"And what happened in class? I didn't see Evan when he got home as I was out with Zane, and then he was gone before I got up this morning."

My heart beat faster, and I rubbed the back of my neck. "Nothing. Just a lesson in self-defense."

"Hannah, what happened?"

I turned to her, heat rushing to my cheeks. "I don't want to talk about it yet. Please don't ask anymore."

She frowned but nodded. "Okay. But I'm here for you."

"I know. It's just weird, like I thought it would be."

"What's weird?" She paused mid-stride to get the cash drawer from the safe.

I looked down, biting the inside of my cheek.

"Hannah?" she prompted.

My words came out in a rush. "I had a date with your brother, and now I'm not sure what I want, and he's probably hurting, and it's my fault." I glanced up at her to gauge her reaction.

She strode toward me and took my hands in hers. "No matter what," she said fiercely, "we are friends. Do you understand me?"

My face softened into a smile as tension left me. "Yes. Perfectly clear."

"Good. Sorry about the cold."

The room instantly warmed to its normal ambient temperature.

"I understand that, too," I said with a laugh.

"Let's finish opening. Old John is already waiting." She turned to go to the office.

Looking out the window, I saw the old man standing on the sidewalk by the front door, his hands in his pockets and face to the street.

"Earlier than usual," I said, and proceeded to pour water into the tank on top of the espresso machine.

A steady stream of customers filled the day, for which I was grateful. The last thing I wanted was time to think about Evan, or magic, or my father. During my break, I saw another message from Jamison.

Please talk to me. There are things you need to know.

Ugh, the guy would not take no for an answer! I blocked his profile and went back to scrolling reels until my break was over.

Jewels had come in during my break, and she was busy making mochas for Donna and friends, laughing and talking to the women. I shook my head and gathered the bus tub from the stand next to the door.

"I don't get it either," Jessica said as I passed by her. "Staid Donna actually likes our punk rocker."

"It's a miracle," I replied.

Since I opened, I left around three in the afternoon and decided to take a bubble bath. It had been ages since I had soaked in the tub. The girls would probably go straight to Jessica's house after closing, and I would meet them there. The hot water combined with the floral scent of a bath bomb soothed my senses. I blasted grunge music, shaved my legs, and washed my hair. When the water cooled, I begrudgingly wrapped a towel around my body and dressed.

If I had to see Evan tonight, I wanted all the confidence-boosting I could get. Black jeans, knee-high leather boots, and a cobalt blue shirt were a good start. Applying some rose lip gloss, I smiled in the mirror. The shirt was just low-cut enough to give a hint of cleavage, and my jeans hugged my hips. I slipped on my black leather jacket, and my armor settled around me.

"Crows-feet be damned," I said, grabbing my purse and strutting out the door.

I let myself into the backyard gate, familiar with my friends' family home. The others were already there, gathered around a ready fire pit. As I latched the gate behind me, Jessica aimed her finger at the wood and sparks caught.

"Am I late?" I asked. I shifted my purse to dig out my phone and check the time.

"No, dear. You're right on time." Sofia smiled genially.

"I ordered pizza instead of cooking," Jessica gestured to the table.

"And closing was quick. As soon as you left, things slowed down, so we did some of the cleaning early," Jewels piped up.

"Ah. Well, good. Thanks." I stammered a bit as Evan's eyes slid up and down my body. When his gaze met mine, it was full of something that made my breath catch.

Act cool, Hannah.

I looked away and picked up a paper plate and chose a piece of pepperoni pizza, settling into the chair next to Jessica. When I glanced back at Evan, he was still watching me with an intensity that made my heart pound. I leaned forward slightly to take a bite of pizza, and his gaze snapped to my cleavage and then to my lips.

"But now that everyone is here, let's discuss tonight's exercise." Sofia said.

At the sound of her voice, Evan gave a slight shake of his head and tore his eyes from me, focusing on Sofia, who rose from her seat and moved to stand closer to the warmth of the fire. A chill permeated the air.

"As I mentioned," Sofia continued, "Susan did a reading for the whole of Willowbrook, as the Council charges her to do every new moon. Her reading showed something big coming, a force on par with Jessica's storm."

Jessica flushed with embarrassment.

"Sofia, that was not—"

"On purpose," Sofia finished for her. "We all know. And most likely, whatever is coming won't be on purpose, either. Having three witches come into their power in less than a year is unheard of." Her gaze penetrated Jessica, Evan, and I in turn. "Having two who get nudges of the future is extraordinary. Have either of you experienced visions of what is to come?"

I jolted when I realized she was looking at Jewels and Evan. Evan had visions? I knew he was empathetic, but this was new information.

Jewels twirled a strand of her pink hair around a finger. "The only thing I see is as if I'm underwater, which doesn't make sense because I'll be in the park when this happens. "I can't envision the island sinking or flooding to cover the roofs." She shook her head. "It's strange."

Sofia pursed her lips. "Strange indeed. Evan?"

"Nothing," he said tersely. "I've been preoccupied, and my futuristic sight isn't very strong."

"Jessica, when Hannah suspended you, what did you see?" Sofia asked, turning to my friend.

She furrowed her brow in thought. "Nothing out of the ordinary. One moment, Hannah was standing in front of me looking terrified, and the next, she was gone, and I dispersed my fireball."

"Evan?" Sofia questioned.

"Nothing," he repeated.

I watched him out of the corner of my eye. He stood completely still, arms crossed over his chest. He had avoided looking at me since his scrutiny when I first arrived. Did he feel conflicted about our conversation like I did? I startled when Sofia clapped her hands.

"Well, we know something will happen; we just don't know exactly what or when. So, we train. Jewels, since your powers are strictly precog, you will take notes in case you see something I miss. Evan, stand over there," Sofia gestured to the edge of the patio, "and be ready to shield whichever one of those two who needs it." She pointed at Jessica and me. "You girls go to the center of the lawn and do the same exercise as before. Jessica, you get to choose what magic to throw at Hannah. And Hannah, your job is to freeze Jessica's magic. Try not to freeze her, just her power. And then I want to see if you can release her like you did at the preschool."

I sighed and reluctantly put my half-eaten pizza aside. "I don't even know if anything I did made the magic dissipate," I said as I took my place across from Jessica.

She grinned. "Let's find out. I love playing with my power."

"That's because you know how to," I grumbled.

"Well," Jessica raised one finger, and a swirl of fire encircled it. "Stop me." She flicked her hand, and the flame shot toward me.

I raised my own hands and said, "Stop."

The fire singed my jacket. "Damn, I like this coat!"

"Stop me," she said again.

This time, a lightning bolt exploded from her outstretched hands.

"Freeze!" I pointed at the flash of light only to have my finger receive a shock that traveled through my entire body.

Jessica turned to look at Evan. "Easy, brother. I'm not pulling out the big guns. Yet."

I glanced toward him and wished I hadn't. He stood there, frowning, hands by his sides in what I thought of as his ready stance. He looked concerned. For me?

Too late, I realized Jessica had readied another burst of power in the form of fire. A ball about the size of a small apple flew at my face. Twisting my shoulders, I barely avoided taking it in the face.

"Seriously, Jess?" I shouted as I righted myself.

"Stay focused," Sofia called.

"Yeah, stay focused." Jessica echoed. A wicked grin crossed her face as she fired another flaming ball at me.

"Enough!" I yelled, waving my entire arm in a circle. I was done with this whole thing. I didn't want to be a witch if it meant getting attacked by fire and electricity by my best friend.

Jessica and her fire stopped moving.

"Finally," I said. "How long do you want me to wait before trying to unfreeze her?"

When there was no response, I looked over to where Sofia stood between Evan and Jewels. All three were frozen in place, Sofia with a large smile on her face, and Evan with a satisfied smirk. Jewels stared down unseeing at the paper in her lap, pen poised to write.

"Resume," I said, frantically rotating my hand to include everyone in the yard.

No one moved.

The fireball's trajectory would take it to the fence, so unfreezing it before someone who could deal with it was a bad idea. I went and stood directly in front of Sofia and flapped my hand at her. "Resume," I said.

Her eyebrow twitched.

"Resume!" I flicked my fingers toward her. Did the gesture matter as much as the word? I had no idea, but I was willing to try anything.

I thought I saw movement in her eyes.

"Sofia?" I asked softly.

Nothing. I suppose there wasn't anything else I could do besides wait for the magic to wear off. I really hoped Sofia could teach me how to draw it back into myself like Jessica did with her weather.

Chapter 23: The Challenge

I t only took a few minutes before everyone went into motion. Almost comically, Evan's suspension mid-stride caused him to stumble forward. He looked around, his eyes finding me. Sofia, though, seemed unsurprised to see me on the patio instead of in the grass across from Jessica, who extinguished her fireball and joined us.

"How long?" Sofia asked.

"Oh, um, I didn't think to time it," I stammered. Of course, Sofia would want to know how long they were stuck in my magic spell, or whatever it's called.

Jewels stood up, pencil in hand. "I think it was about six minutes. Does that seem right?"

My sense of time had never been great, but I said, "Yes, that's close."

Sofia rubbed her chin thoughtfully. "Ten minutes when it was one person, six for four. Do you recall how long the kids were frozen?"

"It couldn't have been longer than a few minutes. Three, at most," I hazarded.

"Then it's safe to say the larger the group, the less time. Did you try reversing your magic?"

I nodded. "I said 'resume' like I did before, but nothing happened. At least, I don't think so. I thought I saw you move slightly, Sofia, but that was it. Then, a minute or two passed and everyone started moving."

"So, it is possible that your panic over being discovered caused you to have more force in your intention when at work as opposed to here, in the backyard where no one can see." Sofia gestured at the high privacy fence and shrubbery.

"And you think I can learn to reverse it, like Jessica does?"

Jessica snorted. "Our abilities are very different." She lifted a bag from beneath the table that I hadn't noticed and pulled out a container of cookies. Opening it, she picked one and took a bite, catching a few crumbs in her other hand.

"True, they are," Sofia said firmly. "But every witch has the capacity to call his or her magic back. It's just a question of how. The best way to figure it out is to train." She checked her watch. "It's getting late, but I want you and Evan to meet every day, if possible. Evan can shield himself from your power while you practice."

"Practice on what? If he's shielded, it won't be him." I didn't want to look at him to see his reaction about having to spend more time with me.

"If I'm right, and I usually am, you can freeze anything, not just dishes and people. Try bubbles."

"Bubbles?" I laughed. I leaned forward to get my own chocolate chip cookie, and the heat from Evan's eyes made me glance at him. He gave a slow smile. My heart pounded, and heat rushed to my cheeks. Maybe this outfit was a bad idea.

"Yes, bubbles." Sofia responded. "Harmless if they get away, but easy to see if they are moving or not. So, practice both freezing and unfreezing bubbles. I think your magic is just a very strong binding power, something unusual but not unheard of."

"Look at it this way," Jewels said brightly. "You won't have fireballs flying at your face."

"Right, but that was part of how she connected to her power."

My eyes darted to Evan. He looked serious and calm; not like he was ready for a fight, but more like he was planning one. It reminded me of training during his class when he saw one of the ladies struggling to get a move down and he needed to find another way to show it to her. What did he want me to understand that I wasn't seeing?

"She has to feel threatened," he continued. "Or feel like something bad will happen if she doesn't stop it. Bubbles won't make her feel like that."

I nodded. "He's right, at least for now." Maybe Sofia would change her mind about making us practice.

"Oh, I didn't forget that part." Sofia's face split into a wide grin. "That's why you'll be doing it in public."

"What? No, I can't."

"Sofia! That goes against the Council!"

"Someone we don't want knowing will find out, and then what?"

"She's not ready."

Sofia held up her hand, and we all fell silent.

"Start with somewhere quiet, like the park early in the morning or the beach. Choose a spot where discovery is unlikely yet possible. The threat of discovery should be enough motivation. Then, as you gain more control, you can go to more public places."

Frowning, I started to shake my head in refusal.

"If you want to learn about your power, you will do this," she said firmly. "Otherwise, you will be on your own."

Jewels crossed over to me. "Hannah, trust me. You don't want to try to do it alone. That's what landed me and Jessica in group therapy."

"Fine," I said. "I'll do it."

Evan, however, didn't voice his agreement. He just looked at me with those unreadable hazel eyes, and I couldn't decipher his expression. He probably wasn't pleased with the arrangement either, but would also do what Sofia said.

"Can I go home now?" I asked.

"Yes, I think it's a good idea if we all get some rest," Sofia said. "I'll expect an update on your progress in three days, when we will train your teleportation powers."

"I'll walk with you," Evan said gruffly. "Jewels?"

"This is still a safe town," I protested. "We will be fine."

"Fine." He turned without another word and went inside.

"I see your conversation went well," Jessica said.

"I don't want to talk about it."

"Well, good night then." She opened the back gate and let Jewels, Sofia, and I out.

"Yes, good night." Sofia turned in the opposite direction and ambled down the sidewalk.

"Wow, the tension tonight! Both the Barnes' are irritated with you."

"Apparently."

"I think Jessica is frustrated that you already had a moment of control. Hers didn't come for quite some time."

"She's jealous of me?" I raised my eyebrows. "I can't see Jessica being jealous of anyone. She has a good life, owns her own business, is a well-respected member of the community, and has a gorgeous boyfriend who adores her. What is there to be jealous about?"

Jewels tilted her head and counted on her fingers as she spoke. "You already have better control over your magic than she did at the beginning, you are also a well-respected community member, but everyone also likes you, you have both your parents even if you don't want a relationship with your father, and it's highly unlikely your powers will destroy the town."

"Jewels, Jessica and I have been friends for a long time. I think if she were jealous of me, I would know. But she wouldn't be. Or if she thought she might be, she would talk to me."

"If you say so." She shrugged. "I'm still new here, so what do I know?"

"Oh, please don't be like that. You've been the most understanding one since Zane's party. I need you."

She sighed dramatically. "I really am the most understanding, aren't I?"

And just like that, she was her carefree self again. She chatted about a suspicion that the Crony Crew were planning a big surprise at the fall festival as we walked the few blocks to home. I tried to show an interest, but I couldn't shake the thought that she was right about Jessica's feelings.

When we got home, she turned the TV on to a cartoon channel and asked if I wanted popcorn.

"I'm good, thanks. I think I'm going to get ready for bed."

"Okay, but no dwelling. As long as you fix things with Evan, everything will be fine." She flashed me her lovely wide smile and went into the kitchen.

I wanted to ask her what she meant, but I was afraid of the answer.

This time, I did not ignore my evening routine and even remembered to use the eye cream. Feeling a little more centered, I slid beneath the plush comforter and snuggled down against the pillows. Then I texted Jessica.

Are we okay?

Her reply came seconds later.

Why wouldn't we be?

I started typing, then erased a phrase, typed some more, and finally hit send.

Because I don't want to see my dad. Because Jewels said my magic is easier than yours. Because your brother is frustrated with me. Pick one.

This time, it took longer for her to reply.

We will always be friends, but sometimes we'll be mad at each other. I'm not mad, but I'm feeling something that is uncomfortable. We'll be okay. I'm sure of it.

Tears welled in my eyes, and I furiously blinked. Jewels was right. How could I be so self-centered and oblivious?

Can I do anything to fix it?

Not right now.

I dropped my phone on the nightstand and turned my head to look out the window. The branches of the old oak tree in the backyard swayed slightly in the breeze. I watched it until my eyes felt heavy and finally closed, my thoughts a whirling mess.

Chapter 24: Arrival

The next morning was another shift at the preschool. I felt bleary-eyed from tossing and turning most of the night, even in sleep. Thankfully, Jewels was still in her room when I left. I didn't want her to worry about me. I sent up another grateful thought when I realized today was art day. Once a month, we combined classes and set up several art stations that the children rotated through. Everything was a project or craft that didn't need much adult assistance. As long as Owen didn't try to be an owl during recess again, the day should be mostly uneventful. I really just wanted to bury myself in my bed with a good book and music, but duty called.

"Good morning, Miss Helen," I greeted the other teacher as I strode into her room. We alternated which classroom hosted art day, and it was her turn.

"Morning, Miss Hannah." Helen sounded as cheerful as ever. I took that to mean she had no idea what had happened the other day.

I glanced around the room, taking in the tables with paint, paintbrushes, and paper laid out. "What else do we need for today?"

"Can you grab the wipes from the cupboard?" Helen placed a stack of smocks on the low table by the door. "I think that's it. Oh, wait. I forgot the flowers."

"I'll get them." We were doing still-life today, and the kids would paint what they saw using vases of artificial flowers on the tables.

Carefully, I took the prepared vases from a shelf in the closet. I didn't want one of them to slip and accidentally trigger my magic. I placed the flowers so that every three or four kids could easily see them, then got the baby wipes from the cupboard. One thing Helen taught me when I first started was that letting the children use baby wipes to clean their hands before washing them dramatically cut down on the mess at the sink and on the floor, counter, tables...basically everywhere little messy hands could reach.

A few minutes later, the first students came in. From then on, a whirlwind of activity took all of my attention. We settled the kids at the tables once they had their things put away. Helen explained the project in a few minutes, which was all the attention the children could muster with tempting art supplies in front of them. Then we told them to start. We walked around the tables, adding paint to palettes and praising the art. Some students studied the blossoms and even tried to mix colors to get the shades of reds and purples right. Others simply smeared paint on the paper.

When I got to Owen, I stifled a laugh before leaning over to admire his paper. "Is that an owl, Owen?"

He grinned up at me and nodded. "Miss Helen said we can paint whatever we wanted with the flowers."

"She did, indeed. But, Owen, where are your flowers?"

His picture was a splash of green and brown feathers and bright yellow beak and eyes.

"Under the owl. I painted them first. See?" He pointed at a spot in the middle of the owl.

I looked closer and could barely make out the circles of flowers under the owl's body. "It's very nice."

During recess, Helen said, "There's always one."

I glanced at her. "One what?"

She smiled and nodded toward Owen on the swings. "There's always one who gets into our hearts more than the others, and usually they are the ones who also cause the most trouble."

I laughed. "He does tend to take more energy than the others."

I headed to my other job as soon as parents picked up the last of the children after lunch. When I saw Jessica behind the counter, facing Donna, I instantly thought that Jessica is Sofia's Owen. The idea made me grin as I stepped up next to Jessica just in time to hear Donna's comment.

"The last time I had one of your cinnamon rolls, I had terrible stomach pains. What is in them? And why are you smiling like that?" She directed her last question at me.

"Oh, nothing. Just thinking about something that happened at the preschool. Have you had allergy testing done? Perhaps there's an ingredient that you're intolerant or allergic to."

Jessica shot me a warning look.

"I don't see how that's your business," Donna replied. She scooped her coffee and pastry off the counter and stomped to a table.

"I thought you two made up," I whispered to Jessica.

"I thought we did, too," she said. "Next time, don't say anything unless you hear the whole thing."

"Sorry, just trying to help."

She sighed. "I know. It just wasn't good timing. Watch the counter, would you? I need to make a call."

"Of course." I managed to smile despite the thickness in my throat.

I took in the room with a glance, noting Donna sitting alone and a group of college students sitting with laptops and books out. Otherwise, the shop was quiet. Opting for the repetitive task of stocking, pulled cups from their storage spots beneath the counter, stacking them neatly by the register. Once the cups and lids were full, ready for the afternoon rush, I started on the napkins and utensils. The chime of the doorbell made me glance up.

A tall man in his fifties, with skin a shade or two darker than mine, strode in and paused halfway to the counter. His dark brown eyes flicked to me, and a strange expression crossed his face.

Not a local, I thought. Even though it was the off-season, we still got visitors throughout the year. I smiled brightly. "Welcome to Over the Moon. What can I get for you?"

My question seemed to jar him from his thoughts as he shook his head minutely before walking closer.

"It's my first time here. What do you recommend?" The timbre of his voice was soothing and somehow familiar.

I knew I had never seen him before, so perhaps someone I knew had a voice similar to this man's. Jessica's dad, perhaps.

"Well, I think it's all good. Do you prefer coffee or tea? Are you looking for a snack?"

His gaze roamed the chalkboard menu on the wall behind me. "Tea, but I'm not sure what type." He gestured to the many canisters on the shelves. "I'm not hungry right now. In fact, my stomach is a little queasy."

I nodded. "The ferry ride. Happens a lot. I know just the thing." Scanning the canisters, I quickly found the one I needed. "Two dollars, please."

"That's it?"

Laughing at his surprise, I said, "We're not like the mainland. And Jessica believes tea heals as much as it is tasty, so she wants it to be affordable for everyone."

He scrunched his nose. "I've had some very nasty tea."

"Then you haven't had the right tea." As we talked, I placed the tea in a bag and slowly poured hot water over it. Steam rose from the cup. "This is green tea with peppermint, ginger, and fennel. Give it three minutes to steep before drinking. It will set your stomach right in no time."

"You know quite a bit about tea. Jessica, again?"

I nodded. "She owns the place. Her mom was a fabulous gardener, and Jessica learned from her."

"Was?"

"Hmm?" I realized I was talking too much, saying too much about Jessica's personal life. Trying to change the subject, I said, "And as Jessica's best and longest friend, I learned a lot from her. I still am, honestly. There is more to tea than just herbs in hot water." I heartily wished someone, anyone, would walk in. Sofia, or even Evan, would be welcome.

As if the universe heard me, the door opened and Evan came in, eating up the distance between the door and the counter with his long strides. He looked amazing in his work jeans and a red t-shirt that was just snug enough to give a hint of the muscular chest beneath it. My breath caught for a moment when he looked at me, a slight smile on his lips, and I almost wished we were alone so I could explain how I felt. Okay, so maybe it would be better if it were anyone besides Evan.

"Hi, Hannah," he said. "Can I get a coffee to go?"

"Uh, yeah. Of course. Your usual?" Why was I stuttering like we'd never talked before?

"Perfect." His smirk grew, and he gave me a wink. "You know what I like."

Was he flirting with me? I attempted a glare, and it must have been pathetic because he just laughed.

With an audible groan, I grabbed a cup off the stack and yanked the milk out of the mini-fridge, pouring it into the frothing pitcher.

"Your name is Hannah?" the man asked.

Evan's stance shifted, and he seemed to put himself between me and the stranger, even though the counter separated me from the two men.

"And what's your name, friend?" Evan asked.

His low tone and even cadence sounded dangerous and reminded me of how he talks to us about attackers during class. Evan had little tolerance for men who hurt women, and it showed in the way he went on instant guard mode the second he thought anyone was a threat. I saw it happen when Zane first arrived in town. But now, that protectiveness was for me, not his sister.

"Jamison."

The frothing pitcher fell from my numb fingers, clattering to the floor and splattering milk.

"Hi, Hannah," Jamison said with a small smile. He tilted his head, looking at me earnestly. "I had to see you."

Chapter 25: Family Drama

W hat happened?" Jessica came from the back room.

I couldn't move. A rushing sound filled my ears.

"Hannah?" Evan ignored the rules and swung his long legs over the counter. He clasped my arms and gave me a little shake. "Hey, I'm here."

My heart raced as my chest tightened. Spots floated in my vision as I tried to focus on Evan. "I can't breathe," I managed to gasp out.

"Match my breath. In, out. Good, again." Evan breathed with me. No, he was breathing for me.

After several rounds, I could feel my hands again. A few more breaths allowed my vision to fully clear.

"Who are you?" Jessica rounded on Jamison.

"Jamison Stewart," he said calmly.

"Ah." Jessica turned to Evan. "Is she okay?"

"She will be."

He gave a worried frown as his gaze roamed my face. When did the gold flecks in his eyes become so pronounced?

"I suppose you thought coming here unannounced was a good idea." Jessica had her hands on her hips as she faced Jamison.

Jamison held his hands up placatingly. "I didn't think I had a choice. And it's important I talk to her."

I struggled to follow the conversation. Dizziness still swept over me, but I shifted my gaze between Jamison and Jessica.

Jamison shrugged, a sheepish look on his face. "I didn't see how there was any other way. Hannah quit responding to my messages."

"For good reason, I'm sure." She glanced at me, her lips tight. At least she had my back despite her personal thoughts on the matter.

"I have a good reason to see her. As I said, it's important."

"Hannah," Evan murmured.

I redirected my focus to him, careful not to turn my head too quickly. The pressure in my chest had eased, but my head felt like a helium balloon.

"You don't have to talk to him." Evan's grip on my arms tensed slightly and then relaxed into a gentle hold. "Just say the word and we'll make him leave."

"Can it be later?" Was that my voice? It sounded hoarse and muted.

Jamison nodded. "Absolutely. Just tell me when."

"I don't know. Just later."

Evan shifted to wrap an arm around my shoulders and faced the other man. "She'll let you know. You should leave. Now."

His dangerous voice was back. I shook my head, making another wave of dizziness float through me.

"I can handle myself," I said. Then, realizing I hadn't said it out loud, I croaked out, "Evan, I can handle myself."

His brown eyes flicked to me. "I know. I taught you." To Jamison, he said, "Now go. She'll contact you when she's ready."

Jamison nodded again and opened his mouth to speak. Jessica held up her hand. "Not another word. Just turn and leave like my brother said before he decides to go back over the counter."

Jamison gave me a worried look before doing as she said, glancing back once when he reached the door. Evan turned and pulled me into a hug, tucking me against his chest and resting his chin on my head. I breathed in his unique scent of sandalwood and leather and cinnamon. My heart rate slowed to a normal steady beat.

"I can't believe his nerve," Evan growled.

I just took another deep breath and closed my eyes, resting against his strength.

"He wouldn't have just shown up if Hannah had talked to him," came Jessica's reply.

"It's her choice, Jess."

"I know, and she made the wrong one."

At that, my eyes flew open, and I shoved away from Evan, twisting to face my friend.

"Just because you had a great dad doesn't mean everyone did. Mine left when I was a baby. And then he thinks he can demand to see me?"

"Hannah, the customers," Jessica began.

"I don't care! Donna, do you care? What about you?" I pointed at the group of college students. They were all staring at us.

"I'm sorry. Family drama, you know?" Jessica said to the room. "Here, free cookies." She pulled a tray from the case and set it on a nearby table. "Take her home, Evan," she said to her brother. The temperature in the room dropped a few degrees. "I'll call Jewels in." She pulled her phone from her pocket.

"I'm sorry, Jessica." I knew I hadn't handled myself well. My friend also didn't deserve to be yelled at when she was just trying to help.

"I know. But you need some space, and I need help closing. We can talk later."

"Come on, Hannah. I'll walk you." Evan gestured to the door.

Sighing, I gathered my belongings and shrugged into my light jacket before following him outside.

"I'm making a mess of everything," I said after a few moments.

He shook his head. "No, you're not. It's not your fault he showed up like that."

Hot tears spilled from my eyes, and I brushed them away angrily. "No, but Jessica is upset with me for apparently not wanting him here and for something to do with magic. I don't even know what that's about. And then the whole thing with you. Jewels is the only one not mad at me."

"I'm not mad at you."

"Okay, maybe not. But I screwed up my chance with you. I've had a crush on you for years, and you finally look at me the way I hoped, and then I blow it." *Shut up, shut up,* I thought. Why was I saying so much? Wait. I stopped walking and glared at Evan. "Are you doing something with your powers to make me talk?"

"What?" he scoffed. "No. I wouldn't do that to you, Hannah."

"Are you sure? What were you thinking as we left the shop?"

"I was thinking that I was worried about you and wanted to help if I could." He started walking again. "Come on, let's talk somewhere else."

"Okay." I took a few quick steps to catch up to him. "But what else? You didn't wish I would open up and tell you what I thought?"

He tilted his head, considering. "No, but I did think that things would be easier if I understood you more. But, Hannah, that's not how my powers work. I can project an emotion, and if someone is receptive, they will feel it. Like calming a room. I can't direct emotions or make someone do something."

"I don't know. Sofia said magic can progress."

"Right, but I'm pretty sure she meant within our current abilities. We don't suddenly manifest new ones. Now, please, let's not talk about this anymore here. Anyone could hear."

"Oh, of course. Keep magic a secret on an island founded by witches and where everyone knows but pretends we don't exist." I nodded dramatically. "Makes total sense."

Evan rolled his eyes. "Come on. Not everyone knows."

As we neared my cottage, the door opened, and Jewels skipped down the steps. She jogged over to me, her pink hair bouncing on her shoulders.

"Hi. I heard there was a scene at the shop. You okay?"

"Yes. Jessica kicked me out, though."

Jewels chewed on her bottom lip and glanced between Evan and me. "I'm sure it will work out. I better go. She's expecting me."

"Wait. Did you have another vision of me?" I wanted to ask her if the one she had before that showed things under water had changed, but didn't want to get too specific.

She shook her head. "No. Just the same one. I had it again a few minutes before Jessica called me."

A few minutes before Jessica called her would have been when Jamison showed up. He couldn't have been there for longer than that, despite the feeling of time slowing. Did his arrival trigger it?

"I'll see you later." Jewels gave me a quick hug and trotted down the street.

"I need to get to work. Are you going to be okay alone?" Evan asked.

I took a deep breath. "I think so. Thank you, Evan. I'm glad you were there." A sudden wave of exhaustion came over me, and I hid a yawn behind one hand.

"I'm glad, too. I'll come by after I'm finished with Dave Brown's back steps." He hesitated for a second then leaned over and kissed my cheek. "See you later."

I stood at the bottom of steps to the cottage and watched as he strode away, hands in his pockets and his head down. He glanced back and waved when he turned the corner at the end of the street. I waved back and went inside.

It felt like the last note of a song hanging in the air— soft, uncertain, but still full of promise.

Chapter 26: Liminal Space

My thoughts tripped over each other in a tumbled mess. Evan and I kept having miscommunications, Jamison was here against my wishes, Jessica was upset with me, and I was no closer to controlling my magic than I was when it began. I started the kettle for tea, but when it started whistling, decided I didn't really want any. I picked up a piece of chocolate from the green ceramic bowl on the counter, unwrapped it, and stared at until it melted on my fingers. Dropping the wrapper in the trash, I washed my hands and paced to the front window. Autumn sunshine streamed across the street, lending everything a soft golden glow.

I grabbed a jacket and headed out the door, leaving my phone on the counter. The island wasn't so big that someone couldn't find me if they needed to, but I doubted anyone would want to. Everyone who lived in Willowbrook loved the sea and the beach, but it held special memories for me. The few times my mother relaxed and actually played with me happened at the beach. I remembered her laughing as we chased the waves back into the ocean, the way her smile lit up her face when I found a bit of sea glass or a pretty shell, and how she scolded me with a grin when I chased the gulls across the damp sand. We spent hours at the beach every day in the summer, bringing picnics and making sandcastles. That was before she became corporate, both in her career and in her relationship with me.

I hesitate for a moment before leaving the sidewalk and stepping onto the sand, feeling the shift from town to sea. As always, I had kicked my shoes off and left them at the edge of the pavement. Only one other pair sat there, and fresh footprints led directly to the edge of the water. I could make out a form on the beach, stretched out on a colorful blanket. I veered to the right, angling my path so it would avoid the other person and take me to the water. If they had left their shoes, they were local, and I didn't want to be drawn into a conversation. The warm sand gave way beneath me and pressed between my toes, sharp bits of shell digging into my soles. Despite the season, the mild temperature and clear skies made it feel like a summer evening. Briefly, I wondered if that was Jessica's doing since rain had canceled the harvest festival for the last three years. It had always been her favorite town event. I shook my head, not wanting to think about her just now. I needed to find solace and grounding in a way that none of Sofia's prescribed magical exercises managed.

When I arrived at the tideline, I dug my toes into the wet sand and let the waves gently wash over my feet. I closed my eyes and felt the rhythm of the ocean, the heat of the sun on my back. I allowed nature to infuse my spirit and calm my mind. This was something my mother and I used to do whenever we had a bad day. She used to tell me that the earth kept us solid while the water washed our cares away. We would stand like this for as long as it took for us to feel serene. Sometimes, it would only be a few minutes for me, so I would quietly move inland and play in the sand, scooping great trenches and making mounds, until she finally moved and came to join me.

I opened my eyes and looked out at the water. Shadows and light chased each other across the top of the waves, and I glanced around, not realizing how long I had stood there. The tide was out, the waterline many yards in front of where I stood. Whoever I had shared this beach with was gone. I turned to glance west and saw the barest sliver of light in the sky. I lifted one foot and rotated my ankle a few times, then the other. I must have stood there for at least two hours, lost in past memories and feeling the sadness dissipate. I inhaled a deep breath full of salt and fish and wood smoke, held it for a few seconds, then exhaled in a rush. My problems still awaited me, but I knew I could handle them.

I made my way back to my shoes and sat on a granite boulder to brush my feet off before slipping into my shoes and walking back to my house. Lights were on in the cottage, indicating that Jewels was home as I had forgotten to turn them on before I left.

"Oh, good. You're home," she said when I walked in. "Were you with Evan?"

I shed my jacket, hanging it on the hook by the door. "No, he had a job. I went to the beach."

"Feel better?" she asked.

Jewels sat ensconced in the chair, one foot up on the coffee table as she painted her toenails an electric blue.

I smiled despite myself. Jewels had only been with us a few months, yet it seemed like she had always been part of the island.

"Yes, actually. Although I didn't realize how long I was there."

"Magic can be found in liminal spaces."

I raised my eyebrows. "What?"

She looked up as she switched feet. "Liminal spaces are places between. They aren't really one thing, but both. Like the beach. Or a doorway. I think magic has been calling to you your whole life, and that's why you love standing there at the edge of the water."

I shook my head. "No, I like standing there because it was something my mom and I used to do, back when she acted like a mom and not a corporate manager of my life."

"Maybe she has magic too," Jewels said with a shrug.

I snorted a laugh. "My mom? Not a chance. She's too rigid." I thought of Sofia in her flowing colorful tops and preference for sweets. The closest my mom came to looking relaxed was when she wore her designer leggings and went to spin class, but even then, she had perfectly done makeup and hair that sweat wouldn't dare ruin.

"People can surprise you. Did you and Evan finally talk?"

"Not about us, but I think we will soon. It wasn't the time after Jamison showed up, and now I think I've missed my chance. All the chances. Every time I try to talk to him, it doesn't go well. For an empath, he's rather dense."

She trilled in her contagious way. "He's still a man, regardless of his magical powers or other gifts." Jewels wagged her eyebrows.

"Well, I'm probably not going to find out about those 'other gifts' now. Ugh!" I flopped back against the couch cushion. "I just wanted to keep living my life. I didn't ask for magic or my dad to show up. And I have to do magical training with Evan. Maybe I'll quit his self-defense class and take up running again."

"I guess you'll have to pretend you didn't have that little romantic interlude." Jewels finished with her toes and leaned back, carefully crossing her feet at the ankles so she didn't smudge the paint before it dried. "And eventually, you'll have to talk to him about how you feel."

Just then, my phone buzzed. I looked at it sitting on the coffee table as if it was a hissing viper. Jewels raised her eyebrows at me.

"You can't avoid the world for forever."

I huffed and picked up my phone, staring at the name on the screen. "It's Evan."

"Just answer like you would before. It will be okay." Jewels gave me an encouraging smile.

Taking a deep breath, I pressed the answer button, pasted a smile on my face so my voice would sound cheerful, and said, "Were your ears burning?"

"What?" Evan's voice sent shivers down my spine even over the airways. Warmth spread through me, and I realized my smile was genuine.

"Jewels and I were just talking about my magic training, so I thought your ears may have been burning."

I kept smiling, even though my heart pounded in my chest.

"Ah, no. I'm just calling to check on you. You sound better."

"I went to the beach for a while. It always helps."

He cleared his throat. "Good. I was worried about you, Hannah."

"I think I'll be okay."

"I'm glad. Speaking of training, do you work at the preschool tomorrow?"

I fiddle with my necklace as I answer, and Jewels motioned for me to stop the nervous habit. "Nope. I have to be at Over the Moon at eleven, though."

"Perfect. Let's meet on the east beach in the morning. Eight?"

I groaned a little. "Can we make it nine? For caffeine's sake?"

I could almost see the grin on his face as he said, "Eight-thirty, and I'll bring coffee."

"Deal."

"See you in the morning, Hannah."

The soft way he said my name almost undid me. I sucked in a breath and managed to get out a goodbye before hanging up. Tomorrow would be a disaster. If I maintained my distance so there wasn't any accidental brushing of shoulders, and so I couldn't smell his spicy, earthy fragrance, I could make it through some training. I doubted I would have enough focus to actually accomplish anything, though.

"You've got it bad," Jewels's voice broke into my thoughts.

"What? What have I got?"

She shook her head at me as if disappointed but smirked. "You're in love."

"No. What? No. I mean, I've had a crush on him for a while, but he has to be more like a big brother now. Especially now. He has to be since we obviously can't make a romantic relationship work. Not with all the other things happening. Well, sure, I still have a crush on him.

Who wouldn't? But it can't be anything more." I realized I was babbling and abruptly stopped talking. I refused to think about how my stomach knotted at the thought of seeing him.

Her chuckle as she stood and headed to her room was not reassuring.

Chapter 27: Beach Bubbles

I stood in a room filled with butterflies. Tropical plants lined the side of the glass-walled enclosure, and blue, yellow, orange, and red wings fluttered around me. A bright blue butterfly landed on my hand, its legs tickling my palm. I brought my hand closer to my face to examine the delicate creature. Suddenly, the air changed from warm and balmy to bone-chilling cold, and my breath misted in front of me. Frost crept over the windows and crawled along the plants. Butterflies dropped from their flight, landing on the stone floor. The one in my hand stopped moving, and I watched in horror as ice coated its wings before it shattered, leaving nothing but tiny blue fragments in my hand.

The alarm blared, and I hit the snooze button and rolled over, staring at the ceiling as my heart rate slowed. Breathing deeply, I focused on the simple grounding exercise Sofia insisted we perform daily. After a few minutes, I felt steady enough to get out of bed and dress. I pulled back the curtain to check the weather and saw a light dusting of sparkling frost. It rarely got cold enough on the island to snow, and frost was unusual. Perhaps my subconscious sensed the change in weather and turned my dream into a nightmare.

I slipped on black jeans and a soft blue sweater that almost matched the butterfly from my dream before padding out to the kitchen. Jewels already sat there with a muffin and a steaming mug of coffee.

"Morning," I mumbled, snagging my own muffin from the box on the counter.

"Morning," she replied. "Coffee?"

I shook my head, sitting across from her. "Evan said he would provide."

"Perhaps he can also provide some information about this weather."

"Hmm?"

"This is not typical of Willowbrook, right? I think Jessica has something to do with it."

In the haze of my dream, I had forgotten that my friend's magic was weather-related along with fire and growing things. Jewels's comment brought me fully awake, and the bite of blueberry muffin turned dry in my mouth.

"I will talk to her," I finally said.

"After your morning date," Jewels's tone went from concerned to teasing.

I wish I knew how to do that; how to live in the moment and not let worry overtake my thoughts.

"It's not a date," I protested. "We're training, under orders from Sofia."

Jewels picked up her mug and looked at me over the rim as she sipped. "Yes, and he's bringing coffee."

"Because we're friends." I glared at her.

"Keep telling yourself that."

I scoffed. "I need to go. I'll see you later." I stood and put the rest of my muffin into a glass container.

"Yep. And I expect some romantic details later."

"There won't be any because this is just training." I emphasized the last word.

"Sure, sure."

Her laugh followed me out of the kitchen as I went to the bathroom to finish getting ready.

I arrived at the beach a few minutes before eight-thirty and scanned the expanse as I slipped off my shoes. With the cold, I wouldn't be walking in the water today, but the sand felt oddly comforting in its coolness. I spotted Evan sitting on some driftwood and headed over to him. He stood as I approached, handing me a paper cup of warmth. I noted he also dressed a little warmer today than usual, changing out his typical t-shirt for a long-sleeved Henley under a black quilted vest. I forced my eyes to remain on his instead of wandering the length of his body. Damn, the man was handsome without even trying.

"How did you get coffee from the shop already?" It opened at nine on Sundays.

His brow furrowed. "Jess didn't sleep much and she went in around seven."

"I wondered if this weather was her."

"Yeah, it's been a while since she's lost control enough to affect the whole island. She's not really talking to me, though."

I sighed. "I think I know what it's about. I'll talk to her."

"Thanks, Hannah."

The relief on his face made me want to reach up and brush his hair from his forehead, but I kept my hand firmly fisted at my side and took a long sip of the coffee instead.

"Hazelnut. You remembered."

He smiled, and the glint in his eyes returned. "It's hard to forget."

I turned away from him and looked out at the ocean, gray and endless. The rhythmic flow of the waves steadied my heartbeat. "Well, shall we get started?" I tried for a light tone, remembering Jewels's advice to keep things normal.

"Yeah. Ready when you are. Sofia said bubbles, so I figured I would blow, and you can freeze, or whatever it is you do."

That brought a burst of genuine laughter from me, and I looked back at him. "Evan, I don't know what it is I do. But I will try."

His answering grin made the heat rise to my cheeks, and I covered my blush with another drink from the cup in my hand. Then I set the cup in the sand, twisting it a little to make sure it stayed upright, and took a few steps back. Evan put his cup beside mine and pulled a small bottle of bubbles from his pocket.

"Okay, so don't worry about affecting me. I'll keep my shield up. Focus on stopping the bubbles."

"And if someone comes along and notices they are stuck in midair?"

He shrugged. "I'll put the shield around you and stop your magic."

"Well, when you make it sound that easy…"

"It worked with Jessica. Sofia explained that it made sense. Jess has superpowers connected to her emotions, and I can sense emotions and block magic. We complement each other. Sofia said it's common in siblings, and it helps to keep the balance of power."

I nodded. "It does make sense. And I guess if you weren't here, then all of our magic would be out of control."

"No, not really. Sofia can also shield. She said there's usually a handful of witches in an area that can. Otherwise, all the children coming into their powers would destroy everything." As he talked, he opened the bottle and swirled the bubble wand around in the solution. "Now, remember, this is the beach most visible from the ferry." He gestured to the dock, the wood still shiny from being replaced that summer. "And a lot of people like to come here to jog in the morning. It is Sunday, so there's a possibility some people will come before church starts at ten. Anyone could see."

"If you're trying to make me feel better, it's not working."

"I'm reminding you that discovery is imminent. So, you need to figure out how to pull your magic back when you do freeze the bubbles."

I rolled my head, releasing a knot in my neck. "Okay. Let's do it."

He lifted the wand, pursed his lips, and blew softly. A stream of glistening bubbles flowed out and floated in the air. I held my hand up and commanded them to stop.

Nothing happened. I tried again, this time saying, "Freeze."

Evan blew more bubbles, and more, pausing between to watch me. I tried pretending the bubbles were Jessica's fireballs.

"This isn't working. I can't do it," I said after several minutes. I stomped over and picked up my coffee, which had cooled.

"I have an idea. Let's make a game out of it. A bet."

"What's the bet?" I peered at him.

"For every bubble that touches the ground and pops, you owe me a pushup. In front of everyone at the next class. And by next class, I mean the next class on the schedule, not the next women's self-defense class."

"I'm going to do pushups in front of, what, six-year-olds?"

He shrugged. "The next class is actually the teens."

"Oh no." I shook my head. "I'm not doing pushups in front of teens."

"You won't have to if you keep the bubbles from touching the sand." When I hesitated, he added, "Hannah, we already know that your magic has to have something to motivate it. At least for now it does. You need there to be a threat. So, I'm threatening to make you do pushups in front of teens."

Huffing, I stared at him with eyebrows raised. He looked back, implacable. I drained the rest of my coffee, dropped the cup on the sand, and finally said, "Fine. Let's do this."

I moved a few steps away from him and rolled my shoulders as if getting ready to defend myself on his mat. I supposed in some ways this was similar. Glancing around, I double-checked that we were still alone on the beach. Besides the gulls squawking and wheeling overhead, it was empty.

"Ready now?" he wore a slight smirk, and his eyes sparkled with amusement.

"I won't let you win this," I ground out between gritted teeth.

"Okay, go." He lifted the bubble wand to his lips and blew gently.

A stream of bubbles flowed out, wafting gently on the breeze. Evan quickly dipped the plastic circle back into the container and blew more bubbles.

I willed my magic to help me. Okay, I wished it would. Desperately. Focusing on the bubbles, I held my palms out like a traffic cop and said, in my most commanding tone usually reserved for rowdy preschoolers, "Stop."

The soapy orbs became motionless.

I cast a triumphant grin at Evan.

"Nice," he said before blowing more bubbles.

"Wait! That's not fair."

"Stop them," came his calm response.

I waved my hand, my chest tight with anxiety. "Stop."

The new bubbles still floated, slowly drifting around, and I watched in horror as one neared the sand. I flinched, and my stomach rolled, the coffee suddenly feeling like a lump.

"No!" I cried out.

Once again, it seemed time stilled, only this time Evan remained unaffected. But the seagulls halted mid-flight. Evan's eyes widened as he took in the scene, his mouth slightly ajar.

"I think your reach is getting bigger," he said.

The excited barking of a dog drew my eyes to the other side of the beach. A golden lab bounded across the sand toward the water. Tracing his path back to the sidewalk, I saw Sandy West in a long blue dress and multicolored scarf. She slowly followed her dog, wrestling to keep the scarf from blowing away.

"Quick, before she sees," Evan hissed.

My breath came in short gasps, and I clenched my fists to keep my hands from shaking. "I don't know how I did it before."

"Try something."

"Can't you—"

"Yes, but I won't until you try."

Damn him. And Sofia for putting us here when I had no clue how my magic worked. I brought up the memory of the playground, of Helen beginning to open the door and of what I said. I recalled how my mother spoke to her assistants when she needed something done immediately. It was a tone that didn't allow for questions and expected quick action.

"Resume," I said in my mother's tone.

At once, the gulls renewed their calls and cries, hopefully not affected by their momentary stillness. Just then, Sandy finished tying her scarf in a knot and looked up at the sky before glancing around. She saw us and waved. We waved back, and then I sank onto my knees in the sand.

"I can't do this again. That was too close." I stared at the ground, tracing circles in the coarse grains with my fingertip.

Evan knelt beside me, and our knees almost touched. "That's the point, remember? Sofia wanted you to have the element of risk."

"I don't understand why. You and Jessica don't train that way. Jewels certainly doesn't."

"I think," he said slowly, "it's because not only do you need a good reason to use your magic, but you need a good reason to pull it back. Jessica's magic needs released, or she loses control, like a kettle that is over-boiling. Mine is more innate, and it's not like I can cause a lot of damage from sensing someone's emotions. Jewels's…well, I'm not sure how her magic works, but it's not as visible as yours or Jessica's."

"I wish I could give it back."

"Hannah, look at me."

Reluctantly, I raised my eyes to meet his.

"You are doing very well for a new witch. You haven't destroyed anything; you even saved little Owen from a broken arm or worse, and you saved Levi from getting hit by a car. We will keep practicing, and you'll get better. You'll find other ways to encourage your powers to obey. While our magic—Jess's and mine—came from our parents, we still had to learn how to work with it instead of against it. It's the same for you, even though magic doesn't run in your family."

His words triggered instant recall of the night I first used magic and what Jessica said about ancestral connection. Suddenly, a flash of memory went through my mind of when I was very little, probably about three years old. I was playing with blocks on the floor, and my mother sat nearby on a chair. A man came out of the kitchen. He seemed angry, and I started to cry. The lights in the house went dark, and my mother picked me up and told the man to leave, declaring he was scaring me. He tried to talk to her, but she turned and took me to the bedroom.

"Oh!" I gasped.

"Hannah?" Evan grasped my shoulder. "What is it?"

"Jamison." I looked at him, my face slack. "My father has magic."

Chapter 28: Explanations

e van walked me home, and I explained about the memory.
"So, you see, I do have hereditary magic." I grinned. "I'm not just a random witch."

"Right. And do you think that's why Jamison reached out? Maybe that's why he left when you were a baby?"

I stumbled to a halt, my breath catching in my throat, and almost tripped. "Oh. Oh! I need to see him."

I whirled, already breaking into a jog toward the inn. Evan's long legs easily kept pace with me. We arrived only minutes later, and I leaned over, panting slightly both from the run and the overwhelming emotions.

"You don't have to stay," I said to him. I wanted him to stay. I needed someone with me who was wholly on my side. And I wanted time to talk to Evan as well.

"I have time."

A rush of calm washed over me, and I peered at him suspiciously. "You can push emotions?"

He shrugged. "Only sometimes, and only to those I really care about." His cheeks looked flushed. I'm sure mine did too after the wind on the beach and the dash here.

"Thanks. Um, I'm going to see if he'll come to the park."

Evan nodded, and I went in, asking the front desk to ring Jamison's room. The receptionist, Carl, told Jamison he had a visitor.

"Thanks, Carl."

"Anytime, Hannah."

A moment later, Jamison stepped into the lobby. It struck me again how similar we looked, and I mentally slapped my forehead at not recognizing it when I first saw him in Over the Moon.

"Hannah? Hi." His voice held a hopeful edge, and he smiled tentatively.

"Hi. I was wondering if you had time to talk." My voice shook a little with nerves and excitement, and I hoped he didn't hear it. "We can go to the park."

"Oh, sure. Let me get my jacket."

I nodded. "I'll be outside."

In the few moments I had alone with Evan before Jamison stepped out, I asked, "What's the best way to approach this?"

"Ask him to tell his story. You'll know what to do after that."

Jamison appeared and hesitated when his gaze landed on Evan. His expression shifted from amicable to something more wary.

"Jamison, this is Evan." I nearly added "my friend," but stopped myself. I wasn't sure how that would land.

Jamison descended the three steps to the sidewalk, his posture loose, but his eyes sharp as he shook Evan's hand. "I remember you." I watched as his grip tightened. "You're very protective of Hannah. I approve. Not that you need it," he added casually.

Evan didn't flinch, but I saw the way his jaw tensed. He released Jamison's hand a second too late, just enough to make a point. "Yes, I've known Hannah a long time." His voice was clear, and there was something pointed about it. "She's my sister's best friend."

An awkward silence descended, and a flicker of something unspoken passed between them. I looked between the two men, trying to decipher the hidden meaning of their conversation. Was there a challenge? I gave a little shake of my head. I wasn't here for that.

Jamison was the first to break eye contact, exhaling as if he was shaking something off. "Right. Well. The park, then?"

Evan nodded, his expression neutral.

"The park is this way." I gestured before turning and leading the way down the block.

"I remember," Jamison said. "Not much has changed in Willowbrook since I was here last."

As we turned to walk, Evan positioned himself just slightly closer to me. What is going on?

In just a few minutes, we were at the park. It was empty this time of day, and we sat at a picnic table under one of the old oak trees, Jamison on one side and Evan and I on the other. Jessica's community garden held some squash and lettuces, but the volunteers had harvested the rest of the vegetables and mulched the berry plants with straw to protect them from the chill winter.

"So, you changed your mind," Jamison said.

I nodded. "I remembered something from when I was little. And I thought I could at least hear you out. What happened?"

Jamison took a deep breath and briefly closed his eyes. It looked like what I did when I was steeling myself to say something difficult. He looked at me, his dark brown eyes meeting mine across the table and also across time.

"It's a long story. Or at least a long journey."

"Start at the beginning. Why did you leave?"

He sighed. "I'll start before that. It will explain a lot." Shifting his weight, he crossed his arms on the table. "My family moved here from upstate during my junior year in high school. My father lived here when he was young and missed the small town life. And my grandparents were born here. It seemed fate kept bringing our family back to the island. Anyway, when I met your mother, I thought she was the most beautiful and exciting woman I'd ever known. We clicked immediately. We liked the same things and loved living here on the island. We went to prom together—both junior and senior—and we were homecoming king and queen our senior year. If a modern fairy tale romance existed, it was us. We never fought. So naturally, when we graduated, we got married. I was content as an electrician apprentice and knew eventually

I could make good money. Charlotte had a knack for advertising and putting together business packages, so she worked from home making flyers and business cards and creating advertisements for the papers for the local businesses.

"When she told me she was pregnant, we were elated. It seemed a perfect thing to add to our perfect lives. You were born, this tiny, delicate little girl, and soon after, strange things started happening to me at work.

"Sometimes, I couldn't get the power to come on to a switch even after my boss checked over my work and said it was correct. Other times, electricity would run through wires that weren't fully connected. Once it blew a breaker, and none of us could figure out how when the power wasn't connected to the main yet. Things like that. Then, one afternoon, I got off work early and went home to find Charlotte cooking dinner in the kitchen and you were in your room. I walked in, and all the lights in the house turned on at once. We thought it was some kind of strange power surge. When I mentioned it to my dad, he told me to talk to Milton Calhoun. He said it must have skipped a generation, but he wouldn't explain."

My head snapped up. "Wait, Milton Calhoun? As in Donna's father?" I interrupted. I filed the information away for later.

Jamison nodded. "That's the one."

"Where are your parents now? Why haven't I met them?"

Jamison's face fell. "My mother died of cancer shortly after you were born. My father passed away when you were five. He was so brokenhearted after losing his wife that he just gave up."

"I'm sorry," I whispered.

He shook his head. "It was a long time ago. Anyway..." He paused, leaned back a bit, and took a deep breath before saying in a rush, "I talked to Milton, and he told me I had magical powers. It seemed crazy to me, but the more Milton explained, the more it made sense."

"I know exactly how that feels." I chuckled.

"So, your magic is related to electricity?" Evan spoke for the first time since the inn.

Jamison looked between us. "This isn't...surprising to you?"

Evan shook his head. "Not really. I suspected something as much."

"What is your last name?" Suspicion colored his voice, and he drew back a little.

"Barnes."

"Ah. You're one of the founding families. No wonder you're not surprised." Then Jamison turned to me. "And, Hannah?"

I gave a rueful smile. "Newbie witch here, learning how to control my powers. Had a lesson this morning, in fact."

"Good. Even with Milton's help, it took years before I could control it. His abilities are related to animals, which is why he makes such a good vet."

Realization hit me. "And that's why Mom asked you to leave."

Jamison gave me a sad smile. "Yes. She couldn't handle the idea of it. And when it started happening around her, and especially around you, she told me to leave until I could control it. Unfortunately, it took so long and caused so much trouble that I never tried to return. Until now."

I mulled that over as silence stretched between us. Finally, I asked, "Why did you come back?"

Jamison did that thing again where he closes his eyes while taking a deep breath. Then he said, "I was worried that you would manifest magic and not have anyone to help you." He smiled at Evan. "Looks like I was wrong."

A sharp heat clawed its way up my throat, burning like a swallowed scream. I pushed back from the picnic table so fast the legs scraped against the concrete with an ugly screech.

"You don't get to pretend this was some noble act," I snapped, my voice trembling with the force of everything

I was holding in. "I probably wouldn't have magic if you hadn't reached out."

He furrowed his brow. "What do you mean?"

My breath hitched, and I clenched my fists. "I mean, I was perfectly happy with my little life here on the island until you messaged me. That's what triggered my magic. It's possible I would have gone my whole life without this...this...problem! This is your fault."

Jamison flinched, but I didn't care.

"Hannah." Evan's voice was calm, careful, but there was a warning there. "You don't know that."

I spun toward him. "I do know that." My voice shook. "Isn't that what Sofia told me? That trauma triggered my magic?" I stabbed my finger at Jamison, my whole body shaking now. "I was fine until you showed up. I didn't have any trauma until you messaged me. You did this to me."

Before either of them could stop me, I turned on my heel and stormed off, my boots striking the pavement in short, furious strides. The cold air stung my flushed cheeks, but I barely noticed. I just needed to get away. Away from Jamison. Away from Evan's careful, knowing looks. Away from how my hands still trembled with all this power I never asked for.

I needed to talk to someone who understood what was happening to me and how I felt. Someone who has always been there for me.

I needed to talk to Jessica.

Chapter 29:
Confrontations

ntering the shop, I went directly to the counter where Jess was blending herbs into a tea canister. "We need to talk."

She peered at me. "Uh, okay. Go in the back. I'll be right there."

As I stomped to the break room, I heard her tell Jewels, "Take over, will you?" and Jewels's assent.

I paced the small room, shaking out my hands and blowing breaths through my mouth.

"What is going on?" Jess said as she entered and shut the door.

"Jamison! That's what. He's a witch."

"What?"

"Yeah, so that's why he messaged me. He wanted to make sure I was okay if I had magic."

"But, Hannah, that's a good thing. It means he cares."

I sliced my hand through the air. "No! No, it means he triggered my powers. I would be normal and happy if he just left me alone!"

Jessica reached out and grabbed my hand. "Hannah, come sit down. Tell me what happened."

I slumped in the chair, crossing my arms over my chest and glaring at the wall. "Evan and I were training this morning, and something he said made me realize that Jamison must be a witch, too. So, I went and talked with him."

"Okay, that's good."

"Yeah, except it's not. It's not good at all. If he would've left me alone, I wouldn't have magic at all. I wouldn't be in this mess of having to train with Evan when I don't know if he really wants to be with me or not, and you wouldn't be mad at me because I don't want to get to know my so-called father."

"Oh, Hannah, I'm not mad at you. I just think you will regret it if you don't get to know him. To be honest, I am a little jealous that you have a father you don't want while I want my father but can't have him. And it's quite possible that something else would have triggered your magic sooner or later. It just happened to be him. It's not his fault."

I shook my head and slunk lower in the chair. "My mother told me it wasn't a good idea. I should have listened to her."

Jessica sighed. "It's almost rush time. I need to get back and help Jewels. Listen, I'll make you some tea. Let's talk more when we close, okay?"

I nodded. "Thanks."

While I waited for the tea, I picked at a loose thread at the hem of my shirt. Jessica brought a bagel sandwich with the tea and left as soon as she told me what was in it: holy basil, passionflower, and lavender. I blew across the surface then took a cautious sip. The herbal, floral warmth spread through me. After several more swallows, I felt my muscles start to relax as the tension left my body.

Grudgingly, I admitted to myself that Evan and Jessica could be right. My magic would probably have emerged eventually without Jamison's contact. I would have to apologize to him, too.

Talking to Jessica after closing didn't do anything to alleviate my anxiety. She did her best to explain her stance; I did my best to listen. But the anger burned inside me. Jamison should have stayed, especially since he knew I could end up a witch. Eventually, Jess sighed and said she hoped I found what I needed, and we each walked home.

I put my earbuds in and turned up the music, letting it drown out my thoughts. My steps matched the beat, yet I couldn't shake the idea that my parents should have done more. Arriving at the cottage, I heaved a sigh of relief upon seeing the lights off. Jewels wasn't home yet.

Once I made it inside, I called my mom.

"Charlotte Stewart," she answered.

I didn't even bother saying hello. "Mom, why didn't you tell me that I could have special abilities?"

"Hannah? What—it's not Sunday."

I sighed again, wishing for patience. "I know. Now please answer me."

Her voice took on the official tone she used with difficult clients. "I'm not sure I understand what you're asking."

"Magic, Mom! I'm talking about magic. You knew. You knew Jamison had powers. And if there was even a chance they would be passed to me, you should have told me. At the very least, you should have asked Jamison to stay until you knew. Don't you think it might be important for me to know? To have help, even if it was from Jamison?"

My mother spluttered, and I heard a muffled sound as if she briefly covered the phone with her hand. "Jamison said the binding would prevent you from having magic."

"What binding?" Once again, there was something other people knew about me that I didn't have a clue about. It made me want to throw something.

"He explained that it would prevent you from developing magical powers. He said it's something typically placed on children, so they didn't use magic before they had the ability to reason." She spoke in a controlled, subdued tone, as though addressing a displeased client.

"Oh, he did, huh?" I paced the small living room of my cottage. "Well, it's a temporary solution. Did he tell you that? Did he tell you that a life-changing or traumatic event could still trigger it? Or that the binding would wear off? It's not permanent."

She fell silent for a few moments then said, "No, he didn't mention that to me. So does that mean you…"

"Have magic? Yeah. And it's caused me all kinds of issues. I can't believe you! As my mother, it's your job to protect and help me. Prepare me for the world. And Jamison should have known better. Or he should have found out. Are you a witch too?"

"Definitely not!" She sounded offended at the idea. "I didn't even know Jamison was one until after you were born. Apparently, your birth was his life-changing event. It started slowly, with strange things with the lights and power. Sometimes a light would turn on or off when he entered or left a room. Then he told me about similar experiences at work, and I told him he had to figure it out. I thought maybe it was just a coincidence. Or maybe the MRI he had when he had shoulder pain when he was younger made his electrical field expand." She heaved a sigh of her own. "I don't know. I didn't believe in magic or supernatural powers. Then one day he came home and said he had talked to some people called the Council and he was to begin training. For a while, it seemed to help reduce the occurrences of his uncontrolled abilities. But then things got worse. All the lights and electrical appliances would turn on or off when he walked into a room. It didn't even matter whether they were plugged in or not. And eventually, I just couldn't take it anymore. I didn't want it around you. It seemed dangerous. I couldn't risk you getting hurt."

"And that's when you asked him to leave," I whispered.

"Yes. And when he went, he had some people come and put the binding on you. Hannah, you have to believe me. I was trying to protect you."

I closed my eyes and pressed my fingers to my temples. I recalled the days we spent at the beach together and how she made sure I had nice clothes and good food. My mother was many things, but she had always loved me as best as she knew how, and I never lacked for anything growing up.

Taking a deep breath, I said, "I believe you."

"Hannah, can I ask…what are your powers?"

"I can freeze things, people. Stop their motion. And I can teleport objects."

"Oh. I can see how that might be helpful."

"Really? I don't know…" I trailed off, remembering the first time when I stopped the glasses from shattering on the floor. Then when I saved Owen from falling and Levi from the wanna-be race car driver. "You're right. They are very helpful. I just need to learn how to control them."

"Like Jamison."

"Like Jamison, and every other witch who isn't allowed to have their powers when they're young."

"I understand you want connection or closure, but please keep your distance from him. His magic isn't safe to be around. He caused the entire island to be without power for almost three days. Who knows what it's evolved to over the years?"

I rolled my eyes. If only my mother knew that Jessica had caused the storm that almost wrecked the island. Then again, my mother would probably demand that I stop being friends with Jessica if she knew.

"I need answers from him. And maybe he can help me with my own magic."

"It's not a good idea."

I hated it when she pressured me. "Mom, I need to go."

"I am sorry, Hannah. Truly."

I blinked rapidly. I couldn't recall the last time my mother had apologized for anything. After managing to squeak out, "I know," I pressed the end button.

Jewels still wasn't home. I vaguely recalled her saying something about going out for a drink after work, though not with whom. Before I talked myself out of it, I quickly pulled up Jamison's number and called him next.

"Hello?"

"Jamison, it's Hannah." I refused to call him "dad."

I heard a quick inhale of breath. "Hannah. Hi. I'm so glad you called."

Ignoring his pleasantries and the obvious hopeful tone of his voice, I said, "Why didn't you come back sooner to make sure I was okay? You knew magic could manifest at any point. Wasn't I important to you?" My chest tightened.

"Of course, you were important to me. You are important to me, Hannah. I didn't want to leave. Your mother made me. She said I wasn't safe to be around until I could control my magic." He sighed. "And I had to agree. I worried I would accidentally electrocute you or something. I didn't know then how my powers affected people."

"Mom said you caused the island to lose power for three days."

He paused before saying, "I did. That was the day she asked me to leave. I loved you both so much that it hurt when your mother pushed me from your lives. And I lost control."

His story seemed similar to Jessica's. Was I also destined to lose control if someone hurt my feelings? I shook my head and resolved not to think about it.

"I'm sorry, Hannah. I should have at least stayed in touch, regardless of what Charlotte wanted."

"What about the binding?"

He sighed again. "She told you about that too, huh?"

"She said you had me bound so I would never have magic."

"She misunderstood. Or she hoped that would be the outcome. I figured if you were bound, you had a chance to grow up before anything happened, if you had powers. That part worked, at least."

I furrowed my brow, thinking. I made sense. I pictured Owen having magical powers and knew that would be a disaster.

"But wouldn't it be better if potentially magical children knew what could happen? Get training earlier?

Maybe they could avoid some of the major negative occurrences of magic."

"From my understanding, that is the case with some children born into magical families. You'll have to ask someone else for clarification. I don't know the specifics. But you haven't caused anything to happen yet, have you?"

"No. But a precog has had visions of something terrible happening." I wouldn't tell him it was Jewels.

"Then it's good I came back. I will do what I can to help you."

"I already have a mentor. But thanks anyway."

"Then can we get to know each other on a non-magical level?" He pleaded.

"I can try," I said. "That's the best I can do right now."

"I'll take it."

We hung up, and I saw a text from my mom. "Now what does she want?" I grumbled.

I mean it, Hannah. Stay away from Jamison.

I shook my head. I refused to make her past trauma my problem. She had to come to terms with what I was and what Jamison did, because there wasn't any changing it. Tired of people telling what to do, I cranked up the volume on the music and settled onto the couch, closing my eyes and ignoring the world for just a few minutes.

Chapter 30: Harvest Festival

T hankfully, I didn't have much time the rest of the weekend to think about my parents. The annual Willowbrook Harvest Festival occurred the first weekend in October.

The planning committee had strategically placed hay bales throughout the park as seating. Bright orange pumpkins in a patch made a cheerful orange backdrop next to the community garden. All of the local businesses had booths, including Over the Moon. Jessica, Jewels, and I took turns in the booth serving hot drinks until midafternoon when we shut it down to participate in the activities. Our small town festival drew people from the mainland, so everyone benefited from one last income boost before winter.

The warmth of the afternoon soon had me tying my flannel shirt around my waist and wishing I had chosen a tank top in a color other than black. Almost everyone in the park had similar outfits on, and it made me giggle to think of it as Willowbrook's harvest festival uniform.

As I walked through the park, the smells of kettle corn and hot dogs drew me to the food court. I hadn't realized how hungry I felt until then. Standing in line, I let my gaze wander over the crowd. I spotted Jewels standing in the kettle corn line with Donna. *Those two seem to be together a lot.* It was surprising to see colorful Jewels with serious Donna. Jewels wore a purple and black plaid skirt and a gold pullover sweater, while Donna wore a long jean skirt with a navy blouse. But perhaps they balanced each other out. Looking at them, I remembered what Jamison had said about Donna's dad training him. I wondered if Donna had bound magic like me.

"Buy you lunch?"

The sound of Evan's voice startled me out of my thoughts. I whirled and almost stumbled. His hand caught my elbow.

"Steady, there. I didn't mean to scare you."

I was sure he could hear my heart pounding. If only he knew the real reason. Thankfully, with the throng of people here, he was probably shielded and wasn't sensing anything from me. I hoped, anyway.

"It's okay," I managed with a smile.

He gestured at the hot dog stand. "So? What will you have?"

"Oh, um, a chili cheese dog, please. But you don't have to buy it."

"My pleasure." He stepped to the window when it was our turn and ordered two chili cheese dogs and lemonade.

When we had our food, we managed to find seats at one of the picnic tables, next to a family with two small children.

"Does it seem busier than last year to you?" he asked.

I quickly chewed and swallowed before answering. "Yes, actually, now that you mention it. Word must be really getting out about our small town."

"Well, between the awesome concert and our fabulous festivals, who can blame them? They can't live here, so they visit, which is the next best thing. And it's good for the businesses."

I nodded agreement. He chatted comfortably, and I wondered if our beach training session had lessened the strain between us. Perhaps today would be a good time to talk to him about our relationship, whatever it ended up being.

"About the other day—" I started.

"Are you going to—" he said at the same time.

We both laughed.

"You first," I said.

"No, ladies first." He smiled, and my heart melted.

I inhaled and slowly exhaled before starting again. "I want to apologize. Both about not giving you more of a chance to talk to me at the dojo and how I acted."

Evan slowly put his fork down and wiped his fingers with a napkin before reaching over and taking my hand. "Hannah, I'm sorry, too. To be completely honest, it hurt that you seemed to just want to be friends. And I shouldn't have done what I did."

I hesitated. I wanted more with him, but I wasn't sure now was the time. "There's a lot happening in my life right now. With learning that I'm a witch to my father coming back, and my mother being, well, my mother…" Trailing off, I extricated my hand from his. "I'm not sure now is a good time to start a relationship."

Hurt flashed in his eyes, and I grimaced. Then he straightened and took a large gulp of lemonade.

"I understand. But, Hannah? You need to decide about us. Soon. I can't be in limbo anymore."

Pressure built in my chest. Evan wanted a decision, which was only fair. But Jamison wanted to be part of my life, my mother wanted me to stay away from him, my friendship with Jessica still felt strained, and I wasn't even close to controlling my magic. I wasn't sure how much more I could take.

"I know. And I will," I finally said. "I just need to figure some of this other stuff out first.

He nodded. "I get it. I can wait a little longer."

Silence descended, and I picked at the edge of the wooden picnic table, running my nail in a crack. I knew what I wanted. I just didn't know if I deserved it.

Evan cleared his throat. "Well, that doesn't mean we can't slay it in the pumpkin carving contest."

"Oh?"

"I have an idea for a design, and I know you love carving pumpkins." His grin was almost his usual mischievous one.

"Let's do it." I stood to throw my trash away.

Evan did the same and led the way to the contest area. I followed, feeling like I had just made another mistake and knowing I would need to fix it. But for now, I would enjoy the festival.

After signing us up as a team with the committee, we wandered through the pumpkin patch, looking for the perfect one. The town imported the squash from mainland farms, so there were a variety to choose from. Each pumpkin was a squat, cheerful globe in colors of dark orange, gold, and peach. Some were still green, and the occasional Cinderella white pumpkin stood out among the darker shades. The scent of hay and earth hung in the air, mingling with the faint aroma of cinnamon from a nearby cider stand. Children squealed as they darted between the pumpkins.

"This one?" I asked, pointing to one the size of a small beach ball.

Instead of answering me, I felt his finger run across a spot on my shoulder, and my skin tingled at his touch.

"I didn't notice you had a tattoo here," he breathed.

I turned my head to look at him. "Yeah, I got it last year."

"And just what does a blue butterfly mean?" He shifted his focus from my shoulder to my eyes.

My cheeks felt warm, and I told myself it was the sunny weather Jessica produced. I had to clear my throat before I could answer. "Transformation and hope," I finally squeaked out.

"When did you get it?" His breath tickled the side of my neck.

I wanted to lean into him but managed to hold perfectly still. "The day I went to see my mom."

"I love it."

Some boys ran by just then, laughing and throwing popcorn at each other. I sucked in a breath, grateful for the interruption.

"About the pumpkin?" I reminded him.

Evan tore his gaze from me and studied it for a moment. "It has a weird flat spot. But look at this one."

He moved a few feet over and hefted a huge pumpkin that was almost perfectly round. Its bright green stem provided the perfect handle for the lid.

"It's great," I said.

He carried it over to our designated table.

"For the design, I thought we could do something that symbolizes Willowbrook."

"Like what?"

"You're good at drawing, right?"

I laughed. "Nope. That's Jewels. You picked the wrong partner if you wanted artistic ability."

He laughed good-naturedly. "Okay, I'll sketch it. But then you have to clean the guts."

"Deal."

He took the pencil and began pressing it into the skin. I watched, trying to figure out what he had planned. He covered one side with wavy lines and swirls, then drew a long line that wrapped around to the other side. As he hunched lower over the pumpkin, his shoulders hid the drawing from me. After a few more minutes, he stood back.

"What do you think?"

I peered at it and walked around the table to see it from all directions. As I did, the scene appeared. "Oh! It's the beach and the pier!"

"Yep. What do you think?"

I grabbed the pencil. "I like it, but it needs some detail. Clouds and birds are in my limited drawing capabilities." I added a few shapes to the upper areas of the pumpkin, making them large enough that we could carve them out.

"We're so taking first place," Evan said as he admired our work. He picked up the knife and swiftly cut a circle around the stem, popping it out and setting it aside. "You're up."

I grinned. "I know some people can't stand the feel of pumpkin pulp and seeds, but I find it delicious. Plus, it's good for the skin."

"I wouldn't know." He smiled bemusedly at me as I dug into the gourd with one hand, holding it steady with the other.

I scooped out a large glop of pulp and dropped it on the newspaper lining the table.

"Well, I do. I learned it from Rita at the Beauty Den."

"So, is that what you and my sister do in the fall? Make pumpkin facials?"

"No, but that is an excellent idea."

"It would probably help." His eyes went wide with shock as soon as he spoke.

"Oh, really?" I pulled out another large chunk of pumpkin guts and threw it at him. It splattered on his chest and neck. "Maybe it would help you, too." I giggled.

He tilted his head. "You did not just do that." With a glint in his eyes, he grabbed a handful of pulp from the table and lobbed it at me.

I turned, but not quickly enough. The slimy substance hit my shoulder and the side of my head.

"I hope pumpkin is good for the hair, too," he quipped.

My mouth dropped open slightly before I lunged for the pile. Evan got there first, and our fingers met in the middle of the goop, scrabbling for what we could. We threw at the same time, and seeds and sticky orange strands found their marks.

Laughing, I wiped some from my cheek. Evan shook his head and stepped toward me.

"You just made it worse," he said.

He used the corner of his flannel to wipe my face, his large hands surprisingly gentle. I longed to stretch up and kiss him but knew it would just confuse things further. From the look in his eyes, I suspected he had the same thought. He cleared his throat and moved back a few steps.

"Well, we aren't going to win any carving contests without carving."

I nodded in agreement, not trusting my voice, and returned to my task of cleaning the inside. Once I scraped it clean, Evan picked up the knife again.

"What happened to you two?" Jessica asked as she approached our table with Zane.

"She started it," Evan said with an affected whine.

Jessica rolled her eyes. "You look ridiculous. Please tell me you're going to clean up."

"Sure, sis. As soon as we win this contest."

"Actually, I'm going to the restroom now. The pumpkin is drying, and it feels a little like glue in my hair." I gestured to the pumpkin. "It's your turn to work, anyway."

"I thought you said pumpkin is good for your skin," Evan teased.

"I didn't say I liked it," I protested.

He laughed and motioned for me to go.

"Looks like you have left the friend zone," Jessica said, walking beside me. Zane stayed behind to talk to Evan.

I shook my head. "Not quite. But we aren't fighting anymore, either." I picked an orange strand from my shirt. "At least not in that way."

"What are you going to wish for when we light the lanterns tonight?" she asked slyly.

The lantern lighting part of the festival was my favorite. Everyone got a paper lantern and wrote things they wanted to release on one side and things they wished for on the other. Then, we all lit the candles at once and let the lanterns float over the town.

"For my magic to go away," I muttered.

She grabbed my arm, stopping me in my tracks. "You can't be serious, Hannah!"

I sighed. "I'm not. But it would make things easier, wouldn't it?"

"I used to think the same thing," she said sympathetically. "But now I think I wouldn't be who I am without my magic."

"I hope I can get to that point. Right now, everything is just too much."

"I'm sorry that I haven't been more supportive."

There were a lot of apologies going around lately.

"It's okay. I understand. I'm sorry if I made things harder for you."

"You didn't. Truly. Grief is a long road." Then she laughed. "This is a total hug moment, but I am not hugging you until you get that stuff off you. Go. I'll wait for you." She gestured to the nearby bathroom.

I smiled with relief to have my friend back and went in. I washed my face and pulled as much of the pulp off my clothes as I could, then dampened some paper towels and ran them over my hair, cleaning it as much as possible. Satisfied that I got most of it, I surveyed my reflection in the mirror. My eyes were bright, and I looked almost happy. A wish settled over me of having more moments with Evan like dancing at the concert and pumpkin fights. I longed for quiet dinners with him, too, and sunny beach days. Maybe I could take a chance with Evan again.

Shaking my head to expel the yearning, I exited the small building and rejoined Jessica. As we walked back to the carving area, I asked her what she planned to wish for on her lantern.

"Oh, probably something practical, like a windfall year, so I can expand the store."

"Not a proposal?" I bumped her shoulder with mine.

Her cheeks turned red. "It's a little early for that, don't you think?" she spluttered.

"Not really. It's been, what, five months? You two are perfect for each other."

She sighed wistfully. "It's so great. I don't want to ruin it."

As we approached Evan and Zane, I heard singing. "Do you hear that?" I cocked my head.

Jessica looked around. "Oh, it's the Crony Crew!" She pointed.

"They started a few minutes ago," Evan said. "They're pretty good, aren't they?"

The four older men had dressed in red and white striped vests and straw hats. They sang On the Sunny Side of the Street, with Old John taking the lead. They even had some small dance moves to go with the lyrics.

"This is a nice surprise," Jessica said. "It fits well with our small town charm."

"Oh, the *Chronicle!*" Zane exclaimed, and he maneuvered through the people encircling the quartet, pulling out his phone to get a photograph.

Evan laughed. "Looks like lover boy almost forgot he's the newspaper."

"He's been distracted today," Jessica admitted. "I'm not sure what's going on. He said he would talk with me later."

"Hopefully, it's nothing serious," I offered.

"Hey, what do you think?" Evan drew our attention to the pumpkin.

The depiction of the pier and beach wrapped around the entire thing, and he even added delicate starfish.

"It's beautiful," I breathed. "I can't believe you did that in the short time I was gone."

He shrugged, but pink tinged his face. "Well, the design itself is pretty simple. Just a few swirls and lines, really. It didn't take much."

"I don't deserve any of the prize when we win. I barely helped."

"You provided the inspiration."

His statement caught me off guard.

"How?"

"Willowbrook wouldn't be the same if you weren't here."

I stared at him as my heart pounded in my chest again. A sting in my eyes warned of tears.

"Well, brother, you outdid yourself," Jessica intervened.

I threw a grateful glance at her.

"Thanks. Hannah, can you stay here in case they start the judging early? It's my turn to clean up."

I nodded and watched him pace through the park.

"Earth to Hannah," Jessica said.

I tore my eyes from Evan's retreating back.

"Jewels is right. You've got it bad. Just tell him already."

"I don't know what you mean."

Exasperated, she said, "Tell him you want to be with him."

"I can't. I don't know if I do. Not yet. There's so much happening—"

My mother's piercing voice interrupted me. "Hannah, darling. There you are!"

Chapter 31: Breaking Point

I turned to see my mother picking her way across the grass, walking on tiptoes to keep her high heels from sinking into the soft earth. Her black pencil skirt and white blouse stood out in the midst of plaid and denim. The sight was so out of place, so ridiculous amid the laid-back atmosphere of the festival, that for a moment, I could only stare.

"Mother? What are you doing here?"

She fluttered her hand in front of her face. "It's very warm today, isn't it?"

I exchanged amused looks with Jessica, knowing she worked some magic to ensure the festival had good weather. No surprise there.

"Yes, but why are you here?" I insisted.

My mother sighed as if my questioning were an unbearable burden. "Well, you didn't respond to my text. I do not want you around Jamison. Do you hear me, Hannah Grace?"

I threw my hands up. "I haven't even seen him today. And besides, it's none of your business!"

She planted her hands on her hips, her heels finally sinking into the ground. "It is my business. You're my daughter. I raised you—"

"Because you told him to leave," I hissed, lowering my voice even as the heat in my chest built. It pressed outward like something alive, something ready to break free. I sucked in a breath and willed my nerves to settle. I did not want to cause a scene today.

"Did we win?" Evan's cheerful call briefly broke the thick tension, and I turned to see him approaching. His broad grin faltered when he noticed my mother. "Oh, hello," he said politely.

My mother flashed him the kind of smile she reserved for clients and business partners—the polished, professional one that meant *you are irrelevant to me, but I'll tolerate your presence.* "Would you two mind?" she asked with a sweet voice. "I need a few minutes with my daughter."

Jessica hesitated, shifting slightly, looking at me as if waiting for my cue. I knew she wouldn't abandon me if I gave her an indication to stay.

"No, you don't." I told my mother firmly. "I'm not discussing this today. Please go home."

"Hannah," my mother said, her voice softening in that calculated way I knew too well.

"Charlotte?"

Great. This is the last thing I need.

Jamison approached us from the other side of the park, hands in his pockets, looking far too relaxed for someone who had unknowingly stepped onto a battlefield.

"I thought I heard you. Been a long time." He sounded fond of my mother, as if the years between them hadn't happened. "Hi, Hannah."

I noticed several townspeople glancing our way. I could feel their curious eyes, their prying ears waiting for a reason to listen in. My heart pounded.

"This is not happening. Not here."

I turned sharply on my heel, heading for the street, hoping—praying—they would follow me, that we could at least move this conversation away from the festival. Jessica and Zane hung back, appearing unsure of what they should do, but Evan walked behind my parents.

"Absolutely not. We will talk about this now. I did not come across the inlet to be told to go home," she snapped.

"Your stubbornness is infuriating," I said, biting out the words.

"You got it from somewhere," she shot back without missing a beat.

I tried the other parental figure. Maybe he would be more reasonable. "Jamison, I know you're planning on staying in Willowbrook for now, but can you please give me some space?"

He sighed, running a hand through his graying hair. "I only came over when I heard your mother's voice," Jamison said. "In my defense, I never loved anyone else."

"Do you even know what love is?" my mother hissed back, her face twisting with something sharp and bitter.

"Do you?" he retorted.

Their words scraped at my nerves, each syllable a tug-of-war between old wounds and fresh ones.

We reached the sidewalk. I stomped toward the ferry landing. "Not here!" I whirled on them. "This is not the time or the place for this conversation." At least everyone was in the park, and we were mostly out of earshot now, if not out of view.

The laughter from the festival seemed distant, unreal. Warm air pressed against my skin like a too-heavy blanket, making it harder to breathe. The scent of roasting apples and cinnamon felt cloying, nauseating. My fingers twitched.

"Hannah's right," Evan said in his steady way. "Perhaps you can plan a meeting for tomorrow."

My mother peered at him. "I'm sorry, but who are you?"

"Evan Barnes," he said. "I'm Hannah's, well, we're not sure yet, but I'm hoping to be her significant other."

"One of the Barnes' children. That makes sense. But this is a family matter, and that does not include you." My mother dismissed him with a flick of her fingers.

Her rejection of Evan, just like she rejected everything I've ever wanted, stung in a way I didn't expect. "Mother! Don't be rude. He's trying to help me."

"Don't talk to me that way, Hannah Grace."

"She's not a child anymore, Char. Give her some credit." Jamison looked at me with sadness in his gaze. "You know, Hannah, I would have stayed if she had let me," he said, voice tight.

"Oh, don't be dramatic," my mother scoffed. "You ran at the first sign of trouble, like you always do."

"I left because you pushed me out!" Jamison shot back. He turned to me. "Hannah, you don't have to listen to her."

"Don't manipulate her," my mother said.

"I'm not manipulating her! I'm trying to be her father!"

Their voices rose, overlapping, buzzing in my ears like a swarm of bees. The words blurred together, nothing but sharp edges and an old argument I wanted no part of. They're standing right in front of me, fighting over me, but not actually seeing me. Why won't they ask me what I want? I covered my ears with my hands and closed my eyes, but I could still hear their bickering. Their words tangled together, each one like a claw scraping against my skin.

"He ran at the first sign of trouble, like he always does," my mother snapped.

"I wanted to stay, but you—"

"Don't rewrite history, Jamison."

Their words hit me like waves, relentless, dragging me under. I squeezed my eyes shut, my breath quick and shallow.

She was unhappy being a mother, and my father abandoned me, however he wanted to veil it in excuses of respecting my mother's wishes.

And now, here they were, arguing over me like I was some prize in a fight neither of them had actually won. Like I was the problem. Like I had to pick a side.

What if I don't want either of them?

This is too loud. Too much.

"Hannah," Evan murmured, his voice softer now. "Take a breath."

But I barely heard him. My hands were trembling. Children shrieked with laughter in the distance. A fiddle played somewhere, too fast, too cheerful, like a taunt. Someone's dog barked excitedly. Music, footsteps, conversations. The weight of it pressed against my skull, suffocating.

Evan was saying something else in his calm and steady way, his hand on my arm. I couldn't hear him over the rushing in my ears.

"All of you, just stop!" I shouted, putting my hands up as if I could physically push the noise away. I squeezed my eyes shut.

The silence was instantaneous. The music, the voices, the rustling leaves—gone.

My eyes snapped open.

My mother's lips were parted mid-sentence, but no sound came out. Jamison had one hand raised as if gesturing. I turned slowly and looked back at the park. A man stood mid-step, his boot hovering above the dirt. Two women hovered over a hay bale, stuck between sitting and standing. A little girl's long hair, caught in the wind, didn't move. Several sparrows hung frozen in the sky.

"Oh, no."

I swallowed hard, my stomach twisting. My breath came fast and shallow. I took a shaky step back, my hands trembling.

"What did I do?" I whispered.

Chapter 32: Suspended Matters

T he silence was more unbearable than the arguing had been. I looked at Evan, and I could see his chest rise with his breathing. He was standing still, but he wasn't frozen like the rest of the island.

"Evan?" I whispered.

"I'm okay." He took a small step toward me, moving slowly. "I had my shields up, so I wouldn't get overwhelmed by the festivalgoers."

"I did this." I made a sweeping motion with my arm. "I ruined Willowbrook."

Cold sweat broke out on my neck. My breath became shallow, and I gasped, unable to suck in enough air. My hands shook, and I gripped the bottom of my shirt to stop them from trembling. Dark spots formed at the edge of my vision as panic clawed at my throat.

"Hannah, look at me. Breathe." Evan shifted closer to me. "You can fix this."

I shake my head frantically. "I don't know how."

Evan reached for my hand, but I flinched away, afraid of what else I might do. My magic had spiraled out of control, and the evidence of my mistake surrounded me, frozen in time.

"Hey," he murmured. "I'm here. You didn't freeze me."

I let him unclench my fist and curl my fingers around his, the warmth from his touch grounding me. My pulse, erratic moments before, steadied slightly.

I shook my head again. "You got lucky because you were already shielded."

He smiled gently. "I think you could have got me, too, if you really wanted to."

Did I spare him because of my feelings for him? I still wasn't ready to admit what they were. But the way he looked at me, steady and unwavering, made my heart ache in a way I wasn't ready to explore.

I peered at my parents, trying to detect any movement. "They should stay suspended for only a few moments, right? If Jessica and Sofia are correct that the number of people affects how long they stay frozen, then everyone should be back to normal in just a few seconds."

Evan nodded. "Yes. So, all we have to do is wait."

I paced a few steps each way, glancing impatiently at the time on my phone with every turn. My steps became quicker, and my breathing shallower. Evan remained where he stood, a small frown furrowing his brows as he watched me. The minutes dragged, my nerves fraying more with each passing second.

Two minutes passed. Then five. Eight. A sick realization settled in my stomach, heavy and unshakable.

The ferry horn sounded, and I realized there would soon be witnesses. How would I explain it? Briefly, I considered running home and hiding until the suspension wore off. If it wore off.

I stopped my pacing next to Evan and looked toward the park. "This is bad, Evan. My magic should have worn off by now. I don't know how to fix it."

His fingers intertwined with mine, and I looked down at our joined hands. The contest between my trembling fingers and his solid grip made my stomach flip.

"Hannah, listen. When Jessica lost control, it was because she thought Zane was leaving her. She couldn't face that loss so soon after our parents' death." He squeezed my hand briefly. "You need to figure out your trigger."

I yanked my hand free and took several steps away from him. "My trigger? My trigger was them!" I gestured to my parents, still frozen mid-argument. "They were fighting over me as if they had a say in my life now. Jamison left when I was a baby and never came back until now. My mother…she never really wanted me. Her ambitions always flowed in the direction of the corporate ladder and didn't leave room for me."

"I think you'll need to go deeper than that."

I glanced at him sharply. "What do you mean?"

"I understand your frustration about their disagreement. Even to me, it seemed like they were continuing a fight from years ago." I opened my mouth to respond, and he put one hand up to forestall me. "Hear me out. Your magic responds to threats, correct?" When I nodded, he continued, "So what felt threatening about this situation?"

"Besides the fact that the entire town could see and hear them? Or how about how my father had abandoned me to a magic-hating woman who would rather be in a board meeting than come to my piano recitals? They both knew the possibility of my magic existed." My voice rose, cracking under the weight of my words. All of my muscles tensed, and my heart rate sped up. Heat suffused my skin, and I tried and failed to take a full breath.

"Abandoned," Evan whispered.

I blinked at him. "What?"

"You felt abandoned. Both by your father because he left without a trace when you were little, and by your mother because she was never really present in your life." He moved closer to me. I could smell the scent of pumpkin on his clothes and mint from his gum on his breath. "And I think you thought I would leave you, too."

A weight pressed on my chest. My stomach churned, and saliva built-up in my mouth. I swallowed thickly, willing my lunch to stay put. I finally managed to drag in a full breath and, shaking my head, I turned away from him.

"You and Jessica have always been there for me." I ignored the flippant tone I used, pretending we were bantering. My voice wavered, betraying me.

"And we always will be. Hannah, please look at me."

I shook my head again, not trusting my voice.

His hands grasped my shoulders and softly slid down my arms to encircle my waist. He pulled me closer, and I felt his mouth against my ear. "Hannah," he whispered, the word sending a flutter to my belly that was not at all unpleasant. "I love you. I'm not going anywhere."

A sob escaped me, and I covered my mouth with one hand. Tears streaked down my cheeks. The tension suddenly left my muscles, and I would have sunk to the ground if Evan hadn't held me. His arms tightened further.

"I've got you."

I twisted slowly, and he relaxed his grip just enough to let me rotate to face him. "I love you, too," I choked out.

He gently cupped my face, and I gazed into his eyes, unwavering in their belief in me. "You're not alone, Hannah. You can fix this."

The words sank into me, dissolving the fear and uncertainty that wrapped around my power like choking vines. Evan was right. My feelings of abandonment had fueled my magic and strengthened it more than ever. Emotion had always fueled my power: the fear of abandonment and the desperate need to protect myself even when no real danger was present. I had lashed out not with intention, but with raw, unchecked feeling.

But now... now, something was shifting. With Evan's arms around me and his quiet, steady presence anchoring me, I felt a shift.

A gasp escaped my lips as a strange sensation filled me. A deep pulse, like a heartbeat, reverberated outward from my core—the very place I had struggled to reach during every lesson, the place Sofia had urged me to connect with, but I could never quite grasp. It was like a door unlocking, a dam breaking, and suddenly, the crushing weight that had pressed down on me lifted.

The world stirred.

A sharp inhale from my mother. My father's quiet, disoriented murmur. The festival, once frozen in eerie stillness, now hummed with life again. I heard the rustling leaves, the distant cry of a seagull, the slow, uncertain shuffling of feet as people regained their awareness, and the music starting up again.

Looking at my parents, I stepped back from Evan but kept my hand in his to keep the connection. I wasn't ready to release the anchor of his presence. My mother's hand drifted to touch her throat, and she frowned as if trying to remember what she was just saying. Jamison swayed slightly before steadying himself, his brows furrowing.

And me? I felt different. The wild, untamed force inside me had settled, no longer thrashing for control but finally, finally, fitting into place. It was still powerful, still vast and unknowable, but it was mine.

"I did it," I breathed out.

Evan grinned. "I knew you could."

Before I could fully process how I pulled my magic back and let time flow again, my mother turned toward me. Her eyes flickered with lingering confusion, then sharpened into something far more unsettling. Recognition. Understanding.

And then something else.

Her gaze locked onto mine, dark and searching, and I felt a shiver of unease ripple through me. A storm was brewing behind her expression, a tempest of emotions I couldn't yet name. My stomach twisted as I realized that whatever had just happened between us—whatever impossible truth she had just experienced—the conversation wasn't over.

Not by a long shot.

Chapter 33: Together

My mother's eyes went wide with confusion and a flicker of fear. "What…what just happened?" Her voice was shaky but held a sharp edge, as if she'd already pieced things together. She glanced first at Jamison and then Evan for an explanation, but her focus snapped back to me. "Did you do something?"

I wanted to laugh or scream at the sky. "Mom, I told you. My magical powers are freezing people and things in place, and teleportation of objects."

She stumbled back as if I were something other, something dangerous. "No. No, this isn't…you can't be—" Her voice wavers, her hands trembling. "This isn't possible. You aren't possible." The weight of denial crushes her voice. She turns to Jamison, accusation in her gaze. "This is because of you."

Jamison grimaced but didn't look away. His jaw tightened, his hands curling into fists at his sides. "You always knew it was a possibility, Charlotte." His voice was quiet, but firm. "You just didn't want to face it."

My mother shook her head, eyes darting wildly as if searching for a way out of this reality. "No, I thought if I kept her away from all of this, if I raised her without any of it, she would be normal." Her voice cracked on the last word, and she turned her gaze back to me. There was something raw in her expression.

I swallowed the lump forming in my throat. "Mom, I am normal. Magic doesn't change that."

She let out a short, bitter laugh. "Doesn't it? Hannah, I watched magic destroy everything. It took Jamison from me. It turned my life upside down. And now…" She inhaled sharply, gripping her arms as if holding herself together. "Now, it's taken you, too."

Her words were a gut punch, but I refused to back down. "You mean you pushed my dad away because of magic. You pushed me away before I even had the chance to know the truth." My voice wavered, but I forced myself to meet her gaze. "You weren't reluctant to be a mother because you didn't want me. You were scared of what I could be."

My mother flinched, guilt flickering across her face before she masked it with frustration. "You don't understand, Hannah. I saw what magic did to people. The risks, the chaos. I didn't want that for you."

"You didn't want me at all." The words slipped out before I could stop them, and the moment they did, a hollow silence fell between us.

For a second, pain flashed in her eyes. But she smothered it, straightening her shoulders. "I wanted to protect you."

"By pretending magic didn't exist?" I threw my hands up but quickly lowered them to my sides. "By making me feel like I was never enough? Like something was always off between us, but I never knew why?"

She shook her head, turning away. "You wouldn't understand."

I took a step forward, my heart pounding. "Then make me understand."

She paused, a first for her. The wall she had built over the years wavered, if only slightly. But instead of answering, she turned her gaze to the ground, her lips pressing into a thin line. I felt Evan's presence beside me, silent support in the midst of this new storm.

Jamison sighed, running a hand through his hair before speaking. "Charlotte, you can't keep running from this. Hannah deserves the truth."

She closed her eyes for a long moment before exhaling shakily. Something I couldn't quite name filled her eyes when she opened them again. Regret? Fear? A mix of both?

"I didn't know how to love something I was afraid of," she admitted, her voice barely above a whisper.

The words cut deep, but they also unraveled something inside me. Because for the first time, I saw the truth behind my mother's distance. It wasn't just rejection—it was fear. Fear of the unknown. Fear of me.

And I didn't know which hurt more.

My mother's words hung over me like a dark cloud before settling into my bones. So many things made sense now.

Jamison murmured, "Charlotte, she's still your daughter."

Her shoulders sagged as she turned toward him. "What if I don't know how to be her mother? What if I've already ruined everything?"

My heart ached. A part of me wanted to yell that yes, she had ruined things, that the years of feeling unwanted weren't so easily brushed aside. I could feel Evan watching me, waiting to see how I would respond. I knew he would be by my side, no matter what I chose. But I didn't want to repeat the experience of losing control of my powers due to unacknowledged and suppressed emotions.

Taking a deep breath, I stepped forward. "I don't need you to be perfect, Mom. I just need you to try."

Her lips parted, and I expected an argument. Her Instagram-worthy life didn't leave room for imperfections. Instead, she nodded. "Tell me how I can."

Shrugging, I said, "Maybe I can call you on days other than Sunday? Perhaps we can do something besides a scheduled dinner?"

She gave me a small smile full of pain and hope. "That sounds good."

It wasn't an instant fix, but it was something.

Then I turned to Jamison. "And you?" I asked, my voice quieter now. "You left because of your magic, but you didn't come back for me."

Guilt flashed across his face. "You're right. I should have fought harder to be in your life. But when Charlotte told me to leave, I thought I was doing what was best for you. And when the years passed...I didn't know how to come back." He shook his head, his voice thick with emotion. "That was a mistake, Hannah. And I'm sorry."

I searched his face for any hint of hesitation, but all I saw was regret. And maybe that was enough for now.

"I can't forgive either of you overnight," I admitted. "But I do want to understand. And I want both of you in my life."

My mother swallowed hard, then hesitantly reached for my hand. It was the first time in years that she had willingly initiated touch. "I'd like that."

The feeling of her hand in mine instantly brought my mind back to the beach when I was small, and we stood together, hand in hand, letting the waves rush over our toes. I gave her hand a small squeeze.

Jamison nodded and took my other hand. "Me too."

"See? I told you that you weren't alone," Evan said softly, placing his hands on my shoulders.

"Hannah!"

I spun around at the sound of my name to see Jewels running toward us, her pink-streaked hair glinting in the light. As she neared, I saw she had silver glitter in it, likely from Beauty Den's contribution to the festival: face paint and sparkle spray. Jewels flung herself into my arms.

"Are you okay?" she asked, panting.

"I'm fine," I said, laughing and pushing a strand of her hair out of my eyes.

"Hannah!"

Looking up, I saw Jessica jogging up the sidewalk, Zane next to her. When they reached us, Jessica wrapped her arms around Jewels and me.

"Where did you go? What happened?"

I laughed, and happy tears slid down my face. "It's okay. Everything is fine." I hugged my friends then extricated myself from the tangle of limbs. "I'll explain everything."

The truth of Evan's words—that I wasn't alone—settled over me like a warm blanket. Despite the fact I had stayed in Willowbrook most of my life, I had never quit searching for a place to belong. I had it all along; I just didn't realize it until now.

Just then, a cell phone rang. Jessica's.

We looked at each other. "Sofia," we said in union, then laughed.

She pulled it out of her back pocket and answered. "Hi, Sofia. We're all together." She grinned at us and rolled her eyes. "Uh-huh...yeah...okay." Pressing end, she turned to us. "Well, it's not a shocker. Sofia wants us to meet at my house immediately. She said she felt the magical disturbance but couldn't react in time before the suspension magic affected her. Apparently, you," she pointed at me, "took her by surprise."

"I'm sorry to interrupt, but who is Sofia and why does she want to see you?" my mother asked in her professional tone.

I quirked an eyebrow at her. "I guess you could say she's my mentor. She's been helping me learn how to control my powers."

"She's not doing a very good job, is she?" she retorted.

I sighed. "Mom, this wasn't her fault. I'm still very new to all of this."

Jamison nodded. "Remember how many months I trained before you finally kicked me out, Char?" When she glared at him, he held up his hands in surrender. "I don't say that to start a fight, but to prove a point. It takes time to learn magic."

"Well, I wouldn't know, would I?" she said primly.

I slung my arm around her shoulders. "Come on, Mom. Let's all go see Sofia. Perhaps she will help ease your mind a bit."

She tensed then said, "But I'll be the only one there who doesn't have magic."

Zane leaned around Jessica, having moved to wrap his arms around her waist from behind her when our group hug disbanded. "Nah, I don't have magic, either.

Eventually, you'll learn that love transcends all that. Plus, there will be cookies and wine. There's always cookies and wine after something like this." He grinned, and my mother gave a small answering smile.

Bless him for including her and making her his co-conspirator.

"Well, as long as I'm not intruding."

We strolled down the sidewalk to Jessica and Evan's house. Zane and Jessica took the lead, holding hands, with Jewels right behind them. My parents followed, and I noticed Jamison leaned in to talk quietly to my mother. Evan and I brought up the rear. I looked sideways at him, enjoying how the late afternoon light played with the natural blond highlights in his hair.

"Like what you see?" he asked with a wink.

"Definitely."

He put his arm around my shoulders, pulling me closer. "No matter what, butterfly, we're in this together."

Chapter 34: It's an Art

We packed into Jessica's living room. I breathed in the comforting scent of cinnamon and warm vanilla from the cookies being passed around as Zane poured us all a rich red wine. My parents sat on the loveseat with their shoulders almost touching. Sofia took the single chair, resting her elbows on the armrests. Zane stood in front of the fireplace, one arm on the mantle. The rest of us found places on the sofa, except for Jewels, who sat on the floor, her sketchpad out and pencil moving as she drew.

"Well," Sofia began, folding her hands in her lap. She studied me with those sharp eyes that always seemed to see more than she let on. "You did well today, Hannah."

I scoffed. "I froze the entire island."

"Yes, but you also reversed it. That's progress."

Evan reached over and squeezed my hand. "We're proud of you."

My dad nodded. "It's difficult to learn magic when you didn't even know it was possible. I'm still sorry for my part in that."

I swallowed hard, my throat tight. "It's okay. I understand why you did it."

Jessica nudged my knee with hers. "But next time, don't panic-freeze a bunch of people."

Jewels looked up from her drawing and grinned. "Or do. Could be fun."

Sofia shot them both a look, but the corners of her mouth twitched.

My mother, who hadn't said anything since I introduced her to Sofia, leaned forward slightly. "What happens now? With Hannah's magic, I mean?"

Sofia's gaze flicked to me. "Now, she practices. She learns control. And she learns to trust herself."

The last part settled in my chest like a warm blanket. Trust myself. It wasn't just about magic. It was about everything.

I glanced at Evan. His calm expression reassured me, and there was something softer in his eyes than before. He gave my hand another squeeze, and I moved to entwine my fingers with his.

"So, are you two a thing now?" Jessica asked with a grin.

Evan raised his eyebrows at me in a challenge.

I crinkled my nose at him with a smile.

"We're a thing. I don't know what yet, but I want to find out."

His grin lit up his face. "Finally stopped running, huh? I thought you were the one with the freezing power."

A giggle escaped me, and I almost clamped my other hand on my mouth until I heard Jessica and Jewels join in. Soon, the three of us were laughing so hard that tears ran down our cheeks. I gasped in a breath and looked at the ceiling.

"I don't understand. What's so funny?" my mother asked perplexed.

That set us off again until Sofia sighed with exasperation and said, "Evan, clamp them down, will you?"

It felt like a bucket of cold water splashed over me, cooling my cheeks and bringing my manic laughter to a halt.

"Is that new, brother?" Jessica asked.

Evan nodded his head with another grin. "I've been working on it. I can dampen emotions. I can't change them, just reduce the intensity."

Jessica groaned. "Where was that power when I thought Zane was leaving?"

He shrugged. "I can't help it if it waited until I needed it." He gave me a meaningful look.

I drew away from him a little. "Did you use it on me before? After I suspended the town?"

His guilty look said it all.

"So, it wasn't me, after all. I didn't pull back my magic," I muttered, looking away.

"Hannah, no. It's not like that. You did it, truly. I just...calmed the panic a little so you could think."

His pleading tone made me glance at him. I knew him too well after all this time to ignore the earnestness in his expression.

"Hannah, dear," Sofia said gently. "Evan's shield can't change what already occurred. Meaning if he shields you before your magic takes effect, it will reverberate off his shield and return to you. But if something or someone is already suspended, his shields won't help." She paused, her gaze softening. "You reversed your magic and released the town. That was you. Evan's ability to assist with high emotions and magical shielding will be invaluable as all of you continue to learn how to control your powers. And, Hannah, he did what he did out of love. Even an old woman like me can see that."

My heart stumbled over the thought. He had said the words, but I didn't really understand the depth of them. I drew in a breath and gently released it. "I know. I guess I'm still too independent to want help."

"That will have to change." Evan nuzzled my cheek.

A comfortable silence settled over the room. For the first time in weeks, everything felt okay. Almost normal.

Then Jewels gasped.

We all turned to her. She was staring at her hands, palms up, her face pale. "Whoa," she whispered.

"What is it?" Jessica asked, instantly alert.

"Look." Jewels pointed at her sketchbook.

It had a faint silver glow. The little cat she had drawn wiggled, stretched, and then, impossibly, hopped off the page. Jewels shot to her feet.

"What the—"

We all stared at the tiny, perfect, and very real black kitten now purring and rubbing on Jewels's ankles.

"Oh," Sofia said with amusement. "Now that is interesting."

Zane scooped up the kitten and held it in the crook of his arm, scratching its ears.

Jewels looked at Sofia, her face pale. "I just made a cat."

Sofia nodded. "Yes."

"I drew a cat. And now it's here."

"It appears so," Sofia said calmly.

Jewels asked frantically, "What does this mean?"

Sofia smiled knowingly. "It means, dear girl, that your magic has changed. We won't know the extent of it until we test it."

"Uh, can I get a little help here?" Jamison broke in.

I looked at my parents to see my mother slumped over the armrest. Standing, I rushed to kneel in front of her. "Mom?"

"She fainted when she saw the cat," Jamison explained.

"I'll get some tea for when she comes to," Jessica said, ever practical, striding to the kitchen.

"Perhaps, Jamison, when she has recovered, you might want to take her home," Sofia suggested.

He nodded. "Yes, that's probably a good idea. Today has been a lot for her."

My mother's eyes fluttered, and she slowly focused on me. "Hannah?"

"It's okay, Mom. Come into the kitchen and have some tea."

Jamison helped her to her feet and kept hold of her elbow as she followed me to the kitchen. I thanked Jessica for the tea—lavender with lots of honey—and made sure my mother had a few sips.

"I'll talk to you both tomorrow," I said before returning to the living room.

Some blank paper sat on the coffee table. Evan stood next to the sofa, and Jewels sat in his place.

She looked up at me with a weak smile. "We're going to do some testing."

"Now, Jewels," Sofia said. "Try drawing something simple. A flower, perhaps."

Jewels hesitated, gripping her pencil. "And if it comes to life?"

"Then we'll know your magic is consistent," Sofia said.

I moved to stand beside Evan and leaned forward, watching as Jewels sketched a small daisy. The lines were quick and simple, but as soon as she lifted her pencil, the paper shimmered.

The daisy trembled, then lifted, fully formed, from the page. It was real—stem, petals, everything.

"Holy shit," Jewels gasped.

Jessica picked up the flower, turning it over in her hands. "It feels real." She sniffed it. "It smells real."

Zane whistled. "That's a little terrifying."

Jewels rubbed her temples. "Okay, okay. This is fine. It's cool. I can work with this."

Sofia chuckled. "You may want to be careful about what you draw, at least until you can figure out how to control this new power."

"Yeah, no kidding," Jewels muttered.

Jessica snickered. "Imagine if you drew a dragon."

Jewels groaned, flopping back onto the couch. "Don't give me ideas."

Sofia patted her shoulder. "Tomorrow, we'll start work on your training. But for now, I suggest you all get some rest." She stood, making her way to the front door.

"I'll walk you and Jewels home," Evan said to me.

"Who will walk me home?" Zane asked.

"You may walk me home, young man," Sofia said.

He grinned and gave Jessica a quick kiss. "Yes, ma'am." He offered Sofia his arm, and they descended the front steps.

I gave Jessica a hug goodbye then looked at Jewels. She was staring at her hands. There was something different in her expression now. She looked uncertain or uncomfortable.

I knew that feeling all too well.

And just like that, I knew. My chaos might be settling, but Jewels's was only just beginning.

Jessica groaned and flopped back against the couch. "Oh, great. Here we go again."

I couldn't help but laugh.

Because somehow, I had a feeling she was right.

Acknowledgements

I had the idea for *Suspended Matters* while writing *Natural Disaster,* and of course life got in the way, and I kept pushing the book to the bottom of the list. This book would not have seen the light of day for another few months, or maybe even a year, if it weren't for some very important people. I started it at a writing retreat in September 2024, and pushed back the publishing date from March 2025 to May 2025, but I'm very proud of writing and publishing a book in eight months, especially when the first one took years to complete.

First off, I want to thank my husband, David. Once again, he quietly supported my efforts and encouraged me to keep going. He reminded me to write and edit my book, and kept me supplied with peanut M&Ms. While neither reading nor writing are his thing, he understands how important it is for me to tell my stories. He's the love of my life and I can't imagine accomplishing this series without his solid presence.

Thank you, Emily, for being my sounding board (again!). Your marketing expertise is invaluable, and your eye for story development really made this book what it is. Every day, I am grateful for the writing community that brought us together and for our friendship. I'd be lost without you.

To my beta readers, Mariah and Holly, who caught the random error, large plot holes, and gave me positive and constructive feedback, thank you. I needed every bit of time and effort you dedicated to my book.

And a special thanks to the women of Spirited Ink Society for their feedback on my scenes when I knew something was off but couldn't figure it out. I'm blessed to be surrounded by very talented women authors who share their individual knowledge.

There are many other people in my life who helped me on this journey. My mom, who would text me encouraging comments when she knew I was writing, following them up with funny videos in the late evening when she knew I was done for the day. The patron at the library who, every time she sees me, asks me when my book is coming out. My library co-workers who gave me their opinions on my cover. The baristas who supplied me caffeine, and the random lady at the restaurant who cheered when she found out I was an author with a book releasing soon. Every soul that touched mine during this process assisted in some way.

Thank you, thank you, thank you.

About the Author

Alena Orrison is an award-winning author and a freelance writer and editor. She holds a Bachelor's Degree in English, with an emphasis in Creative Writing. She started writing stories when she was three years old by telling them to her mom, who wrote them down. She has been editing professionally since 2015. Alena has several articles and stories published online and in anthologies.

Alena currently lives in North Idaho with her husband, four children, two grandchildren, mom, three dogs, five cats, and a varying number of chickens. When she is not spending time with family and friends, gardening, boating, hiking, or at the gym, she is reading and writing. Alena also likes to crochet and spin yarn for some downtime. Some of her favorite authors include Anne McCaffrey, Elizabeth Cunningham, Elizabeth Gilbert, and Erin Morgenstern.

You can visit her at alenaorrison.com

The following is an
excerpt from:

Natural Disaster

Witches of Willowbrook
Book One

Alena Orrison

Chapter 6: Curiosity

T he door chimed, and several women with shopping bags approached the counter. I stepped to the sink, washed my hands, and asked for their orders. Only after I began ringing them up did I realize Donna Calhoun was part of the group. When it was her turn to order, I made sure to be extremely polite so there would be nothing she could fault me for. She still sneered as she ordered an extra-large drip coffee, black, and a peanut butter brownie.

Gah! What is her problem? I fumed.

I made the requested drinks, placing them and the snacks on a tray, and took everything to the table the ladies had commandeered. "Holler if you need anything else," I said cheerily.

"There is one thing," Donna said. "When are you going to use better coffee beans? These make terrible coffee."

I took a steadying breath. "These beans are single origin, organic, fair trade, and from Madagascar. Where do you get your beans from?"

Let Donna act like a stuck-up brat to me in front of her friends. I'd be the friendliest barista they had ever seen, and she'd make a fool of herself.

She took a slow sip of her coffee. "Hmm. Perhaps it's the way you make it."

"There's a new way to make drip coffee? I haven't heard of that. I visit Seattle every six months and talk to other baristas from all over the country, but no one has ever said there's a new way to make it. I'll have to jump on the message board and ask." I grinned, but there was an edge to my voice. The sunlight streaming through the windows suddenly dimmed. I cast a quick look out the window. Dark clouds gathered and appeared ominous. My attention was caught for a moment on Zane standing by the register, glancing at me and then his wristwatch. "Do you need anything else? I have other customers who need my attention."

"No, Jessica. This is lovely. Thank you," Larissa Malcom stated.

I left the women to their gossip and pettiness. Still fuming, I stomped around the end of the counter to face the reporter. He was tall, almost as tall as my brother. I could tell by the fit of his clothes that he worked out. "Hi, what can I get for you?"

"I think I'll have a blueberry scone and the..."

A crash of thunder drowned out the rest of his response. He gave a start and gazed thoughtfully out the window. His attention returned to me when I politely asked him to repeat his order. As I made his coffee, Zane settled at the table by the window again and pulled his laptop out of his briefcase. Once the special of the day was ready—a blue Lotus with huckleberry and coconut— I carried it out to him.

"Here you go." I put the plastic cup and a warm blueberry scone on the table in front of the businessman.

Without looking up from his laptop, he said, "Thank you."

Leaning a little on one hip, I glanced around the coffee shop. All the customers seemed content for the moment, so I decided to satisfy my curiosity. "What are you here to report on?"

"I didn't say I was here to report on anything." Zane barely took his eyes off his screen.

"Okay." I laughed a little. "So, why are you here?"

"Sorry, Jessica. I'm really too busy to talk right now." He pushed his dark hair away from his forehead as he focused on me. His gray eyes held a note of displeasure.

"Oh, right. Sorry. Let me know if you need anything else." I gave him a tight smile and went back to the counter.

From there, I could observe Zane without being obvious. He was in a blue button-up shirt open at the neck, pressed black slacks, and shiny black shoes. The fact that he had kept looking at his watch as I talked to Donna irritated me. I gave excellent service, and in a small town, that service included catching up on a bit of the news. Yesterday, when he first came in, I assumed he was an insurance adjustor or investment manager here to meet a client, but a book and coffee shop is a strange place for a business meeting.

I shrugged dismissively and wiped the counter.

"Excuse me." Zane stood at the counter, briefcase in hand.

"Yes?" I dried my hands but didn't raise my eyes to meet his. His brusque tone earlier irritated me more than I wanted to admit.

"Where is the restroom?"

"Down the hall to the left." I gestured toward the back of a magazine rack. I gave a little sniff in surprise as he turned away without another word. "Someone's moods change faster than mine," I muttered under my breath.

Glancing around the shop, I noted the tables that needed busing and realized the reporter still had part of his scone and an almost full cup of coffee on the table. He left his suit jacket hung over the back of the chair, so he obviously meant to return, but he had taken his laptop to the restroom with him.

Refusing to look at the laughing women, I went to a bookshelf and straightened a few copies from the *A Song of Ice and Fire* series. That one was still popular because of the recent television series adaptation. By the time I finished my circuit of the bookshelves, the sky outside appeared to be clearing again. Zane was back at his table, hunched over his laptop and reading something intently on the screen.

"Freak spring storm, eh, Jess?" Old John said from his usual spot as I passed him.

"Yeah, that one came out of nowhere," I said.

He gave me a knowing wink, turning back to his cronies to add his opinion on the building moratorium the city council recently passed.

I shook my head. Old John had been acting crazier than normal lately. He'd always been eccentric, but now he had taken to making strange remarks about the weather, followed by a wink or a little smile. I wondered if I should mention it to his wife, Laura, the next time she came by with a casserole or to put out her knitted drink cozies.

When Hannah returned from her break, she took one look at the room and headed straight for me.

"What did she say this time?"

"That my coffee isn't any good. And when I told her where it came from, she insulted how I made it. I wanted to blow up at her but managed to stay calm." I shrugged. "I basically asked her if she knew more about the coffee business than I did. She didn't answer, but Larissa looked amused."

"Donna acts like she's better than anyone else around, but she's not and she knows it. I'm surprised she still has friends."

"There must be something admirable about her, otherwise Larissa and the others wouldn't keep inviting her out."

"And what about Mr. Handsome in the center?" Hannah asked.

"Oh, he's in a mood today. He's barely talked to me. And yesterday, he was so friendly. I haven't quite figured out his story yet. But," I lowered my voice even more, "he took his laptop to the bathroom. Who even does that here?"

We laughed, and Hannah went to lower the blinds when Old John's group complained about the bright light coming into the front window.

The rest of the morning passed quickly, and the afternoon rush went as expected, with high schoolers arriving to chill with their friends or do homework. Through it all, Zane sat at his table. Once in a while,

Hannah or I would stop by to ask if he needed anything. Besides ordering the special again and a bagel sandwich, he seemed engrossed in his work.

Since Hannah opened in the mornings, I closed up in the evenings. I usually stayed open until seven o'clock but would sometimes close earlier if it was slow. She was off the clock at two, but she hung around and nursed a small tea.

A little after three p.m., Evan pushed open the door and strode in. I noted the way Hannah's eyes lit up.

"Now what do you want?" I gave my brother a pretend glare.

"My afternoon usual, please, sweet sister." He turned to Hannah while I prepared his caramel mocha. "Hi, Hannah. I thought you would already be home."

"Oh, uh, yeah. I was just finishing my tea." She blushed.

"Well, if you want to wait a few moments, I can walk you home."

I tried not to smirk at him while I finished his drink with a swirl of whipped cream. "I thought you had another class?" I asked, handing his coveted caffeine over the counter.

"Not today. I have a personal training session in about an hour, so I have time to kill. Ready, Hannah?"

I gave her a wave and an encouraging smile and watched Evan hold the door open for her. *I hope he's not leading her on*, I thought.

The shopaholics in the corner gathered their things, and I felt relieved they were leaving. I also noted, with a frown, that Donna didn't clean up her dishes or garbage. We served eat-in orders on ceramic plates and in ceramic mugs, crafted from the local pottery artist down the street. The least that woman could do was put her plate in the bin.

As Donna walked by the counter, she didn't say a word to me, unlike her friends, who all offered a cheerful farewell or thank you. "See you next time!" I called after them.

I would not let her get the best of me. I took a few deep breaths and moved to clean their table. There was a napkin under Donna's plate with writing on it. Curious, I read the note.

You are not as exceptional as you think.

My jaw clenched, and I threw the napkin in the trash can, along with the remains of her brownie.

"Easy, girl." Old John put a hand on my shoulder. "There's no need to be so worked up."

I turned and looked into the kind, wrinkly face of my most frequent customer, aside from my brother. "I don't know what I ever did to Donna, but she hates me."

A tear slipped down my cheek. John reached up and brushed it away. "You didn't do anything. She's jealous of you, and those kinds of emotions can make people act in ways they usually wouldn't."

"Jealous of me? Really? I don't think so. No one wants to be me. I'm the girl who lost her parents and moved home to take care of their estate." My tears were flowing freely now.

Old John pulled me into a hug. He smelled of sawdust, but I didn't mind.

"There, now. Cry it out for a bit. Everything will be okay," he soothed.

"Thanks, John." After a moment, I sniffed and wiped my eyes.

He released me from his embrace but kept hold of my shoulders. "Now, you listen to me, girl. You are unique. There's a lot you don't realize about this town, but you'll learn. Just keep your chin up." He gave my shoulders one last squeeze.

I nodded uncertainly and glanced around to see who noticed my meltdown. Only Zane was still here, head bent to his computer. I went to the bathroom to splash cool water on my face. The last thing I wanted was blotchy cheeks. When I came out, sunlight streamed through the windows while rain came down in sheets. *John is right; the weather is definitely strange lately.*